I0782427

SHELTERED IN THE STORM

A COZY ALIEN ROMANCE

THE FORTUSIAN MATES
BOOK 1

LISA EDMONDS

Ebook ISBN 978-1-963525-16-8

Paperback ISBN 978-1-963525-17-5

Edited by Grey Moth Editing

Cover Art By Lindsey Staton (@honeyy.fae)

Cover Typography by Megan Van Dyke

Vos and Calla Portrait by FlavulousArt

Chapter Headers and Interior Art by Carly at BookishBeasts

All stock photos licensed appropriately

Published in the United States

By Storybook House, LLC

This one's for the hopeful romantics.

CONTENT NOTES

This book, as with all other titles in this series, contains scenes that depict violence, death, sex, and some topics that may be disturbing to some readers.

The epilogue contains a pregnancy and can be considered optional for those who prefer to avoid the topic. The final chapter before the epilogue can be treated as an ending.

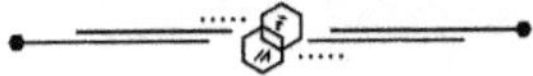

A complete list of content notes can be found on my website at **https://www.lisaedmonds.com/contentnotes**

ALSO BY LISA EDMONDS

The Fortusian Mates Series

Sheltered in the Storm

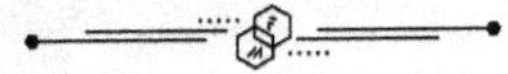

The Alice Worth Series

Heart of Malice

Heart of Fire

Heart of Ice

Heart of Stone

Heart of Shadows

Heart of Vengeance

Heart of Lies

Heart of the Pack

Heart of the Damned

Short Stories and Novellas

From the Ashes

Just For One Night

Blood Money

Ghosting 101

Perfectly Magical

Alice Worth and the Elite Death Machine

The Alice Worth World Novels

Mortal Heart

PROLOGUE

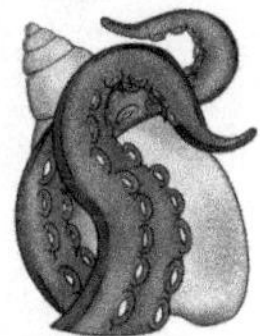

VOS

The ambassador was a dead them walking.

From my hiding place inside an air duct, I watched through the metal grate as the Kurutan ambassador N'vors emerged from their transport, ambulating on four oversized flippers. They clacked their six-fingered claws in greeting to the five trade delegates and well-armed embassy guards who had gathered to welcome them.

My wrist chronometer showed 1400 hours. Right on time. Kurutan considered arriving early or late to be unconscionably rude. An admirable trait, but one that made them an easier target, even with the embassy's extensive security measures, which were some of the best I had ever encountered.

But not nearly good enough to keep an elite assassin out, or to save the ambassador from their fate.

Nor would N'vors's thick, insect-like carapace protect them. Attempting to shoot the ambassador through the tiny gaps between the plates of their exoskeleton would be difficult if nearly impossible, so I had discarded that method as a means of attack.

Instead, I readied my weapon and waited for N'vors to finish their traditional dance of greeting and speak. My heartsbeats remained steady, my breathing slow and even. Quick kills and speedy exits were my trade, and I was very good at my trade.

I had gained entry during the night, in the wake of a diversion I had paid a street gang to create near the embassy's entrance. My body ached from my long, silent wait inside this duct, from the tips of my human fingers to my webbed toes, squeezed inside heavy boots that were part of my worker's disguise.

Even my tentacles twitched and ached, though I allowed them to stir and explore the interior of the duct as far as they were able to reach. I was a large man, powerfully built and two meters in height, with four large tentacles each as long as I was tall growing from my back. This duct was not designed for someone my size, much less my tentacles. The people of this planet, Bordians, were much smaller and often ran on their feet and hands. At least the slick, almost frictionless fabric of my coveralls helped me slide through the duct fairly easily.

I expected the ambassador's transport to depart as soon as N'vors got out. Instead, a small Kurutan child, so young their carapace had not yet hardened, hopped from the transport's open door and padded on tiny flipper feet across the stone floor to their parent's side, claws clacking in excitement.

The ambassador paused their elaborate greeting dance to chitter at the child. I did not speak Kurutan, but a scolding tone needed no translation. The child leaned against their parent and chirped softly in reply. N'vors caressed the little one's head and resumed their dance. The other ambassadors bobbed their heads in acknowledgement of their colleague's greeting.

Damn it to all the hells. I lowered my weapon.

The poison gas dart I had prepared was deadly only to Kurutans. The gas would not harm the other delegates, which was essential to my mission. It would, however, kill the ambassador's child if they inhaled it.

My intel had said nothing about the ambassador bringing their child to the negotiations. My employer's intel was never wrong. Too many lives—mine included—depended on its veracity. The Silent Guard could not afford to lose one of its best and most experienced assassins because of poorly vetted information.

These few minutes in the embassy's foyer would be my only opportunity to dispatch N'vors before the delegates moved to the embassy's ultra-secure meeting room. My brief stated the ambassador must die before they began negotiating for export rights. My life depended on fulfilling my mission. The Guard demanded extortionate prices from its clients in return for a guarantee of success. That guarantee only held up if there were no failures.

I had received my latest update on N'vors's movements only an hour earlier when the ambassador was already on their way to the embassy. The Guard *must* have known about the child.

Unlike many less scrupulous guilds of assassins, the Guard prided itself on its precise kills. While their clients might not care about collateral damage, the Guard's commandants did. Collateral damage drew the attention and ire of planetary leaders, the Central Alliance Defense, and various federations and interplanetary coalitions. Neat, surgical, *quiet* kills were not just the Guard's point of pride—they were a necessity for its ongoing existence, while other, more careless organizations came and went.

I could count the number of times in the past five years my hearts had raced before or during a mission on one tentacle. Twenty standard years of training, conditioning, and service in the Guard had rendered me all but indifferent to danger and death, even my own.

But when the ambassador's child rested their head against their parent and sighed in contentment, my heartsbeats—normally so steady and even during a mission—pounded in my ears. My vision turned silver around the edges, and my glowing eyes reflected in the metal duct.

I did not kill children. Not even if it would mean my own life were forfeit. Not even on my last mission prior to my retirement.

Most of my fellow Guard assassins would not have hesitated to pull the trigger. And perhaps I would have had a difficult time explaining why after all the death I had dealt over the past twenty years I could not bring myself to end a single child's life.

The child's happy sounds and the way their wide eyes peered worshipfully at their parent had reached perhaps the last, tiny part of my primary heart that had not turned to stone.

On the other hand, if I left N'vors and their child alive, made it out of the embassy, and fled, the Guard would hunt me across the galaxy. They would bring me to their headquarters and make a spectacle of my death. All Guard assassins would be called in to witness the consequences of failing to complete a mission and trying to leave the Guard before a contract term ended. No greater suffering or horror existed in Alliance space.

I might put little value on my life, but I did not want that kind of death. I did not want my pain to be an exhibition. I had spent my life in service to the Guard; I would be damned if my death would be used to keep my brethren in line.

Also, the sight of this little Kurutan family filled my belly with bitterness. The genetic manipulations on my homeworld of Fortusia had given me extra speed, senses, and strength, along with my gills and tentacles, but they had also eliminated the dangerous and potentially costly biological instinct to seek and find a partner. I had been created to kill, not to love or treasure a mate. I would never know that kind of belonging. My life, if I reached my retirement and none of the ghosts or enemies of my past found and killed me, would be a solitary one.

But a lonely life would still be a good life, one I had wanted since my youngest days. Freedom was a dream for someone created to serve in the Guard. Few assassins survived the dangers of their twenty-year enlistments to reach retirement. I had not dared to even hope to reach mine until just this year.

I had not fought so hard for so long to reach this moment to have the only dreams I allowed myself to chase ripped away by one child and my own soft hearts.

I raised my weapon again and took aim. If I timed my shot perfectly, I might be able to get the dart to pierce the back of N'vors's throat. The gas would kill in moments. Embassy security would likely get the child and other delegates to safety. The child might not die from the poison—

—But they would see their parent die. If I recalled correctly, a Kurutan child was not likely to survive without its parent, especially if they witnessed the death.

The decision was impossible, but that did not prevent me from having to face it.

My human hand tightened its grip on my weapon and my index finger rested lightly on the trigger. The mechanism was so precise that less than three pounds of pressure activated the dartgun.

Time slowed.

N'vors finished their dance of greeting, bowed deeply, and opened their mouth to speak. I took aim at the soft pink inside of their throat.

In my peripheral vision, I caught a flash of movement from the doorway at the other end of the foyer that led to the landing platform and the busy street beyond.

The energy field guarding the opening flickered and died. Two black spheres flew into the embassy's foyer and landed on the stone floor about a meter apart. The embassy guards shouted the Bordian word for *bomb* and dove for cover, but the enormous lobby offered few places to hide.

Fear and adrenaline washed through me, turning me cold before my training kicked in. I dropped my weapon, scrambled back from the grate, and tapped my wrist cuff to activate my personal shock-absorbing field.

The shockwave rolled through the building with a deafening roar and a rush of crackling blue lightning. The embassy shook violently and plunged into darkness as the foyer collapsed. My lungs filled with smoke and dust. The ringing in my sensitive ears drowned out all other sounds.

Around me, the air duct sagged and buckled as the building rumbled.

A single thought cut through my disorientation: *This is how I die: alone, unknown, buried under megatons of rubble on a planet light-years from my homeworld.*

I expected grief or bitterness to overwhelm me. Instead, my gut felt hollow, as if I had nothing to lose and therefore nothing to regret. Nothing to fight for.

Nothing to leave behind, and no one who would mourn.

The hollowness gave way to rage, and my rage propelled me toward the metal grate as the duct crumpled under the collapsing weight of the building. If I were to die today, I would at least be on my feet.

I deactivated my forcefield cocoon and pulled up the collar of my coveralls to cover my nose and mouth. I also breathed through my gills, allowing them to filter out the smoke and dust particles that clogged my airways and threatened to reduce me to uncontrollable coughing.

A glance behind me confirmed the duct had collapsed in the direction of my initial entry. My only escape would be through the foyer—or what remained of it.

As my hearing returned, the first—and only—sound I heard other than low rumbles of falling stone was a high, thin wail.

The explosion had reduced the embassy's foyer to rubble. The ceiling had collapsed, revealing what appeared to be the roof of the building five stories above. The doorway that led to the landing platform had collapsed as well, but my enhanced eyesight made out a sliver of daylight that offered what might be my only hope of escape. Assuming, of course, I could get through it and disappear before emergency crews arrived.

From the rubble, the thin wail faded to a weak, warbling cry that compelled me to *move*. I gripped the grate with my tentacles, twisted, and pulled. The grate tore away with the sound of shearing metal and broken bolts.

I tossed it behind me deeper into the vent and clambered through the opening, careful not to cut myself on the sharp edges. I did not want to leave any trace of myself at this scene of carnage.

Regardless of my own feelings on this disaster, my training demanded I take note of every detail for my report. At a glance, I determined the guards and delegates were all dead, including Ambassador N'vors. Who had chosen to end these trade negotiations before they began in the messiest, most cold-blooded way possible, I did not know. The Guard was not the culprit—of that much I was certain. Equally certain was the fact others besides the Guard's client, whoever that was, had reason to prevent a trade deal. The Guard would conduct their own investigation using operatives trained for that role. My job now was to leave immediately and report back to my superiors.

My final Guard assignment had not ended in the way I had intended, but it *had* ended. The daylight at the far end of the foyer beckoned, offering escape and a path forward to the retirement I had yearned for.

Another wordless, fearful wail came from under N'vors's bloody corpse. In an ultimate loving sacrifice, the ambassador had covered their child with their own body and died protecting them from the blast. I was in no way prepared for the force of anger and grief that rose within me at that realization.

"*La La,*" the child cried. "*La La? La La, La La!*"

A child's plea was a universally understood sound.

My enhanced hearing caught the distant howl of emergency sirens. My window of time to escape without being questioned was dwindling quickly. I let out a hiss. The building rumbled as something else collapsed. Maybe an exterior wall nearby.

A small pincher on a long, thin arm appeared from under N'vors's body, clacking helplessly. "*La La!*" the child wailed.

What was my survival worth if I left the child to die?

With a grunt of effort, I hefted N'vors's massive body with my human hands and arms just enough to scoop the child up in my tentacles, covering their eyes so they could not see their parent's body. Then I dropped the ambassador's corpse back on the rubble and clambered over fallen stone toward the sliver of daylight.

I had never held any child, but I had no time to process the emotions of the moment. N'vors's child fought my grip with surprising strength and pinched my tentacle that covered their eyes hard enough to draw blood. Cursing, I climbed the pile of rubble and reached the fresh, salty air that blew in through the opening.

Several pairs of webbed hands appeared and voices called out in alarm: a small group of Bordian citizens trying to help survivors. Not emergency services or embassy guards, though those would surely arrive within moments. Generally speaking, Bordians were a kind people, to a fault. No doubt only the likelihood of another collapse kept them from rushing en masse into the building.

With N'vors's body now safely out of sight, I uncovered the child's wide, wild eyes. Through their bright blue tears, they stared up at me in fear and wonder. And thank all the gods above and below, they finally released my bloody tentacle from their pinchers.

"*La ka na?*" the child asked, their voice trembling.

I had no idea what the child asked—I heard only their hopeful tone. For that reason alone, I nodded.

The child's silent blue tears spilled over and became sobs.

The volume of voices outside the opening increased and the half-dozen webbed hands moved frantically. The Bordians must have heard the child crying. I thrust the child into their waiting hands.

"*La ka na!*" the child wailed, reaching toward me.

My hearts lurched. The building rumbled once more. The rescuers retreated with their young charge, leaving me alone.

As the child's wails faded into the distance, I pulled a cap from the pocket of the maintenance uniform I had donned as my cover and put it on to hide my white hair. I changed the color of my tentacles to match my gray coveralls and make them less noticeable. Hopefully, the chaos outside would allow me to slip unnoticed through the onlookers and make my way to a chartered ship bound for Guard Headquarters on Fortusia.

Once I filed my reports, I would be free.

I slipped through the opening in the rubble and into the shadows, moving slowly until I reached the edge of the crowd. And then I walked away, heading to the closest port—

—And my future, whatever it might hold.

CHAPTER 1

CALLA

ONE OF THESE DAYS, A DEEP SPACE RAIDER WOULD BE THE DEATH of me.

"But not today, you soulless bastards," I said aloud over the reassuring hum of my long-range fighter's single remaining engine. "Not today."

At least I'd kept both myself and my ship in one piece, despite the raiders' best efforts to blow me to atoms. I might be limping back to Outpost 60 on less than half power, with no comms, minimal shields and weapons, and life support hanging on by few frayed wires, but I was in better shape than the three raiders who'd attacked me. They were, I assumed, currently in the presence of whatever gods they worshiped, explaining how one lone human pilot managed to kill all three of them and live to toast their deaths.

I raised my flask of moonshine once more to their memory,

took a swig, coughed, and screwed the cap back on so I didn't drink too much. Need to stay sober enough to get myself back to base. One of my squadron mates came from a long line of Probytian moonshiners. She knew how to turn a few ingredients into liquid fire that could strip the coating off my fighter's hull and had a kick like a Gandarian mule ox.

With a groan, I rolled my stiff neck, returned the flask to its hiding place under my seat, and tried to let the adrenaline rush seep away. Even for a pilot with more than a hundred missions under her belt, that was a tall order after a prolonged battle.

Not that long ago, routine patrols along this stretch of frontier rarely turned out so exciting or potentially deadly. Local raider squads had recently instituted a bounty system for killing Defense pilots and destroying or capturing their ships. The bloodthirsty attacks had turned our quiet zone into a shooting gallery. To pilots in our squadron, the bounty system meant patrols should consist of two ships instead of the customary single pilot per mission, but the Alliance Defense brass had yet to approve that measure. They reacted slower than a Foridian slug these days.

And since Epsilon Squad Captain Proos wouldn't take a shit without orders from one of the Alliance Defense admirals, I'd had no backup when these raiders showed up. I planned to get in his face about it the minute I got back to Outpost 60.

"Pompous little green asshole," I muttered, and pictured my fist making contact with the center of Proos's eminently punchable face.

Even for a Raxian, Proos was particularly insufferable. The fact he'd managed to achieve Squad Captain rank despite his utter lack of courage or initiative made me think he had some kind of blackmail material against one or more of the admirals. I would have put money on it. No other explanation made sense. Now his refusal to double up patrols in the wake of the raiders' bounties had damn near gotten me blown to bits.

A quick check of my navigation system revealed I was approaching the planet Jakora. While the planet wasn't part of the Galactic Alliance, its neutrality and location near the edge of Alliance space allowed for pilots of various allegiances to land for shore leave and maintenance as long as they followed the planetary laws.

Hmm...I *could* at least get my comms, shields, and weapons systems repaired and send a report to Captain Proos about the attack. I didn't like the idea of having neither defense nor offense and no way to call for help if I ran into another raider on the way back. Those mangy sons of bogworms had gotten brazen and turned up even in strong Alliance systems.

Come to think of it, I had some leave saved up. I recalled a particularly nice resort near the Jakoran port where the drinks flowed freely, the lavender ocean offered safe swimming day and night, and pilots of all sexes and genders could easily find bedmates to ease the stress and loneliness of the job. After all, Captain Proos could hardly complain about the delay if my ship couldn't make it all the way to Outpost 60 on one engine. All I'd have to do was bribe a mechanic to report my ship as not space-worthy and claim a backlog would delay repairs, and I'd be free to enjoy some well-earned rest.

Decision made, I slowed to near-planet cruising speed and prepared to enter Jakora's thick atmosphere.

The universe, of course, had no intention of letting me off that easy today.

An impact sent my ship careening off course and spinning away from the planet. Alarms blared and red lights activated. Icy shards of terror ripped through me from fingertips to toes.

My training kicked in, shoving my fear aside as I fought to regain control of my ship using the manual control joysticks. Through the cockpit's windows, I caught whirling glimpses of stars and Jakora's purple-white atmosphere through a shower of sparking chunks of debris I recognized as parts of my ship. Half of my starboard wing had sheared off. I must have clipped something floating in orbit around the planet.

And then my ship's main power flickered and died, leaving me in darkness and silence.

"No," I said, my chest tight with horror. "No, no, *no*."

No one answered my pleas. I'd learned long ago that space had no mercy—not for me, and not for anyone else.

My ship spiraled away from Jakora and veered directly toward one of the planet's many moons. Without navigation, I had no idea which one. Not that it mattered, I supposed, other than it would likely be my unmarked grave.

"Fuck that," I stated, just to hear something other than the ominous silence of my cockpit. "I'm not dying today."

Far from a lifeless sphere of rock, this moon appeared to be almost entirely purple ocean surrounding a few dark, irregularly shaped masses of land. I glimpsed enormous swirls of thick clouds that indicated multiple massive hurricanes all happening at the same time. The moon wasn't nearly as hospitable as the planet it orbited, that was for damn sure. Jakora rarely experienced hurricanes.

Still, I'd still take a hurricane-riddled ocean moon over barren rock and no atmosphere any day.

With the manual control joysticks, I fought like hells to gain some control of the ship's flight, but even my emergency power system had apparently taken severe damage and left the joysticks next to useless. I could do little to slow the out-of-control spin or manage my descent.

All too soon, my ship reached the moon's gravitational pull and began its fall toward the surface with a sickening lurch. Gravity—never around when I needed it, and always showing up when I didn't.

The ship bounced, shook, and screamed its way through the atmosphere. I clung to my manual controls with a white-knuckled grip, for all the good it would do if my battered ship broke apart, and held my breath until I made it through to open air.

Wind and rain buffeted my ship as I fell. Far below, on land, I could just make out small clusters of lights sparkling in the night. So this moon was at least sparsely populated.

Nausea twisted my insides, but hope sparked in my chest. If I could level off my trajectory and manage to end up on land instead of the middle of the damn ocean, I had a chance to survive. A very slim chance, but a chance.

My life had been nothing but a series of slim chances. I supposed I shouldn't have expected anything different today.

"Stay in one piece, baby," I coaxed through gritted teeth, my palms sweaty on my controls. I even fired up my landing damper in an attempt to slow my fall, but it had only minimal power and couldn't do much this far off the ground. "Just get me down alive—that's all I ask. Please get me down alive."

The ship—what was left of it—groaned and shook. I couldn't tell if that was just the strain of the descent or a reply to my plea. In any case, the moon's surface continued to approach all too quickly.

Fate had offered me one favor, at least: I seemed to be hurtling toward relatively shallow water just off the coast of a large land mass dotted with lights. Some of the impact might transfer to the water, increasing the possibility I'd survive. I'd take all the odds I could get at this point.

Some part of me was screaming in terror, but all my Alliance training—and really, all the combat training I'd received since the age of three—allowed me to keep that fear at bay and think clearly, even as I faced the grim reality and sickening feeling of plunging from the moon's upper atmosphere all the way to its surface.

I'd faced many opponents in the arena, and many more since I'd become a pilot. I went into this battle with the same attitude as if I were facing any other adversary: you're not taking me out. If it's going to have to be one of us that goes, it's not going to be me.

I squared my shoulders, tightened the harness that held me in my pilot's seat, and glared out the front window of my fighter. Fuck you, pretty purple ocean moon, and whatever the hells I hit up in space. Lieutenant Calla Wren wouldn't go down that easily.

Miraculously, some of the ship's main power flickered on about five hundred meters from the surface. I yanked on my manual control joysticks and used my landing damper to almost level off and slow my descent. With the wind and rain, only one functional wing, and a sparking instrument panel, I didn't have much control over the ship's trajectory, but I did my best to aim for that shallow water, a safe distance from a small cluster of lights. No sense taking out one of the moon's few settlements with my crash landing.

My heartbeat thundered in my ears. What were my chances of survival if I hit water at this speed? One in ten? One in a hundred? Not good enough to even be a sucker's bet.

My front window showed nothing but dark water now. "Come on, come on." I pulled on the manual controls again. The damaged landing damper whined and sputtered, straining to soften the impact. That was all I could do to give myself a chance to survive.

Everything grew hazy as my calm and training gave way to fear. An overwhelming sense of helplessness turned my gasps fast and shallow.

Fighting against adrenaline and instinctive hyperventilation, I forced myself to breathe more slowly and deeply so I didn't lose consciousness. I *wasn't* helpless—I was still fighting. I would fight until the very end. My will had been forged in the arenas of Ganai, and I didn't break for anyone or anything.

If I were to die today, I'd at least do it sitting upright in my pilot's seat, facing forward with my eyes open.

And with that, peace and calm settled over me like a mantle.

As the water rushed up to meet my ship, I chanted my flight instructor's mantra: "Land like a bird, not a rock. Land like a bird, not a rock. Land like a—"

Unfortunately, the ship struck the surface of the water very much like a rock. Then all was darkness and silence.

CHAPTER 2

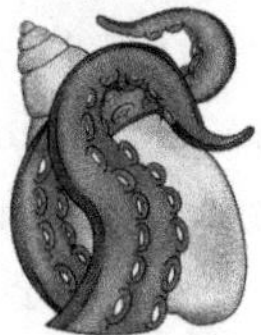

VOS

On the surface, the water frothed and churned, tossed by the winds and rain of a *nuoia*—the locals' term for a strong storm not as large or powerful as a hurricane.

But here in the ocean's dark, purple depths, I drifted in contented silence.

The swift, deep currents carried me parallel to the shore. Even in my relaxed state I had to be mindful of how far I journeyed along the sea floor before I turned and swam back against the current toward the inlet that was my habitual spot to enter the sea.

All too often, the more troubled my thoughts, the further I ended up traveling before I noticed the distance I had covered. Tonight, I had drifted farther than was safe. The ambassador's child had reappeared in my dreams lately, their endless calls of *"La ka na!"* stealing the comfort of sleep.

When I roused myself from my meditative state and opened my eyes, I found myself less than half a kilometer from the camp set up by a group of about a dozen interplanetary raiders.

The bastards had cut down trees to build their base, from which they launched their half-dozen ships that went on day- or week-long runs attacking ships passing through the area. As if that were not bad enough, they had placed mines in the sea only meters from where I now floated. I hated them for that, and a thousand other reasons. The sea was my solace, but they had transformed its beauty into a deadly trap.

I would have killed them all if I did not think it would attract too much attention from their brethren throughout the sector. Solitude and anonymity were more valuable to me than anything—even ridding this otherwise quiet area of murderous raiders and their deadly traps.

So, once again I hissed in the direction of the mines, then slowly turned and rose from near the sea floor to midway to the surface for the journey back to the inlet. My tentacles swirled around me, stretching and preparing for the long swim.

BOOM.

The force of an impact on the surface rolled through the water. I scarcely had time to realize what had happened before it reached me. Ears ringing, vision reduced to gray mist, and limbs heavy as lead, I sank to the ocean floor. I did not lose consciousness, but disorientation left me dazed and lying in the sand.

The first coherent thought that drifted through my cottony brain was, *Had I been closer to the surface, I might have been killed.*

The realization of how close I had come to death just now barely elicited an emotional or physiological response—much as my earlier proximity to the raiders' deadly sea mines had not. The Guard's indoctrination, or my own apathy about my life? Could I even distinguish between the two?

Lingering discomfort and some residual dizziness aside, I seemed uninjured. My need to monitor my environment and identify potential threats compelled me to find out what had crashed. My tentacles stirred, undulated to relieve their aches, and propelled me from the ocean floor to the surface.

Given my proximity to the raider camp, I suspected the object was one of their ships. But when my head rose above the water's surface just enough to see the debris, I found I had been wrong.

The ship was unmistakably an Alliance Defense long-range fighter, or what was left of it.

The nose and one triangular wing of the fighter had crumpled on impact, tearing open the cockpit. The starboard wing was gone entirely, as was most of the tail section. The damage might have occurred during the ship's passage through the atmosphere, or in the attack that had left telltale scorch marks on both sides of the fighter's hull. The once-proud fighter—a Delta Seven model, if I was not mistaken—had been reduced nearly to scrap metal, save perhaps some of its inner workings.

My tentacles swirled in irritation. Of all the oceans in the galaxy, this fighter had chosen to crash into mine.

If the pilot had managed to send a distress call before crashing, or the ship had an automatic emergency beacon, the Alliance would send a rescue team and investigators to retrieve the pilot's remains and the wreck.

I had chosen Iosa as my home for the same reason the small group of raiders created a base here: the moon attracted so little notice, even as a satellite of a popular planet like Jakora. Its violent weather patterns ensured it had no risk of becoming a tourist destination and its sparse population density allowed for solitude.

As the site of a Defense fighter crash, however, Iosa would be of definite interest to the Alliance Defense. Highly motivated to find out what had caused this crash, they would investigate the area and immediately find the raider camp. If they arrested the raiders and destroyed their ships, I would find that agreeable.

My homestead was far enough away that I might avoid their notice. My best hope would be to retreat to my home and keep my head down until the inevitable investigation ended and the Alliance Defense departed with their wrecked ship and dead pilot.

The sound of engines and shouts drew my attention to two boats approaching the wrecked fighter from the direction of the raider camp. During daytime I would have slipped beneath the surface and disappeared. In the dark and rain, I doubted they would be able to see me with only the top of my head and eyes above the surface of the water.

The raiders approached, navigating through their minefield to the wreckage. The fighter would likely sink soon. At the moment it remained afloat, tossed roughly by the waves. The cockpit had been badly damaged and broken open. If that had happened in space or in the atmosphere, the pilot would certainly be dead. If it occurred on impact, though, they might have survived. Not likely, but possible.

The raiders would want to salvage what they could from the wrecked ship and disable any distress beacons. Indeed, one of them—an enormous red-and-black Atolani male, wearing leather from collar to boots and sporting large gold rings on his horns—stood at the front of the lead boat, holding a scanner probably designed to detect signals.

The Atolani let out a shout, tossed the device into the boat, and pointed at the vessel. It sounded like he had not detected any signals. This was welcome news to me as well.

Boarding wave-tossed debris from small boats was no easy feat, but the raiders managed to throw hooks on long ropes and tether their vessels to the wreck. In moments, three of them had clambered onto the fighter. The smallest of the group jumped immediately into the cockpit.

I was about to leave them to their salvage operation when more shouts rang out. The urgency in their voices drew me closer—enough to see clearly, even in the rain and dark, that they were struggling to lift something out of the cockpit.

It was the limp, bloody body of an unmistakably human female pilot.

One of the blue-skinned raiders on the fighter shouted a word to the Atolani in the boat, who might have been their leader. The language was Ymarian. I knew only a little Ymarian, but I recognized the word the raider had shouted. The word meant *alive*.

The pilot had survived the crash—and now she and her ship were in the hands of raiders. At best, the raiders would try to keep her alive and ransom her. At worst...well, she would certainly wish to be dead.

Like the crash, her fate would not be my concern if it were not for the probability it would draw attention to this quiet corner of Iosa.

The raiders shouted back and forth in Ymarian, debating how to get the badly injured pilot to one of the boats. Finally, the Atolani leader called out a command. Two of the Ymarians aboard the fighter tossed the pilot's limp body across three meters of water and into the waiting arms of the Atolani—who promptly dropped her on the boat's metal deck and shoved her out of his way with his foot.

Their casual cruelty and callousness toward a defenseless person set my sharp teeth on edge. My human hands clenched into fists and my eyes glowed. My tentacles trembled with their own anger. I had not felt such visceral fury in...years? Not in recent memory, for certain. Even the sight of the raiders' sea mines spoiling the beautiful ocean depths had not generated this much rage.

After more shouting, the Ymarian raiders on the fighter unhooked the rope that tethered the Atolani's boat to the wreck. The Atolani reeled up the line, shouted one last command to the other boat, and turned his vessel around, heading for the shore and the camp with the pilot. The raiders left on the fighter set to work stripping what they could and tossing the salvaged parts to the three remaining raiders in the boat.

I should swim back to the inlet and return home. The fighter and its pilot were not my responsibility, and I preferred not to draw any notice to myself.

But by all the gods above and below, I hated these raiders. I did not want them to benefit from the crash. If I could sink the fighter—or even better, destroy it using one of the raiders' own mines—they would end up with nothing. If I could do so without leaving clues as to who was responsible, I should take the pilot from them as well and bring her to the closest hospital. No one needed to know who her benefactor had been.

When the Atolani's boat was well out of sight, I swam underwater to the wreck. I surfaced next to the fighter on the opposite side from the raiders' boat and out of sight of the Ymarians working to extract usable items.

Just as I began formulating a plan to bring one of the raiders' mines to the surface to dispatch the fighter, the wind changed direction. Through the rain, I caught a scent that blanked my mind and made me freeze in place.

The smell was unmistakably human blood, but it was a universe more than that.

The scent was of home, hearth, and safety. I had never had any of those things, but I knew this scent in my soul.

While my human brain struggled to grapple with this feeling, all four of my tentacles, moving instinctively and entirely of their own accord, tried to forcibly haul me up the side of the freighter toward the cockpit—the source of that entrancing scent. Each tentacle had its own small brain that controlled it without conscious commands from my central humanoid brain.

I roused myself enough to pull back into the sea before the Ymarian raiders spotted me, but my tentacles would not relinquish their grip on the fighter's crumpled hull.

My body sang of comfort and belonging.

My mate was here.

No, I had no mate. *Could not* have one. A member of the Silent Guard could not have distractions. Sex, yes. Pleasure, yes. But no mate…or so I had been told. So I had believed until this very moment. But with every cell in my body, I *knew* more surely than I had known anything in my life that my mate had been in this fighter.

A chill swept through me, and right behind it a rush of warmth that both terrified and thrilled me all the way to my core.

And behind it came *rage*—white-hot, all-consuming rage.

My mate was bleeding and terribly hurt. Possibly dying. And the raiders had yanked her unconscious and vulnerable from her pilot's seat, flung her carelessly over a stormy sea, and tossed her onto the hard deck of a boat like trash while they carefully handled the parts they pulled from her fighter. My fury was so great my body trembled and my vision tunneled, turning dark red around the edges.

As long as the fighter remained afloat, the Ymarians would stay to fill their boat before heading for their camp with the first load of plunder. The other boat would be halfway to shore. Once my mate was within the camp itself, extracting her would be far more difficult.

Continue with my plan to sink the fighter and kill those left behind, or head straight for the Atolani's boat?

The decision was so easy and instinctive it was not a decision at all.

Quivering in fury and anticipation of the fight to come, my tentacles relinquished their grip on the fighter's hull. I plunged into the water and took off in pursuit of my mate and her captors.

CHAPTER 3

CALLA

My entire existence was pain. The sheer magnitude of its iron grip on every muscle and bone rendered me incoherent.

Rough voices ebbed and flowed through my delirium, the words indistinct. I tasted salt water and blood and smelled rusted metal.

My leaden body slid helplessly around on a smooth surface, hitting hard corners and what might be several pairs of legs and heavy boots. Sizzles of agony through the fog told me I had many broken bones.

My stomach roiled and lurched as if I were subject to violent yawing and up-and-down movement. Could I be in a boat? I dimly recalled aiming for a crash-landing in water, but had no memory of the actual impact or anything after.

Normally choppy water wouldn't have affected me much, if at all; a fighter pilot's training and years of flying tended to eliminate all forms of motion sickness. But these waves were enormous—to the point the boat repeatedly surged atop waves and then plunged meters through the air before hitting the water's surface. I might have vomited from the endless rise and fall if my body could have organized its inner workings well enough to regurgitate anything.

I slipped away into soft darkness again.

Some blurry time later, I woke to calmer seas, the unmistakable sensation of heavy rain, and voices around me speaking Ymarian. One loud male voice didn't sound Ymarian, though. Whoever he was, he bellowed orders like he was in charge.

Agony made it difficult to think, but this time I stayed conscious instead of immediately passing out again. My foggy brain suggested these people had rescued me from my ship in what felt like a small boat. Maybe they were taking me to shore, to a hospital?

My eyelids felt welded shut and I couldn't make any sound but a moan, but I managed to slide my hand across the deck toward the voice of the man who might be the leader. If they knew I was conscious, they might offer me water to drink, or something to dull my pain—

A heavy boot came down on my hand, crushing it to the deck.

Even as half-numb, half-conscious, and maybe half-dead as I was, this new, piercing agony ripped a wail from me that didn't sound human. I tried to pull my hand away, but the boot ground my fingers against the corrugated metal deck. I gagged in pain. Laughter erupted around me, barely audible over the ringing in my ears.

And then one of them screamed.

The scream turned into a gurgle, and then it cut off abruptly. A couple of wet, fleshy *thuds* on the boat's deck made me flinch. Warm liquid splattered across my face.

Weapons fire, shouts, and more gurgley screams filled the air. The foot that had crushed my hand suddenly moved, freeing me. Boots pounded the deck and plasma bolts burned into the metal around me.

A sudden, startlingly clear thought cut through the fog: *Damn it to all the hells, I didn't survive a crash just to die thanks to a stray shot from a plasma gun.*

Less than a minute after that first scream, the number of voices around me had dwindled rapidly, but the fighting continued. In the chaos, a heavy boot brushed past my head and someone stepped on my leg. I moaned.

Gentle hands pushed me away from the fighting and into a small, enclosed space. Maybe a nook under a long bench seat. The rain no longer pelted my face, but I lay in a pool of seawater. The wild weapons fire might have punched holes through the bottom of the boat.

If the boat sank, there was no way I could swim to shore with broken limbs. I'd sink like a stone.

My eyelids fluttered open.

A blurry, shadowy figure with several long tentacles ripped a Ymarian in half. Viscera splattered the interior of the boat, which was already covered in blood and body parts.

The creature flung the Ymarian's remains over the side. In the dark and rain, little of his body was visible except human-like arms and legs and a pair of glowing silvery-blue eyes.

Someone grabbed my arm and hauled me out from under the seat. A fresh wave of agony made my vision go hazy.

I faded in and out, only marginally aware that I dangled in the grip of an enormous, snarling, red-skinned Atolani male clad in a leather vest and pants. He held me up with one arm wrapped under my arms, dragging me toward the boat's stern as he fired at the creature who'd apparently killed everyone else on the boat.

The creature evaded each bolt of plasma fire, moving faster than I could track in my dazed, pain-addled state. What the hells was he?

With what sounded like a curse in his native language, the Atolani braced himself with his feet wide apart as the boat rocked. He shoved the glowing barrel of his plasma gun against my temple. Searing pain. I moaned.

At the other end of the boat, the creature went still.

A bolt of lightning revealed that we were surrounded by scattered body parts, but not enough to account for the number of voices I'd heard. Most of the remains must have been washed or tossed overboard. The head of a Ymarian lay at my feet, their three lifeless eyes fixed and dull and expression frozen in horror.

The flash of light also allowed me a glimpse of a male humanoid body with four long tentacles, glowing eyes, long white hair, and dark purple skin that almost blended in with the night except for its iridescent sheen. Blood in various colors covered every part of him I could see. He didn't appear to be wearing any clothing, but his coiled tentacles hid everything below his waist. When the lightning faded, only his eyes remained visible, shining in the dark.

"Fuck off, or she dies," the Atolani snarled at the creature in Alliance Standard.

That voice had barked orders earlier. Maybe he was the asshole who'd stepped on my hand.

The sea creature hissed and lowered his human arms, as if my life mattered to him. But why would it? He'd ripped everyone else in the boat to pieces.

Whose side was I on here? The Atolani who'd rescued me from my wrecked ship but found my pain amusing? Or the tentacled sea creature who'd just killed a half-dozen men or more, apparently for the hells of it?

Neither, I decided. I was on *my* side. Maybe they'd kill each other. Then I'd try to pilot this leaky boat to shore. At least I'd have a chance to rescue myself instead of being some Atolani's toy or a sea creature's dinner.

With no weapons and no ability to fight, I did the only thing I could: I bit the Atolani's bare forearm with all my might. With a bellow, he ripped his arm out of my mouth. I spat out nasty dark blood and a gobbet of flesh.

I caught a flash of movement out of the corner of my eye just before a body made of what felt like solid muscle crashed into us. The Atolani lost his grip on me and fired wildly as he stumbled. The bolt of plasma singed my hair and missed my head by centimeters.

The sea creature's fist punched straight through the Atolani's chest and ribcage with a thick, meaty crunch. More blood sprayed across my face. Oh, gods. My stomach heaved, and that agony made me start to fade out again.

The sea creature's tentacles wrapped around me with surprising gentleness, drawing me away as his hand withdrew from the Atolani's chest. The Atolani went down hard on the deck, convulsing and spitting blood in his death throes. I would have kicked him if I could.

I fought to stay conscious. Sleep meant I'd no longer hurt so much, but I wouldn't surrender to this creature or be his plaything or prey. The gentleness of his tentacles around me meant nothing. I'd seen these same appendages rend bodies into pieces. His fist had punched straight through a man's chest. The fact the Atolani might have deserved his fate didn't make it any less monstrous.

The rest of the creature's tentacles swept me up and cradled me against a surprisingly warm chest. Not wanting to be torn apart or eaten, I fought his grip as best I could.

The lack of light and my own hazy vision made it difficult to see well. Up close, the creature appeared almost human, but with purple shimmery skin. His eyes gleamed soft and silvery, like starlight.

A humanoid body and four very octopus-like tentacles. He might be Fortusian, but who the hells knew. Out here on the edge of Alliance space, anything was possible. The universe was vast and we knew only the tiniest fraction of the beings who lived within it.

I would have given anything to have a blade or gun, or even for one of his tentacles to be within biting distance. Either on purpose or not, he kept them out of reach of my teeth. I had nothing to threaten him with but my words.

"Let me go," I said, or tried to say. The words came out slurred. I doubted he'd understood even if he spoke Alliance Standard. At least I'd managed to sound threatening. I tried again. "Let me go, or I'll kill you."

His eyes darkened. A strange kind of ripple passed through his tentacles. I tensed, expecting to be crushed or torn apart. Instead, he made a low, sweet sound.

Inexplicably, my body relaxed, as if my insides had turned to warm honey. My fury, pain, mistrust, and fear all but evaporated. When my head started to fall back, his tentacle supported my neck and nudged my head so it rested against his chest. The intimacy of the way he cradled me and my helplessness made me angry, but even that emotion felt muted, as if he'd emitted some kind of relaxing pheromones. Like a predator trying to subdue its prey.

So help me, I had not survived all the horrors of my life to be eaten by a sea monster, no matter how beautiful he was.

Beautiful? Where the hells did that word come from? He wasn't beautiful. He was death incarnate.

Through the hard muscles of his chest, I heard three distinct heartbeats: one in the center and then two right after.

Lub-dub. Lub-dub-dub.

Lub-dub. Lub-dub-dub.

The rhythm soothed me almost as much as that strange coo, and that made me angry too. He'd slaughtered a half-dozen men in less than three minutes and his heart rate wasn't even elevated.

"Let me go," I repeated. This time my voice was pained but clear.

"Raiders," he said in Alliance Standard, his voice rough.

I followed his gaze to the leather-clad Atolani, who'd finally gurgled one last time and gone still. Raiders, here on one of Jakora's moons? No way they'd set up a base anywhere near a popular tourist destination. These men were likely just settlers, and my new captor had killed them all in what seemed like cold blood.

But before I could accuse him of lying, his glowing gaze met mine. "Deep breath," he commanded me.

His imperious tone immediately set my teeth on edge. The only person I took orders from besides myself was Squad Captain Proos, and that was only because I *had* to. This monster, whoever the hells he was, didn't get to order me around.

"No fucking way," I ground out. If only my voice wasn't so full of pain. "Let me go. You're not taking me anywhere."

He'd slaughtered a half-dozen people without batting an eyelash, but he flinched at my words or tone, or both.

Lightning fast, his human hand covered my mouth and pinched my nose. His tentacles encircled me completely, pressing me tightly to his body so I couldn't move.

And then he dove out of the boat and plunged us headfirst into the roiling sea.

CHAPTER 4

VOS

THE MOMENT WE HIT THE WATER'S SURFACE, MY MATE LOST consciousness again, probably from pain.

My hearts ached at her suffering, but perhaps this was a blessing in disguise. Unconscious, she could not fight my attempts to care for her—or give me looks of hatred that cut me to the bone more deeply than any blade. In all my years, I had never felt such hurt.

I longed to swim in the deep with her, but unlike me, she did not have gills and could not breathe in the sea. I surfaced again immediately, holding her head above the water with my human arms.

Even almost drunk on her scent and the feeling of her body in my arms, I knew I must cover my tracks.

My tentacles found a damaged section of the boat and ripped the rusted metal apart. The boat, along with the bloody pieces of the raiders' bodies, disappeared into the inky depths. The creatures of the deep would consume the body parts quickly, leaving no trace of what I had done. As for the torn remains of the boat, the sea contained many large and dangerous predators. They rarely ventured this close to shore, but they would be the likely suspects, not I.

Trembling with fatigue and happiness in equal measures, my tentacles encircled my mate, drinking in her taste and scent through every sensory cell. Her intoxicating, rich, and unique perfume had drawn me to her from the moment I had first caught its traces in the cockpit of her fighter. Its soft notes reminded me of desserts I had enjoyed years ago on faraway planets, but she was no mere sweet. Her scent, her body, her voice, her ferocity when she bit the Atolani and enabled me to get her away from him—everything about her was a wonder.

My desire to take her to the safety of my homestead was nearly all-consuming, but I stole a few rain-soaked moments to float on the ocean's surface, reveling in the feeling of my mate in my arms.

Even unconscious, she flinched in obvious discomfort. Purely on instinct, I let out that strange coo again. She relaxed against me with a sigh.

I had never made that sound before in all my years, and I had made it without conscious thought. I could comfort her and ease her pain and fear with my own voice. She must be my mate. No other explanation made sense.

Gently, I brushed her wet hair from her face so I could see her better. Even pale, battered, and bloody, she was truly lovely, with full lips, striking features, and enticingly thick lashes. Her long red hair was braided, but many strands had escaped and hung loose.

Her uniform, far more utilitarian than flattering, covered a soft but unmistakably strong body that stirred longing in my heart and sent blood rushing to my cock. I set those desires aside for now.

Lightning illuminated a bloodstained badge on her uniform

above her left breast. I read her name, sounding out the strange syllables in Alliance Standard.

"Lieutenant Calla Wren." I repeated her first name more loudly because I liked how the sound of it felt on my tongue. "*Calla*, my mate."

She moaned. Her eyelashes fluttered, revealing pain-filled green eyes that met mine for a heartsbeat before her lids closed once more and she lapsed back into unconsciousness.

My mate. In my arms. My mind reeled with the enormity of it.

My makers had told me in no uncertain terms that those created to serve in the Guard had been genetically engineered to eliminate the innate desire for a mate. Why would I have studied the details of the most wondrous aspect of being Fortusian, when my makers had made me incapable of it? Doing so would only have poured salt on the wound.

As such, I knew only the basics of Fortusian true mate physiology. My body had recognized a partner with whom I would not only be biologically compatible, but whose very being—mind, heart, and soul—complimented and resonated with my own in every way. None of these concepts had meant much to me before tonight, beyond the bitter knowledge that I would never have such joy.

Whether by error or design, after a lifetime of mourning for what my makers had denied me, I *did* possess the ability to know and treasure a true mate. To say my world had tilted on its axis would be an understatement to the extreme.

Even so, my many years of Silent Guard training and conditioning held powerful sway over my actions and instincts. They warred with my new, deeper need to heal and keep her.

My tentacles, though, were not undecided. They knew only the desire to protect. They tasted her sweet skin and fiery human blood and cared nothing for what the Guard would have instructed me to do—had *indoctrinated* me to do. Eliminate the threat. Conceal the evidence of the fighter's crash. Leave the pilot to her fate. Survive to kill another day.

As if *surviving* were enough.

A long time before I had completed my requisite twenty years of service to the Guard, I had wanted more than mere survival. I wanted to *live*, even if I spent my days in hiding far from the Guard's headquarters on a sparsely populated moon of a planet on the very edge of Alliance space. And by all the gods above and below, I had tried to live, but memories invaded my waking thoughts and twisted my dreams.

I had passed each day of my retirement with little thought to what my future might hold. Until this moment, I had never considered what it might mean to want to live for another.

Calla moaned softly. I drew her closer, offering the warmth and comfort of my body heat. As if by instinct, she rested her head on my chest over my primary heart. Did that simple gesture signify something? I did not know.

Her breath gurgled in her chest. The sound filled me with fear and sharpened my focus. I must take her home quickly and tend to her injuries.

I had no map for what would come next, nor any idea how Calla would react to me when she woke with a clearer mind. She had seen me kill the raiders but did not know why. Her horror at my actions was obvious. She did not know the truth of who I was, or that my existence, like my hearts, now belonged to her.

She did not even know my name.

For now, I could do only what I believed was right: keep her alive. Tend to her injuries. Stay at her side for whatever time we had together and hope she saw something in me I did not see in myself.

Leaving the other raiders to plunder the fighter, at least for now, I turned and swam for home.

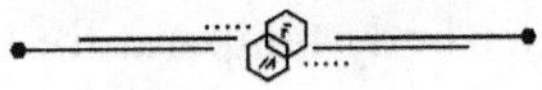

I HAD NEVER BEEN ONE TO CURSE OR PRAISE GODS, MUCH LESS plead with them, but I murmured prayers for much of my long swim back to what I had come to think of as my inlet. Calla's breathing had become far more labored. Fresh blood ran from her mouth and trickled from her nose. I held her as gently as possible during the journey, but her injuries were severe. She might die in my arms before I could get her home.

The dread in my belly gnawed at my insides and filled me with fear.

Normally, I swam underwater using my human arms and legs together with my tentacles, or just my tentacles. But in deference to my Calla's inability to breathe underwater, I had to swim against the current at the surface, holding her body in my tentacles to keep her head out of the water, leaving my arms and legs to do nearly all the hard work. The going was slow, and as strong as I was, my muscles ached terribly.

Had I not floated so far, my return would not have been nearly so long or exhausting. But also, had I not traveled such a distance, I might not have seen or heard the fighter's crash. My mate would now be in the raiders' cruel hands, and I would not have known of her existence—much less hold her.

The last hundred meters of the swim dragged on interminably. On another night, I would not have minded my tiredness. The exhaustion from a long swim and treacherous walk to my homestead would likely have gifted me a rare night of deep, dreamless sleep.

But sleep was not waiting at home for me tonight. I must take my mate to safety and tend to her wounds before she succumbed to them.

By the time I reached the familiar tiny inlet that served as my hidden, habitual entry point to the sea, Calla shivered uncontrollably and her body temperature had dropped notice-ably. She had gone into shock.

Finally, I emerged from the water with aching arms and legs. The muddy bank sucked at my feet until I reached firmer, grassy ground. At least the rain had turned to a drizzle as the worst of the storm passed.

Each time I had climbed this bank, I had immediately missed the sea. This time, the moment my human feet touched firm ground, I ran for home without thinking of the water's warmth and comfort, and without looking back.

My homestead was nearly two kilometers from the inlet—two kilometers of swamp filled with predators and other hidden dangers. Normally I traversed the distance with caution, treading lightly to not alert the enormous, venomous, and perpetually ravenous reptilian kaory to my presence. They were vicious and difficult to kill even when my arms and tentacles were free of burdens. I could not afford any delays, much less to have to fight one—or gods forbid, more than one—while holding and protecting Calla.

Despite the dangers of predators and the need for a quiet journey, I murmured to Calla as I ran, ducking under branches and leaping over pools of brackish water. I told her my full name, my homeworld, the name of this moon, and where I was taking her. I promised she would survive and I would care for her until she recovered. Talking to her helped distract me from my exhaustion, and I wanted her to hear my voice and sense she was safe with me. I did not want her to fear or hate me.

She had looked at me on the raiders' boat as if I were a monster. I feared she was right. I was a killer many times over, and some of my targets during my service to the Guard had not deserved their deaths. I could not delude myself into believing otherwise.

No woman could love a monster, or a man who did

monstrous things. And yet I hoped if I showed her kindness that someday she might.

If I had not kept myself in the same peak physical condition as during my service to the Guard, and Calla's life had not depended on me doing so, I could not have carried her and swum so far so quickly—much less run from the inlet to my homestead after. As it was, I had moments of desperation when I was not sure I would make it to safety before Calla's injuries took her from me.

When my home finally came into view through the trees, I let out a ragged sound of relief.

As if she had heard me or sensed my exhaustion, Calla whimpered and moved uneasily in my tentacles' gentle embrace. Unlike my legs, they did not ache with tiredness. They knew only the joy of her.

I pressed a kiss to her clammy forehead. "We are home, my mate," I said, daring to speak above a whisper for the first time. The kaory rarely ventured near my homestead. I had left the unburied bones of their dead brethren around to warn others away. Even primitive reptilian brains recognized a threat of that kind. "Rest, Calla. I will care for you."

She murmured something I did not understand and went still again except for shallow, raspy breathing that sent chills down my spine.

The cold assassin I had been when I served the Guard would not recognize the man who stood here now in the rain with his hearts in his throat. Would he feel ashamed of me for my fear, or bless my chance at happiness? Perhaps both.

I had built and maintained a tall wall topped with sharp metal shards around my homestead to keep out the venomous serpents that called the surrounding wetlands their home. My Anomuran companion and I dealt with larger predators who occasionally got over the wall.

As I approached the front gate, it swung open. A trio of long eyestalks peered at me over the top of the wall before the entire figure of my companion scuttled into the gate's opening. Her enormous moss-covered shell blocked my way, and she clacked her claws together in obvious anxiety.

"Poe?" she asked, her voice quavering. Her briny smell increased sharply to signify her distress.

"Let me by, Poe," I said sternly. "Calla is badly injured and may die. I need your help."

Poe flickered her long antennae, stirring the air so she could better smell Calla through the chemosensory hairs that covered them from base to tip. Even wet from rain, her senses of smell, taste, and hearing remained sharp. As a guardian of our home, she had proven herself more than adequate, especially against kaory, serpents, and other predators. Her claws were as deadly as my tentacles.

She also had an uncanny sixth sense for both danger and fate.

"Poe..." she murmured. Her eyestalks drooped. She moved aside with a quiet keening.

My stomach clenched. I recognized that sound. She did not think Calla would live.

I left Poe to close the gate and ran to the house. My residence was a three-room capsule home, sturdy and designed to withstand Iosa's weather. I had purchased it sight unseen from its previous owner and renovated it myself with materials purchased from nearby villages. No one but Poe or me had crossed this threshold since I had made it my home nearly five years ago.

Utterly unconcerned by the amount and smell of the muck I was tracking into my otherwise tidy house, I unlatched the door and hurried inside. Poe followed me in, still keening as she gripped the short rope in her clawed hand to pull the door closed and latch it against the rain and wind.

Rather than take Calla to my bed, I placed her on my kitchen table to tend to her injuries. Her comfort came second to efficiency at the moment. I did, however, take the time to place folded towels under her feet to help ensure blood flow to her head and turned on all the lanterns in the kitchen and living area.

Mindful of Calla's need for heat, I lit a fire in the fireplace to banish the chill from the room in addition to the radiant comfort from the thermal spring under the house.

As I finished my preparations, Poe brought both my medical kits from the bedroom, carrying them in her claws by their handles.

"Thank you," I told her, taking the heavy cases from her.

"Poe," she said sadly.

"She will live," I stated, as if by saying it aloud repeatedly I could make it true. As if Calla's blood had not already puddled on the table and her skin was not so pale it appeared almost gray.

With a knife, I cut away her uniform, hissing as I saw the extent of her external injuries firsthand. She had many deep lacerations and bruises from her head to her shins, some of which I thought might have occurred as a result of the way the raiders had extracted her from the fighter's cockpit and their carelessness aboard their boat. Her left arm was broken, as were her right hand and both lower legs. Someone on the raider boat had left the distinct impression of a boot print on her right hand. Judging by how badly it was crushed and scraped, they had stomped on her hand and ground it into the metal deck.

I recalled the pain-filled wail I had heard just before I leapt into the boat. This injury might have been the cause of that cry, which had filled me with such rage that I barely recalled killing the first two raiders.

Now, seeing how badly they had hurt her, I wished I could go back and kill them again—this time, much more slowly. My tentacles lashed the air, and I let out a long hiss.

Poe clacked her claws nervously. She knew I was no threat to her, but her instincts ran deep. I reined in my rage for her sake.

As bad as Calla's lacerations and broken bones were, her internal injuries might be worse. My hands and tentacles, normally very deft and skilled, turned unexpectedly and quite uncharacteristically clumsy in my rush to take my medical scanner from the kit, calibrate it for a human, and pass it over Calla's body.

The grim results left me nearly unable to breathe.

The list of broken bones, damaged organs, and sources of internal bleeding filled the scanner's screen, along with triage instructions on which to treat first.

I leaned against the table, my human hands gripping the wood so tightly that it creaked, while my tentacles ran over Calla's body. Their suckers plucked at her skin in worry, leaving small red marks as they moved.

"Poe," Poe murmured. She could not read the scanner's screen, but she did not have to. Perhaps she had already discerned the extent of Calla's injuries, or maybe my body language and the way I stilled told her all she needed to know.

Then my Anomuran companion did something completely unexpected: she clamped her claw onto my human hand and pinched my fingers hard. The pain jolted me out of my despair.

"Poe," she snapped, her antennae waving rapidly. She tapped one of the medical kits and then shoved the case at me across the table. "*Poe.*"

Her directive was clear: *You have a mission. Get to work.*

And so I did.

CHAPTER 5

CALLA

I drifted in and out of consciousness for what felt like a very, very long time. Everything around me was blurry, in slow motion and fragments.

Whenever my eyes opened, the beautiful sea monster was at my side, eyes glowing softly and voice kind. Despite the horrors I'd witnessed on the boat, I didn't fear him. I was only grateful that though I suffered terribly, I wasn't alone.

Sometimes fever left me floating in a delirium. Icy cloths cooled my forehead and wrists.

At other times, heated blankets covered me from chin to toes as I shivered from cold that seemed so deep and profound that it had turned my bones to ice.

Often, he held my hand and told me stories—first of his homeworld and his childhood in the sea, and then adventures on planets and outposts and aboard deep-space vessels traveling in parts of the galaxy I'd never seen, or even dreamed of seeing.

Sometimes I couldn't understand a word he said, but the

murmur of his voice and a strange but beautiful coo soothed me, even when waves of agony crested so intensely that I screamed. I might have threatened that if he ever told anyone I'd cried, I would feed him appendages-first to a Hardanian bogworm, but I might have imagined that part. I lost track of what was a dream and what wasn't.

Drops of some sweet liquid passed my lips a few times, always accompanied by a coo that eased my pain and fear and then soft darkness.

At some point the agony faded into milder pain and discomfort. Someone carried me in their arms and then lowered me into wonderfully hot water, where soft caresses cleaned my aching body. I shivered as they hummed quietly. Eventually, I fell asleep in the water with my head resting on someone's warm chest.

The next time I became aware of my surroundings, I was no longer in the water or lying on a hard surface. Instead, I was wrapped in something warm and soft and curled up on my side on what felt like a bed. It had been so long since I'd known such comfort that I cried again—but this time, in relief instead of misery.

Gentle fingertips wiped my tears away, and a soft coo made me sigh and snuggle deeper into the warmth of the bed.

I slept.

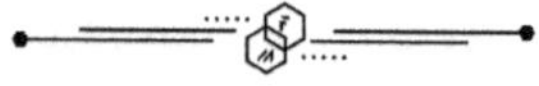

By all the gods, every part of my body *really* fucking hurt.

But also by all the gods, I was glad to be hurting, because that meant I was alive.

I woke up warm and secure, wrapped in strong arms, with my back pressed against a very muscular, distinctly male, and entirely unfamiliar body.

Wait...

Wrapped in *multiple sets* of strong arms. What the hells?

When I inhaled sharply, all the arms tightened around me. "Be still," a man's voice said quietly in Alliance Standard, his mouth near my ear. "You were concussed and your injuries have not yet fully healed."

His words took a while to process, so a concussion was a definite possibility. I remembered my ship falling toward the surface of an inhabited moon, but not the impact itself or much of what happened after.

My instincts told me to fight to free myself. And I damn sure tried to get away, but I couldn't move at all, much less escape the grip of his arms—any of them. Was I weakened by blood loss or was he simply that much stronger than me? Or both?

"Who are you?" My voice sounded hoarse, as if I'd been unconscious for a very long time.

"My name is Vos Turek." He said it very formally, as if giving me his name held some special significance to him. That was definitely possible. I didn't know what species he was. Some cultures held the sharing of names, especially full names, as highly meaningful. For a few, it was as intimate as copulation—though hopefully that wasn't the case here.

"I'm Calla Wren," I said, in case his people interpreted a refusal to give my name as an insult. I was in no shape to defend myself if this man got angry. "Lieutenant Calla Wren of the Alliance Defense."

"I am most pleased to hear your name," he said, his voice warm. So maybe I was right that his people considered names important.

With introductions over, I asked the obvious question: "Where am I?"

"My home. Your ship crashed. Do you remember?"

His words brought back more fragments of memories of an

accident in space and plunging through a moon's atmosphere and a raging thunderstorm toward dark water.

I recalled being carried in someone's arms as they ran very fast through trees in the rain, and then lying on a hard surface, and something sweet on my lips, and lots and lots of pain. But I could not remember this man's face—only a shadowy figure and a pair of silvery eyes.

More vague memories surfaced then: a group of men laughing at me and some kind of violent struggle. But here in this soft bed, those scenes seemed as distant as if they'd taken place in another lifetime.

My recollections might be hazy and my thoughts sluggish, but I had the impression this man—Vos—had cradled and cared for me very tenderly, which was odd because we were strangers to each other.

Despite my aches and pains, I should be far more injured than I felt. I recalled broken bones and internal injuries. I doubted a sparsely inhabited moon of an outer rim planet had an Alliance-standard hospital, and Vos's home—or what I could see of it from the bed—appeared humble.

The bedroom wasn't large, but it seemed comfortable, especially compared to my tiny shared quarters on Outpost 60. The large bed was a vast improvement on my narrow bunk, for sure. Heavy rain thrummed on the roof and what sounded like a window behind me. That was lovely. I hadn't heard rain for years.

Through the open doorway, I caught sight of a simple kitchen, dining table, and part of living area with a chair and sofa and a nest made of branches. Several large medical kits were stacked on the table. Lanterns provided light throughout the house.

Very belatedly, I realized he'd wrapped me in numerous blankets, but I was naked beneath them.

Now that I'd taken stock of my surroundings and gotten my

bearings, I asked, "What's the name of this moon? How long have I been here? *And where the hells are my clothes?*"

"This is Iosa, the fourth moon of Jakora," Vos said. The sets of arms around my body loosened and seemed to caress me before growing still once more. "You have been unconscious for three days. I am sorry that your uniform is no longer able to be worn. I had to remove it to treat your injuries, and it was badly torn to begin with."

I'd never heard of Iosa. And I certainly *felt* like I'd been unconscious for days. He could have said a month and I might have believed him.

As for my lack of clothes…

"Even if my uniform is ruined, you didn't have anything else to put me in?" I scoffed.

He didn't reply at first. "My own clothes would not fit you," he said finally. "I am much larger. My body is not like yours."

That admission cleared my brain as if someone had used their hand to sweep away the fog. "*What* are you?"

When he didn't reply immediately, my stomach knotted. Who or what the hells was I in bed with?

"Let me look at you," I demanded.

"I do not advise—"

"I *said*, let me see you." Now angry as well as uneasy, I pulled against his grip, though trying to get away sent a bolt of pain through my abdomen. "Let go."

If he'd wanted to kill me, he would have already done so. And he certainly wouldn't have invested his time and resources to save my life or warned me not to re-injure myself. But now more fragments of memories were surfacing of what had happened after I'd crashed…and they featured a monstrous sea creature and a bloodbath.

When he finally spoke, his voice sounded strained. Maybe I'd offended him with my tone. At the moment I didn't care.

"I started to say that I do not advise making sudden movements." Vos's arms loosened and the bed moved as he made room for me. "Turn slowly."

As motivated as I was to see him, I did as he suggested and rolled from my left side to my back and then to my right side very gingerly, making sure I stayed fully wrapped in the blankets. He'd presumably already seen all of me there was to see, but he wouldn't be getting any more peeks if I could help it.

My first clear view of him by lantern light explained a lot of things—including the sensation of being wrapped in more than the usual number of arms and why his clothes would not fit me.

But most especially I saw why I recalled the shadowy silhouette of a sea creature.

Vos's body was humanoid, with a wide, muscular torso, long white hair and lashes, dark eyes, and purple skin covered with green-and-white circles. His flesh had a lovely iridescent sheen that caught the dim light and seemed to glow. His hair shimmered.

On either side of his chest, gills fluttered as he breathed, though he seemed to breathe through his nose and mouth as well. My gaze moved from the gills to two pairs of long, multicolored tentacles on his upper and lower back. These were no doubt the extra "arms" that had cradled me so gently but firmly.

Colors and patterns rolled through his skin, along with pulses of bioluminescence. The waves of light moved across and down the length of his body to his waist, where he'd wrapped a blanket around himself.

I couldn't tell exactly how tall he was at the moment, but he was at least two meters tall versus my very reasonable one-point-seven meters, and so solidly built he must easily tip the scales at twice my weight.

He watched me look him over, as if waiting for some kind of reaction. I couldn't help but fear him, but I tried not to show it. He could tear me in half as easily as he'd dispatched the men in the boat.

Since he seemed to be waiting for me to speak, I said, "So, you're Fortusian."

"Yes." He blinked, clearly bemused. Maybe because I didn't recoil or seem shocked.

I would never have admitted it, but it helped that he was both breathtakingly muscular and devastatingly handsome.

"You are not horrified by my appearance?" he asked, his brow furrowed.

"I was stationed on Fortusia for two years," I explained. "Your people combine humanoid DNA with DNA from animal and plant species from across the galaxy."

"Yes." His tentacles reached for me, as if they wanted to wrap around my blanket cocoon again, but he drew them back. They quivered in what might be agitation.

Part of me wanted to tell him it was okay to hold me again because he made me feel warm and secure, and the other, more logical half of me remembered a bloodbath created by those same tentacles.

Also, there was the fact I had a squad and a shitty, useless squad commander back on Outpost 60 who all probably thought I was dead. I was a lieutenant in the Alliance Defense, not some rich tourist wandering the cosmos without responsibilities. I had no business wanting to be held by a gorgeous cephalopod man on the fourth moon of Jakora.

I needed to send an SOS to the outpost and request rescue. If I didn't do so immediately, the Alliance Defense brass would consider me a deserter. I'd be dishonorably discharged and thrown in prison.

Vos stilled his tentacles, except for their quivering tips, which swayed in my direction. The movement caused his blanket to slip. I glimpsed more bare purple and green skin before he drew the covers up over his hips again.

"Why the hells are you naked in bed with me?" I demanded.

His bioluminescence pulsed more quickly. "I have not

touched you in any way other than as a medic," he said, a bit stiffly, as if hurt or offended that I might think he'd taken liberties while I was unconscious. "On my honor, I swear this."

"But you're naked," I persisted. "Maybe you have no clothes that fit me, but don't tell me you don't have clothes for yourself." My eyes narrowed. "Were you expecting sex from me as a thank you for saving my life?"

Now he seemed to swell with disgust. "Of course not."

"Then why?"

"It is...difficult to explain." His tentacles plucked at the bedding, but I wasn't sure what emotion caused their restlessness. "I swear I will never touch you without your permission and you will not be subject to the sight of my body without covering. Will you drop the matter—at least for now?"

His obvious discomfort and evasiveness made me a thousand times more curious, but the note of pleading in his voice diminished my suspicion and mistrust. Whatever the reason for his nudity, he seemed...self-conscious about it rather than being up to no good.

"Okay," I said with a sigh. Despite my misgivings, I was curious about him. "So, back to your biology. If you don't mind me asking, you have three hearts, four tentacles...and I'm assuming camouflage and color-changing abilities?"

"Yes." His tentacles reached for me again. This time, he let them rest on top of my blankets, and I let them stay there. "Also, I have accelerated healing abilities. I can survive extreme temperatures and at vast ocean depths."

"How strong are your tentacles?"

"Very." He tilted his head. "But I assure you, you have no reason to fear them."

I had damn good reasons, but I didn't say that aloud. "So how did I end up at your house? Did you see me crash?"

His eyes took on that silvery hue I recalled from the night of the crash—the one that had terrified me shining in the dark.

"I was swimming in the ocean when your fighter crashed nearby."

"Oh." I touched my temple and winced when my fingertips found a painful spot that felt like a burn. "I don't remember actually crashing, but I recall being in a boat with some men." I met his dark gaze. "And I remember you killed them all."

"I did." He said it simply, as if he'd told me he'd made breakfast. "They hurt you when they took you from your fighter, and hurt you again on their boat. I am sure they intended to do more harm to you when they reached their camp."

His tone made it clear what kind of harm he meant. My stomach churned. Still, I wasn't convinced a wholesale slaughter had been necessary. "Who were they?"

"A group of raiders who have a camp near where you crashed. Vermin who pay little attention to those who live on this moon, but kill and steal from travelers who pass through the system." His eyes glowed. "For the harm they have visited upon innocents, and what they did to you and likely planned to do, they earned their deaths many times over."

The cruelty of the Atolani and his crew supported Vos's explanation, and more to the point, his earnestness seemed utterly genuine. I had no more use for raiders than he and wouldn't mourn their deaths.

I had one final question, and it was the one I had to steel myself the most to ask. "How badly was I hurt?"

Rather than tell me, he handed me a medical scanner that had been sitting on the windowsill and let me process the information for myself. I read through its scans and records, growing colder by the moment.

Before I finished reading the full list, I let the scanner fall from my hand onto the bed. Vos's tentacles vibrated in obvious alarm. My nausea and chills of horror made it difficult to wonder why he seemed to care so much about me and how I felt.

"How am I alive?" I asked, my voice barely a whisper. "I should be dead. *I should be dead.*"

Vos flinched as if I'd struck him. His tentacles wrapped around my blankets and started to draw me toward him.

Angrily, I pushed hard on his chest. He let out a soft coo that somehow made my body relax and my anger and fear dissipate. My hands slid down his chest and landed on the bedding.

As good as it felt, I didn't want anyone controlling me in any way. Not anymore.

"Stop," I said, though my voice was ragged instead of furious. "Don't do that—whatever the hells you just did. Don't take away my feelings. You have no right."

He flinched again. The coo faded. "You must not exert yourself too much."

"I want to know how you kept me alive without a hospital." I wanted to punch him for keeping secrets about my well-being, and I might have done it if I didn't know it would do me far more harm than him. "Just tell me. And don't lie."

"I would never lie to you," he said.

His voice and the way his gaze held mine told me he meant it, but that didn't lessen my anger. "Stop stalling and talk."

He took a deep breath and let it out. "My medical kits are more well-stocked than most. I am highly trained in triage care."

"Nothing in those medical kits could have saved me. I want the whole truth or…" What could I threaten him with? I was injured, I had no weapons, and I was pretty much at his mercy. All I had was a pathetic "Vos, *please.*"

His tentacles caressed me again in a vain attempt to comfort me. "I told you I heal quickly." He raised one of his beautiful tentacles, then let it curl back around my blanket cocoon. "My healing ability is carried in my blood. I shared it with you and used it in combination with conventional medical procedures to treat your wounds."

I recalled that sweet and unfamiliar taste I thought had been part of a dream, or some kind of medicine or food in liquid form. My stomach roiled.

His *blood*. In my mouth, down my throat. On my wounds and into my bloodstream. While I lay unconscious and helpless.

While I lay *dying*.

For most of my life, I'd had no control over my life or my body. I had sworn never to lose that control again, and now I had. The reasons mattered less than the memories that crashed over me like waves.

Almost blindly, I pushed his tentacles away and tried to roll over to put my back to him, but agony seared my middle. I let out a cry of pain.

"Please, Calla," Vos said, his expression equal parts grave and grieving. He held me still with his human hand on my shoulder. His touch was warm, but I wanted to knock his hand away. "You will hurt yourself again. Even if you needed it, I cannot offer you more blood to heal until—" He cut himself off.

"Until what?" I demanded.

His dark gaze met mine. "Until I have replaced what I shared. I gave you all I safely could, and then some."

How the hells much blood had he given me?

I didn't know what to say. I wanted to scream at him for what he'd done, because he'd done something invasive and I couldn't stand anyone doing anything to me without my permission. But if he hadn't shared his blood with me, I would be dead. If he hadn't killed the raiders and taken me home, I'd be dead. If he hadn't been swimming in the ocean when I crashed, I'd be dead.

No matter which way I looked at it, I owed him my life, and yet I hated that fact because of *how* he'd saved me. I made a little sound and closed my eyes so he couldn't see my unshed tears.

"Calla," he said quietly. "I am truly sorry. I have done you a great wrong. I swear I did not intend to do you harm."

I barely knew him, but I did believe that. I took a shaky breath. "I get it. You wanted to save me."

"Yes, but I am also selfish. I could not watch you die."

I opened my eyes so I could see his face. His expression was earnest.

"Why not?" I asked. "You killed a bunch of raiders to get me away from them and then drained half your blood to keep me alive. I don't get it. Who the hells am I to you? I'm nobody."

"You are *not* nobody." Vos's eyes blazed with anger. "Please do not say that."

"Is it because I'm a woman, then? Or at least a living being who isn't a raider? You can't be *that* hard up for companionship."

"I have never sought companionship, until now." His tentacles tightened around my blankets but didn't try to draw me closer to his body. "If I tell you the whole truth, it will not make the situation any better."

His expression went from guarded to a hard mask—the kind I'd only seen on mercenaries and soldiers. His body language also changed, becoming tense, as if ready to attack.

The cold efficiency with which he'd killed the raiders, who were vicious, well-trained fighters themselves, should have clued me in that Vos wasn't an ordinary man who'd chosen to live on a lonely moon on the edge of Alliance space. I blamed my injuries for not thinking about the implications of his slaughter of the raiders beyond the fact he'd simply wanted to save me from their clutches.

Fear chilled my heart. Who *was* this man?

Maybe his nudity had far less to do with sex than making himself appear less threatening, or even vulnerable.

Which might have worked if not for the fact those tentacles could kill me without much trouble. He might have no weapons on him, but he himself *was* a weapon. And no one would mistake his cold eyes for anything but those of a killer.

Still, I wanted the truth, whatever it was. I deserved that much.

"We're both naked in your bed," I pointed out. "Whatever your real reasons were for everything you've done, lying to me will make the situation worse. I respect truth more than lies any day."

Vos's expression didn't change, but his tentacles caressed me again through the blankets. "Calla…"

Why did his voice sound so much like a coo when he said my name? And why did those two simple syllables melt something in my heart?

"You smell like my mate," he said.

If he'd told me I was the long-lost queen of his homeworld, I would have been less shocked.

"I do not know how this is possible," he continued as I gaped. "Because I was created to serve the Silent Guard, I was made to not need a mate, or so I was told by those who created me."

The *Silent Guard?*

If he'd served in the Guard, he'd been one of the deadliest assassins in the galaxy—and probably still was, if he'd survived to serve out his enlistment. Now the killings of the raiders made all the sense in the world.

I was naked in bed next to a cold-blooded, highly trained killer who just happened to be one of the most beautiful men I'd ever laid eyes on, and who happened to think I was his *mate*.

"I never imagined such a situation for myself," Vos continued. "It is not unknown for a human to be the true mate of a Fortusian, but it is rare." His dark eyes searched my face. "I have horrified you."

"No," I swallowed hard. "I'm not horrified. I don't…I don't know *how* to feel. We don't even know each other. And I'm a pilot in the Alliance Defense. I planned to reenlist for two more years. I want the bonus."

If Vos had been alone a long time, maybe his body had

simply reacted to me as the first biologically compatible being he'd encountered. Even as I thought that, though, I didn't believe he couldn't tell the difference between sexual attraction and the call of a true mate.

Thanks to my time stationed on his homeworld, I understood enough about Fortusian biology to know what that meant. If I left him, he would pine for me for the rest of his days. He could find physical pleasure with others, but never true comfort or the sense of belonging to another who also belonged to him.

The concept of a true mate had always revolted me because I believed it eliminated my power or right to make a choice for myself. But at this moment, I wasn't revolted by him or his claim. Apprehensive, overwhelmed, and fully aware I couldn't desert the Alliance Defense, but not revolted. Was that the concussion talking? I wasn't sure.

"Is that why you didn't want to explain why you're naked and holding me?" I asked. "Because you think I'm your mate?"

"Partly. You also experienced intense nightmares and did not lie still in your sleep." He remained expressionless, but his voice sounded more gentle now. And he'd relaxed a little, possibly because I hadn't tried to punch him for calling me his mate. "I needed to keep you warm and prevent you from rolling off the bed."

"You could have done that with your clothes on," I pointed out.

"Perhaps I wanted to see your reaction to my body." His gaze stayed on my face, searching for some clue as to what I thought of the situation. "If you were repulsed by me, you could not be my mate."

I felt many things when I looked at him—too many to process all at once—but repulsion was not one of them.

What could I say? He'd gone to so much trouble to keep me alive. By admitting he thought I was his mate, he'd made himself vulnerable to me in a way that must have gone against every bit of training and indoctrination the Guard had imposed on him.

But none of that was on me. I *did* owe him for saving my life, even if he'd done it in a way I didn't want, but I didn't owe him *me*.

For that matter, if I didn't reenlist in the Defense, I wouldn't receive my hefty bonus for completing my second full term of enlistment. I counted on that money to fund my settlement on some world I hadn't chosen yet, where I could work and save up more to travel the stars.

Iosa wasn't in any of those plans. Neither was Vos.

Better to tell him now so he didn't get his hopes up. Just because I didn't want to be his mate didn't mean I was ungrateful or I wanted to be cruel.

"You need not say it or explain." His voice was quiet. "I see your answer plainly." His expression closed off as if he'd flicked a switch. "Then, if it is what you wish, I will set this strange feeling aside and simply say I did not want you to die nameless and alone on this moon."

But there was no un-ringing that bell.

Despite his offer to pretend otherwise, he clearly believed, or knew through some extra sense, that I *was* his mate.

I'd find some way to compensate him for everything he'd done. He'd saved my life at great risk to his own. That was worth a chunk of my savings, since now I might live to replenish my account instead of, as he'd said, dying nameless and alone on this moon.

I wanted to be asleep instead of watching a powerful man struggle to come to terms with the most profound of rejections, but if I was too much of a coward to face him now, I probably didn't deserve to have survived the crash.

"I'm sorry." I cleared my throat so I didn't sound shaky when I added, "It's probably for the best if I send a communication immediately to my squad commander requesting rescue."

He said nothing for a long moment. "There are no interplanetary communications stations within fifty kilometers," he said finally. "Except for the equipment at the raider camp, and we cannot go there."

I was shocked speechless once more. A nice, quiet homestead was one thing, but fifty kilometers to a town large enough to have interplanetary communications? Who would want to live such an isolated life?

A man who lived in hiding, who'd had his fill of the ways of the worlds and alliances beyond this moon.

"When you are better healed, I will travel to the closest communications relay station and send a message to your squad commander," Vos said. "I will not leave you here alone until you can protect yourself. Even running, I would be gone for many days. I have no motorized transportation."

"You're not going to run fifty kilometers by yourself to send an SOS on my behalf," I said, my voice sharper than I'd intended because the thought of anyone offering to do that for me was beyond ludicrous. "We'll have to wait until I'm well enough to travel with you. My squad commander will just have to understand I couldn't call for help right away."

Mentally, though, I snorted at my own words. Proos would probably be insufferable and irate about my long absence rather than relieved to hear I'd survived both the raider battle and the crash. At least my squadron mates would welcome me back to the outpost, even if Proos yelled at me for hours and assigned me to cleaning duty in the mess hall.

I caught glimpses of a half-dozen emotions in Vos's eyes before he regained his hard mask. One of them might have been hope, though I could have imagined it or misread his expression.

"It will take weeks or months for you to heal enough," he said. "But I will do my best to help you recover your strength, if you will trust me."

Trust. After everything I'd been through, that was a *much* bigger ask than he could possibly realize.

I did believe he'd help me recover and make the journey to a town where I could contact the Alliance Defense—but I also believed he thought these weeks or months of healing might give him a chance to persuade me to stay.

I should tell him there was no chance, but for some reason, the words wouldn't come out.

CHAPTER 6

VOS

IF ONLY FOOLS CLUNG TO FAINT SHREDS OF HOPE, THEN I WAS A fool.

Even the Vos who had secretly dreamed of having a home and happiness someday if he survived his service to the Guard would have scoffed at the tiny flame in my heart that refused to be extinguished by Calla's rejection.

Perhaps I should douse that fire with cold resolve. I should accept that no human woman would want to stay with a killer, or live on an isolated moon, and even less want to be the mate of a creature so different and alien from herself. But I could not bring myself to extinguish my little fire of hope. Nothing in my life had warmed me like its tiny flame.

If I had only weeks or months to spend with my mate before she left me forever, then I would make her as well and safe and treasured as I could. Perhaps we could become friends. Share quiet, happy moments. I could pretend that would be enough.

Calla bit her lower lip—a habit I found endearing. I did not think she was aware she did it. "Vos, I..." Her cheeks turned pink. She moved a little and winced. "I'd like to go to the bathroom."

I started to get up, then remembered I had promised she need not see my body without clothing. "If you will close your eyes, I will rise and dress," I said.

"You don't need to get up," she argued. "I can walk there myself."

My mate—no, *Calla*—was a strong, determined human, but will alone would not get her on her feet. "You cannot," I said gently. "You are not strong enough, and the bones in your legs have only knitted together. I must carry you."

Anger flashed in her eyes. "I'm not helpless."

"No, you are not," I agreed. "But you cannot walk yet, and if you try, you will fall and re-injure yourself. It will delay your recovery time."

Her obvious frustration and humiliation made my hearts ache. My tentacles caressed her through the blankets, desperate to feel and taste her skin and bring her comfort.

Finally, she set her jaw. "All right. But once I'm in there, you can leave me be until I'm ready to come out."

"Of course." There was no reason for me to point out that I had been caring for her needs for many days, as anyone would for their injured mate. She must know that. But now she wished to regain what independence and dignity she could, within her physical limitations.

With a resigned sigh, she closed her eyes.

I moved quickly to the edge of the bed. My tentacles tried to cling to her bedding. I forced them to release the blanket. I could not distinguish between their unhappiness and my own.

Her eyelashes might have moved when I stood, but I must have been mistaken. She had no reason to try to peek at me.

I dressed in my usual home attire: a gray tunic with openings for my tentacles and green pants I cinched with a drawstring. I left my feet bare. She had not flinched at my sharp teeth or tentacles, so my webbed toes were not likely to disturb her.

When I looked back toward the bed, this time I felt certain her eyes had been open until the moment I turned. But if she preferred to pretend she had not stolen glances at me, I would let her pretend.

"Are you ready?" I asked.

She opened her beautiful green eyes. "Yes."

When I reached for her, though, she flinched.

"I'm sorry," she said when I tilted my head. "It's not you or your tentacles. I..." She swallowed. "My stomach and chest really hurt." She clearly struggled mightily to make that admission.

"To be injured is not to be weak," I said. "You do not need to convince me of your strength. I have seen your courage from the moment we first laid eyes on each other."

"You don't need to flatter me," she said, with a faint smile that turned into a grimace. "Just go easy when you pick me up."

She was my heart—or she was meant to be. I would never treat her as anything less.

"I will be gentle," I assured her. "I cannot promise moving will not hurt, but I will do my best to ease your discomfort as best I can."

"Thanks." She braced herself.

As delicately and slowly as possible, my tentacles slid under her little cocoon of blankets. Her every flinch felt like little stabs in all my hearts.

When I lifted her, her ragged gasp made me freeze.

"I'm okay," she rasped, which was clearly untrue. "Go ahead. I can take it. I've had worse."

Rage turned me cold. "When?"

She stilled and looked up at me, pain and memories shining in her eyes. "A long time ago, a long way from here. Basically another lifetime. It's nothing you need to be concerned about. I don't need anyone to slay monsters for me. I grew up and learned to slay my own."

I was so enraptured by the fierceness of her statement that it took several beats for the implication of her words to sink in.

She had suffered such pain *as a child?* Rather than ease my fury, this only doubled it.

"Vos, I said to let it go. We're in a hurry." She jerked her chin at the doorway leading to the washroom. "I don't want to embarrass myself. This has all been quite embarrassing enough," she added under her breath.

I did not *let it go,* as she had ordered, but I set my anger aside to attend to her more immediate needs.

When we reached the washroom, her face fell. "There's no mirror."

I frowned. "You require a mirror to use the facilities and wash yourself?"

She glared at me. I did not like to be on the receiving end of her angry stare, but her fierceness was as beautiful to me as everything else about her.

"I want to see my whole body," she snapped. "I need to see how bad it is. Surely that makes sense to you."

It *did* make sense. I would have made the same demand in her place. "I have a reflective surface in my kitchen," I said. "It is not as clear as a mirror, but it will suffice."

"Then take me there, please."

"Do you need to use these facilities first? I do not wish to move you more than is necessary."

She sighed. "Okay. Just put me down and I'll lean against the washbasin until you're gone."

I did not believe she could stand well enough to lean, but she clearly did not agree. She would fight her limitations with every breath and action.

So I steeled myself and did something I did not want to do: I started to put her on her feet, knowing how much pain it would cause her. The moment her feet touched the ground and took some of her weight, she crumpled in my tentacles with a ragged cry.

Gently, I picked her up once more. "Will you trust me to tell you what you can and cannot do, at least for now?"

"I don't trust anyone," she said bitterly. "But maybe you weren't lying when you said I couldn't stand up."

I wanted to hear why she mistrusted everyone and who had hurt her—and better yet, find those who had mistreated her and show them their own innards before they died—but she needed my immediate help, not promises of retribution.

She allowed me to unwrap her blankets and place her so she could relieve herself, and she obviously hated every moment of the process. To give her what privacy I could, I retreated to the bedroom and closed the door behind me.

A long time passed. I realized I was pacing and sat on the bed.

"Are you well?" I called when the silence had stretched into minutes with no sounds from the bathroom.

"I'm fine," she said, very quietly. Then she laughed. The sound had no humor in it, and its harshness made my tentacles quiver in distress.

"No, I'm not fine," she rasped. "Of course I'm not fine. I'm a gods-damn *mess*. I look like I got chewed up by a Hardanian war-pig and then spat out into a food waste processing unit. And that's just my *legs*." She coughed, but it sounded like she'd done so to try to cover another sob. "You'd better show me the rest of me. I might as well take all the punches at once."

She was capable of slaying her own monsters—or she *would* be, weeks or months from now, when she fully recovered—but I would have taken every last punch for her if I could, and if she would have let me.

When I opened the bathroom door, the pain, anger, grief,

and frustration in her eyes when her gaze met mine was a formidable punch to my gut in itself.

As I watched, all that faded, replaced by grim determination. "Okay." With a pained sound, she reached for me with both hands. Her arms trembled. "I'm ready."

Perhaps *I* was not ready for her to see the extent of her remaining injuries, but I must be as courageous as my mate. "Do you want me to wrap you in blankets?"

She gave me a strained smile. "Not much point being prudish or modest anymore, is there?"

Even so, I gathered up one of the blankets to make a kind of nest in my tentacles, then I picked her up as if she were the most delicate Fylorian crystal. She flinched initially, then sighed with what I hoped was relief as I tucked the blanket around her.

I carried her to the kitchen, where the metal side of my chilled food storage unit offered a reflective surface.

Calla looked straight at the metal and studied herself for a long time.

It had pained me to do so, as her hair was so lovely and long, but I had shorn a few areas of her scalp to treat deep lacerations. Her face had also suffered deep cuts and bruises and remained swollen, especially her right eye and jaw. More half-healed wounds covered her torso, arms, and legs. Areas of dark discoloration showed where her internal injuries had been most serious and would have been ultimately fatal if not for the restorative and healing properties of my blood.

I saw all her injuries, and they made my hearts ache, but I also saw her without them, healed and healthy. She was full of fire, my beautiful, fierce Calla.

She had said quite clearly she was not mine, but my hearts, soul, and body clung to the belief even if my brain insisted otherwise. I had no right to claim her unless she claimed me as well.

And yet my flame of hope endured.

"Okay," she said, though again her words did not match her expression.

"Do you want to see your back?" I inquired.

She took a deep, shaky breath that must have hurt. "Is it as bad as my front?"

"Not as bad," I assured her. "Your pilot's seat helped protect you. There are cuts and scrapes and bruises, but I suspect they occurred as a result of the raiders' mistreatment rather than the crash. Does your back pain you?"

"Everything pains me, Vos. I'm one big blob of pain." She rested her head against my shoulder. She was probably just tired, but that simple act warmed my hearts. "The only time I can tell one pain from another is when I move and it feels like my guts are full of broken glass."

I longed to return to the bedroom, curl around her, and press my lips to her hair. Instead I asked, "Would you like to lie down again?"

"Not yet. My body feels like I've done nothing but lie down for days—which is exactly what I've been doing, I suppose." She bit her lip. "Do you think I can sit on the sofa?"

"I am not sure." I considered. "We can try, if you wish."

"I do wish." She shivered. "Thank you."

I went first to the fireplace to open the valve that controlled the intensity of the flames, then brought her to the sofa.

As soon as I started to set her down, she winced and her grip tightened on my arm. "I take it back. Can you sit and hold me?"

I could not think of anything else I would rather do. "Of course."

I settled on the sofa and arranged her as comfortably as I could, wrapping her blanket around her to cover her body and ensure she stayed warm while the fire heated the room.

Her pallor made my stomach churn with worry. "Which injuries pain you most?" I asked.

"I know you're trying to help, but honestly…" She sighed. "Can we talk about something else besides how injured I am?"

I tilted my head. "What do you want to talk about?"

Calla gestured in the direction of Poe's nest. "Does something live in that, or is that yours?"

I grimaced at the thought of sleeping in that pile of branches and moss.

"The nest belongs to Poe," I explained. At her raised eyebrows, I added, "She is an Anomuran. They are large, shelled beings indigenous to this moon."

She smiled. "You have a pet?"

I shook my head. "Not a pet—a companion and friend. Poe is intelligent and kind, and she can communicate to a limited degree. She is also quite a fierce protector. She is outside guarding our home."

Her smile faded. "What does she need to guard it from? What's lurking out there?"

Her next question remained unspoken, but I saw it in her expression: *What might attack us while I am unable to defend myself?*

"The raiders do not cross the swamp," I said, since she likely would think them the biggest threat. "I have nothing worth stealing, so they do not bother me."

"If they figure out you killed a bunch of them, including that Atolani who might have been their leader, they might make an exception," she said, her expression and tone grim. "I hope you had time to cover your tracks."

"I did." I hesitated, then added, "I also ensured what remained of your fighter was destroyed and its debris sank to the ocean floor so it could not be plundered by the raiders."

"My poor ship." She took another shaky breath. "I understand it had to be done. But how did you manage it?"

I explained that I had returned to the site while she had slept and used one of the raiders' own sea mines to destroy the fighter.

This news seemed to trouble her, for reasons that became clear a moment later. "I thought you were with me the whole time." She said it so quietly that I thought she might be talking to herself.

"Poe guarded you while I was gone," I said. "I did not wish to leave your side, but you were stabilized, and I believed you would not want the raiders to profit by your accident."

"Well, you're right about that." She rested her head on my shoulder once more. "I hope the raiders leave us alone, then. Is there anyone else who might come around?"

I shook my head. "I live many kilometers from the closest village. No one wanders here. The swamps and marshes contain enough dangers to make crossing them inadvisable. If a villager wishes to reach a safe beach, there are closer places to go."

Calla flicked her gaze up at me. She opened her mouth, closed it, and said something else. "Tell me about these swamp dangers, then."

I wondered what she had started to ask before reconsidering, but did not press her about it. "The largest predators are reptilian and amphibious, as you might expect from a moon that is mostly water and experiences a long rainy season. The most common danger is the kaory. They are large and scaled, with a venomous bite and barbed tail. They are also quite fast."

She made a face. "Lovely. What else?"

I told her about other dangerous creatures and how best to avoid them. She seemed to take the information in stride, as I might have expected from a fighter pilot who had been stationed on several worlds with dangerous native species.

But the moment I began to describe the kinds of venomous and constrictor serpents of the swamp and marshlands, her scent changed dramatically, and her fingers slipped into my hand.

I broke off mid-sentence and looked at her hand where it rested, so small, bruised, and seemingly fragile in my own much-larger one.

Much to my disappointment, she pulled her hand away the moment she realized what she had done. "Sorry to get squeamish," she said. "I promise I'm not a coward."

As if I would ever have thought so.

"I really don't like snakes and serpents," she continued. "I got bitten by a deno'lia on Fortusia and damn near died. Ever since, I just can't stand anything that slithers. Not your tentacles, though," she added quickly. "They're fine. Quite comfortable, actually. Anyway..." She cleared her throat. "I need to know what's out there, I guess, so keep going."

"You may hold my hand if you need to," I said, trying not to show how much I wished she would do exactly that. "I am no more a fan of serpents than you, though I have chosen to share their habitat."

Calla's eyes narrowed. "Is that your way of saying you're kind of afraid of snakes too?"

It was my turn to clear my throat. "I do not fear them. I simply take great pains to avoid seeing or encountering them."

For the first time, her lips turned up in a real smile. My hearts seemed to stutter in my chest.

"Oh," she said, her tone light and mocking. "Well, that's totally different, then." She settled into my tentacles' embrace with a wince. "Go on about the local serpents, then, Vos the Fearless."

Coming from anyone else, such a flippant remark would have enraged me, but nothing could take away from the fact I wanted that smile and her casual nickname for me to be the centers of my existence.

Minutes later, as I described the hunting habits of the area's largest and most deadly constrictor, her breathing pattern changed, becoming slow and deep. I let my voice trail off.

Careful not to touch any of her cuts or bruises, I brushed stray hair back from her face. My mate let out a soft sigh, her body warm, still, and fast asleep in my embrace. Heavy rain fell on the roof and ran in sheets down the windows, but inside we were warm and dry.

I rested my chin ever so gently on the top of her head and lost myself in her scent.

Save for her injuries and the knowledge she did not intend to stay with me, this was the most perfect moment of my life. If I could have frozen time, I would have done so without a second thought and lived in this moment for eternity.

I drifted in quiet happiness for a long time, until my own restless thoughts shattered my peace.

Surely the universe would not send me a true mate, only for her to leave again. Not even the most capricious gods would wish me such pain—not after all I had already suffered.

Perhaps somehow sensing my disquiet, Calla murmured in her sleep. I cooed until she relaxed and went quiet again. But the magic of the moment was lost.

What had I ever done to warrant the gods' kindness? I was a killer. A monster. I had more blood on my hands and tentacles than Calla could have dreamed.

A chill swept over me.

Perhaps I had earned this punishment. Perhaps with every beat of my hearts and every ember of that tiny flame of hope, I added to my own suffering. Fire provided light and warmth, but fire also burned. Fire destroyed and turned living things to ash.

How could I be so careless and complicit in my own suffering as to want Calla, to the point I was ready to make her my universe, when every moment I spent with my arms around her did nothing but add pain on top of pain because she planned to leave as soon as she was able?

She had described her injuries as feeling like broken glass. I understood that feeling now, because that was how my gut felt looking at her face—at her long lashes, soft cheeks, and lips I wanted to kiss. That mouth would tell me goodbye as soon as her body had healed enough to walk to the regional capital and its interplanetary communications relay.

To stay or not was her choice; whether to be hurt by her departure was mine. I had suffered enough in this lifetime. I did not need more pain.

Carefully, I rose and carried Calla to the bedroom. I placed her on the bed, then wrapped her in blankets and rolled up several more to secure her in place.

Still asleep, she murmured and extended her hand as if reaching for me.

I thought you were with me the whole time, she had said when I had admitted I left her just long enough to sink her fighter. She had sounded sad, as if the thought I had left her side bothered her.

Was it possible she felt something for me, despite her determination to return to her squadron? Did she feel the call of a true mate, though she was human?

No, of course not. She simply did not want to be left alone when she could not protect herself.

I tucked her hand and arm under the covers.

Then I turned and walked out of the bedroom, out of the house, and into the rain.

CHAPTER 7

CALLA

I woke up alone.

Vos had made me another blanket nest, this time banked on both sides with more folded blankets so I couldn't roll over in my sleep and hurt myself. I thought at first he might be lying close to the window again and simply giving me space, but when I managed to turn onto my back, I found the bed empty.

I lay still and listened for signs that he'd gotten up to make himself food or do something in another room. The only sound in the house was the heavy rain on the roof and windows. I couldn't see him in the kitchen or in the living area.

Vos's absence was as profound of a feeling as his presence had been the first time I woke in this bed with his tentacles around me and his calm, kind voice telling me not to move because I'd been badly hurt. I didn't like this feeling of loneliness. I had no business feeling abandoned, but that was how I felt nonetheless.

Then I got angry at myself.

Damn it, I woke alone in my bunk at the end of every single

sleep shift on the outpost. I shared my quarters with another pilot and we weren't lovers. If ever one of us needed privacy for intimate activities, we let the other know to stay clear. I tended to meet lovers in their own quarters or occasionally at one of the outpost's hotels, where pilots and passengers from passing ships stayed aboard the outpost for a few days or a week. I told them my bunk was too small and squeaked, but that wasn't true. Well, it *did* squeak, but that wasn't the real reason. I preferred to sleep alone. Less chance of developing emotional attachments that just led to hurt.

So why in the name of all the gods above and below did I miss waking up next to Vos?

My concussion, I decided. I was a pile of broken bones, cuts, and bruises wrapped in blankets on an ocean moon in a house surrounded by venomous reptiles and more serpents than I cared to think about. Of course I'd find even a stranger comforting in this situation.

No, you wouldn't—you never have before, my brain tried to argue, but I ignored it. It was muddled by a concussion and didn't know what it was talking about.

I was arguing with my own brain. I was a mess in every way.

Plus, Vos had every reason to think I didn't want to be held while I slept. Hadn't I argued with him about it and demanded explanations like an inquisitor at a trial? If the landing crew on Outpost 60 gave me as many mixed signals as I'd given Vos, I would end up landing my fighter in the mess hall instead of the hangar.

Not that I had a fighter anymore. That hurt too, though not as much as my chest and stomach.

As if on cue, my stomach growled very loudly. When had I last eaten? I had no clue. Without Vos, I was as helpless as a newly hatched Hardanian lava squid.

I opened my mouth to call out just as an enormous creature with a moss-covered shell, three eyes on long stalks, six triple-jointed legs, and pincher-tipped arms appeared in the bedroom doorway. At the moment, the pinchers were clasped as if my visitor was fretting.

"Poe?" she asked anxiously.

"Um, hi." I struggled in vain to rise up on my elbows before pain forced me to sink back into my pillow. "You must be Poe."

"Poe," the creature said agreeably. "Poe?"

"Poe," I repeated. "I'm Calla."

"Poe." The Anomuran female entered the bedroom cautiously. "Poe?"

The latter was unmistakably a question, and I got the feeling this was the limit of her vocabulary.

"Where is Vos?" I asked.

She clacked her pinchers together. Her eyestalks leaned toward the window. "Poe." Her tone was sad.

Outside, then. In the pouring rain. If Poe was inside, maybe Vos was on guard duty. I hoped he was steering clear of serpents and reptiles.

I rubbed my grumbly tummy. "I'm hungry."

"Poe," the Anomuran said, waving her arms. She disappeared back into the other room.

I sighed. She'd probably bring me back a tree branch. Or a chair. Why hadn't Vos outfitted her with a translator? Even with her limited vocabulary, a translator would probably help make communication easier.

Poe startled me when she returned carrying a tray. She set it at the foot of the bed and approached with arms and pinchers outstretched. "Poe," she said briskly.

I shied away. "Um, Poe? No offense, but I don't think I want you to grab me with those."

She waved her arms. "Poe." That time she sounded disgruntled.

I didn't know anything about Anomurans, but I sure as hells

didn't want to make one angry. Those pinchers looked capable of cutting off one of my limbs.

"Okay," I said uneasily. "You're the boss. Well, Vos is probably the boss, but you're the boss's companion. Just please don't pinch me."

"Poe," she said. And that was definitely a reproach.

With surprising dexterity, strength, and gentleness, Poe raised my torso with one arm and slid several pillows and blankets under my head and back so I was upright enough to eat.

"I apologize, Poe," I said when she finished. "You are an excellent helper."

"Poe," she said, tapping her pinchers together. Maybe that meant she was happy. At least she didn't seem angry at me anymore.

The tray contained a bowl of soup that was mainly broth, with some vegetables and meat. Next to it was a slice of bread and a cup of water.

As hungry as I was, I eyed the soup. How badly did I really want to know what was in it?

"Kaory," Vos said from the doorway.

I jumped. My movement caused pain to flare in my abdomen and tipped the glass of water on the tray.

Vos moved so quickly that before I could react, he'd crossed the distance between the doorway and the bed, caught the cup, and set it upright. Not even a drop had spilled. Wow.

And then he stepped back from the bed, his expression a hard mask.

"Kaory is bland but easy to digest," he said. "As are the vegetables and broth. I used only light seasoning. Ideal for a sensitive, healing digestive system. Bread may be less ideal, but you need grains and carbohydrates as well. We will monitor how your body reacts to the bread, and if it does not cause discomfort, you may have more. And of course you must drink water. It is filtered and safe."

Not one word had the slightest bit of inflection or emotion. I'd interacted with primitive computers with more emotion in their voice.

My last memory before falling asleep was of lying wrapped in a blanket, held gently but firmly by his tentacles, as he discussed the local serpentine residents. His voice was full of a smile even as he talked about creatures neither of us liked. My head had rested on his muscular shoulder. I'd felt as close to comfortable and secure as I had in a very long time, despite the situation and all my aches and pains.

He'd called me his mate. And now I might have been a stranger.

Which is what I am, I reminded myself before my emotions got carried away. We'd spent a few days under the same roof, but only spoken for a few hours. Yes, he'd cared for me and our first and only conversation had become emotionally intimate in some ways, but I'd made it clear I couldn't stay here with him. So maybe he'd come accept that, or maybe he'd realized his feelings were attraction rather than a physiological imperative.

Either way, it was a relief. It *was,* I told myself sternly, even if some bruised corner of my heart hadn't quite gotten the message yet.

I tried to keep my thoughts off my face and gave him the kind of smile I would have given him if none of that earlier conversation had happened. "Thank you. It smells delicious."

If he could tell that was a bit of a fib, he didn't let on. "If you want more soup, just let Poe know. There is a pot on the stove. She will provide as much water as you need."

I wanted to know if he'd sit with me while I ate, but I figured if he wanted to, he would have offered rather than suggest I speak to Poe if I needed anything.

He turned on his heel and went into the living area, out of my sight.

Well, okay then. Maybe he just didn't want to be in the same room as me unless he had to.

It was for the best. I wasn't leaving anytime soon. We'd find a way to be at least friendly. I'd seen how warm and caring he really was under that hard mask. Things were just...very complicated right now.

At least thinking through all that distracted from how much my body hurt, but my tummy growled again to remind me to pick up my spoon and sample reptile and vegetable soup and then take a bite of fresh-baked bread.

Both were delicious, but my stomach didn't stop hurting even when I was full. I recalled that lengthy list of injuries on the scanner. I'd be hurting for a long time. I'd been wounded enough times to know the road to recovery often presented as much if not more pain than the initial injury. So I had that to look forward to. Another reason to hope Vos and I could forge some kind of friendship.

I could probably face the coming weeks and months alone if I had to, but I didn't really want to.

Nothing had to be figured out today but the necessities and what I could do to start my recovery within the limitations of my body. I had a mission, and the first phase of my mission was to get myself strong and healed enough to get up out of this bed on my own.

In the meantime...

"Poe, can you ask Vos to help me to the bathroom?" I asked the Anomuran as she picked up my tray.

"Poe," she said, then paused and leaned closer. Two of her eyestalks swiveled toward the other room, while one stayed focused on me. "Poe," she murmured, conspiratorially and—I might be losing my mind here—almost suggestively.

I cursed that my translator had gone to the bottom of the ocean when Vos blew up what was left of my fighter, because I *really* wanted to know what Poe had just said.

"Are you trying to play matchmaker?" I whispered.

"Poe," she whispered back, her eyestalks bobbing.

I'd been around the galaxy and had some wild adventures, but I'd never had a giant alien hermit crab try to fix me up with a broody cephalopod man.

I chuckled—and immediately regretted it when pain lanced through my abdomen. My hands flew to press against my stomach and I couldn't muffle my gasp.

Once again, Vos appeared in the bedroom doorway as if by magic. His expression remained clinical, but I caught a flash of worry and anger in his eyes. "Calla? Have you hurt yourself?"

My name didn't sound like a coo when he said it, but neither was it as impersonal as when he'd talked about the food.

"No, I just moved in a way I shouldn't have." I grimaced and rubbed my stomach gingerly. "But since you're here, mind taking me to the bathroom?"

Maybe Poe could have managed it...somehow...but Vos's tentacles looked ever so much more comfortable than her thin arms and those pinchers.

I looked forward to the day I could take *myself* to the bathroom on my own two legs. Until then, I had to rely on help, and I had to be objective and logical—as logical as Vos was being. Nothing personal about it.

Nothing personal about it, I repeated in my head as he approached and ever-so-gently scooped me and my blanket up with his tentacles. *Nothing at all.*

CHAPTER 8

VOS

I HAD MADE A WAGER WITH MYSELF OVER HOW LONG CALLA would wait to actively begin her recovery. I had bet it would take one week.

I lost my own bet by a margin of three days.

On the fourth morning after she first woke in my home, I entered the bedroom after breakfast to find Calla propped up with pillows, gritting her teeth and muttering curses as she lifted heavy cooking pots with each hand as weights.

Despite my resolve to remain as distant as possible, a chill swept over my body. "Calla!" My sharp tone made her jump. "What are you doing?"

She dropped the pots on the bed and glared. Beads of sweat ran down her face. "Practicing low-altitude flight patterns. What does it look like I'm doing?"

Poe must have brought Calla the pots. I had not specifically instructed my companion not to do such things, but I had thought both she and Calla would have better sense than this. Clearly, I had been mistaken.

I stalked to the bed, fully intending to confiscate the pots. "It looks like you are causing yourself pain and risking re-injuring yourself."

She tightened her grip on the pan handles. "Yes, it hurts a little. Exercising hurts sometimes. I know that as well as you do. I've been working out every morning of my life."

I started to speak, but she cut me off. "Don't treat me like an infant, Vos. And don't act like you know my limitations better than I do. I'm not going to overdo it on day one of what's probably going to be a long process. I'm also not going to just lie here like a Barmian wood slug anymore either, listening to the rain and daydreaming of the beaches on Jakora. Treat me with some respect."

Stung, I folded my arms across my chest. Even as I kept my expression cold, my tentacles swayed with a combination of worry and their never-ending desire to hold her like the treasure she was.

"I have nothing but respect for you," I countered. Thankfully, my voice was steady, if not entirely clinical.

"Funny then that the first thing you did when you walked in here was bark at me and assume I can't tell when I've done enough versus when I've done too much." She took a deep breath and flinched. Her abdominal and chest injuries were taking the longest to heal. "I know you see me as injured and weak because that's all I've been since you met me, but I've been fighting for my life *all* my life. I'm tougher than you think. *This* —" She gestured at her body "—is not who I am."

"I have never seen you as weak," I countered. "I recognized your fortitude aboard the raiders' boat when you bit the Atolani and gave me a chance to kill him and free you." I let myself look on her with gentler eyes. "Since arriving at my home, you did over-exert yourself a few times, have you not? And felt pain as a result?"

"Okay, yes." She let go of the pots and flexed her fingers with a grimace. "But I haven't done that since that first day, right?"

"That is fair." I regarded her. "I apologize for 'barking' at you, and for assuming unfairly that you would not know your limitations."

"Apology accepted." Calla sighed. "Sorry I lashed out. Nobody's really cared whether I got hurt…well, ever. Except my squadron mates, I guess, though they'd probably egg me on rather than tell me to be cautious." She slid the pots aside. "Please don't take them away yet. I can do a bit more once we get done in the bathroom. I'd like to bathe as well, if that's not too much trouble. A good soak in hot water would really help with all the aches."

That request caused me concern, as she could not yet stay upright without something or someone propping her up. If she slid down, I was not sure if she could sit up or get her head above the water.

Still, I could not with a good conscience refuse her cleanliness or pain relief. "I will draw a bath and ask Poe to help you," I said. "To ensure you are safe in the water."

She tried to hide it, but disappointment flashed in her eyes before she forced a smile. "Thanks."

Calla liked Poe and had formed a friendship with her—as their whispered conversations would seem to prove—so why would she not want Poe's assistance?

Puzzled, I started the bath, added minerals and some sprigs of local foliage that made the water smell pleasant, then went in search of my Anomuran companion.

The rain had slowed to a drizzle. I found her outside in the yard, tending to her garden with two eyestalks swiveling at the surrounding forest and one on her plants. "Poe, Calla needs help with her bath."

"Poe," she said without looking at me. Her tone and body language seemed dismissive.

Frowning, I tried again. "She is not yet strong enough to be left alone in the bathroom and will need help sitting up while in the bathing tub. I can keep watch on the house."

She turned to me and waved her pinchers before using one to point at the house. "Poe," she said firmly, her eyestalks bobbing and waving, which I had long ago learned meant she was disgruntled.

"Are you refusing to help her?" I asked, now thoroughly befuddled. "Did she anger you?"

Her eyestalks dipped, meaning no, but she didn't budge. "Poe," she repeated, and pointed again at the door.

"I would prefer not to help her in the bath," I said in an undertone. I doubted Calla could hear me but I did not want to risk hurting her feelings. I needed to keep my distance from her emotionally, but that did not mean I wanted to be unkind.

"Poe." This time she sounded frustrated.

"I bathed her when she was unconscious, but the situation is different now," I said. "She is awake. She is...complicated."

I did not want to be in the water with Calla. Even being in the same *room* tested my resolve, which was why I slept and stayed in the living area and spent most of my days and nights outside. Water was my home. Bathing Calla would be intimate. I was not sure I could pretend otherwise. Even if I stayed outside the tub and simply held her upper body above the water's surface with my tentacles, I feared my determination to remain distant would crumble like poorly made bricks in the Iosan rain.

I did not know how to explain the situation to Poe in a way she would understand. She clearly wished Calla and I to become a mated pair. Calla's rejection and the reasons for it—much less my own decision to keep her at arm's length—would be beyond Poe's comprehension.

Poe barreled into me with enough momentum to make me stagger. "*Poe,*" she said with finality in her tone. She turned back to her garden with a huffing sound.

Left with no choice, and as angry with Poe as I was with myself, I went back inside. I took my time toweling off in the kitchen, though I was likely to be at least partially in the water again momentarily…with Calla. The thought was a dream, and a nightmare.

Was I stalling? I was no coward. I did not *stall*. With a scowl, I tossed the muddy towel into a bin and strode back into the bedroom.

Calla saw me and set her pan-weights aside. "What's wrong?"

Gods, she was beautiful.

Everything is wrong, I wanted to say. *Everything is wrong but you.*

"Poe is busy working on her garden," I said instead. "Are you content to bathe with my help?"

Her gaze searched my face. A myriad of emotions flashed in her eyes—among them, sadness.

"Not if it bothers you," she said finally. "I don't think you want to help with that. I can wait for Poe to get done."

She had offered me a way out. All I needed to do was agree to wait until Poe came inside. The bathwater would stay hot thanks to the thermal spring beneath the house, and as stubborn as Poe could be, she would give in and help Calla…eventually.

For days, my determination to keep Calla at arm's length had not wavered. This would be the most significant challenge yet to that resolve.

"It will not bother me," I said.

Calla's mouth twisted up at the corner. She knew that was a lie. And she knew I had not made much effort to hide the fact I had lied. Because I could not *really* lie to her. My hearts would not allow it.

She held out her arms. "Then we'd best get to it. I'm ready to be clean and less achy, and I'm sure you have better things to do than be my bathtub lifeguard."

I might, but at this moment I could not think of a single one.

"How is your pain today?" I asked as I scooped her up and carried her sheet-wrapped body to the bathroom.

Her smile made my hearts skip a beat. "I feel better today."

After her anguished reaction to my confession that I had used my blood to save her life, I had not raised the topic again. If my decision to share blood with her still upset her, I did not see it.

"I am glad." I sat on the side of the tub with Calla cradled in my tentacles. "I do not know if my blood has continued to heal you or not, since I have never used it to heal someone else."

"You haven't?" She blinked up at me. "Then how did you know it would work?"

"I did not know. It simply had to work." I tested the water's temperature with my hand. "Is this too hot?"

"Vos." Calla reached out, as if she intended to put her palm on my chest, then lowered her hand back into her lap. "Thank you for saving my life. I know I was angry when you told me how you managed it, but I need you to believe me when I say I'm grateful."

"I do believe you." I let myself rest my hand on her much smaller one. "Do you believe I am sorry that my choice upset you?"

"Yes." Her smile returned, and it was like the clouds parting. "I don't know why I feel like I can be so honest with you, or why I seem to believe you when I've always assumed anyone who talks to me is lying."

Before I could ask her why she felt that way, she cleared her throat. "Anyway, bath time." She touched the water and yanked her hand back. "Ooh, hot."

I reached for the cold water spigot. "I will cool it."

"No, no." She stopped me. "It's perfect."

I frowned. "Your reaction indicates the water will not be comfortable for you."

"I want to be pink when I get out," she said, adding to my confusion. "I need a good scalding. Just go with it, Vos. It doesn't have to make sense."

I unwrapped her sheet and set it aside. Bruises and lacerations still marked her body almost from head to toe. The more serious internal injuries would take much longer to heal. Despite the medical scanner reporting they were no longer life-threatening, I worried about unexpected complications, especially if she insisted on exercising.

Should I offer to share blood with her again? I had replenished much of what I had given her a week ago. Another treatment might heal her completely, or close to it.

Then again, I had no idea if sharing my blood had side effects. I had already risked it once. If I harmed her, even without intending to, I would never forgive myself.

"Vos," Calla said, her gaze searching my face. "You're staring at me."

"I apologize. I was checking the condition of your injuries. You appear much improved." With my tentacles, I lowered her very carefully into the water.

She groaned and flinched. "Go on, go on," she said when I stilled. "It's way too hot, and it feels *so good*."

Perhaps everything would be easier if I ceased trying to make what she said make sense.

The sea was my soul's true home, but any water cradled and caressed me like a mother—or like I imagined a mother might hold a child. I had no memories of the woman who had given birth to me, pleasant or otherwise.

I settled Calla into the tub, holding her with two tentacles curled under her arms to keep her from sliding beneath the water's surface. The other two traitorous tentacles tried to haul the rest of me into the tub until I forced them to relinquish their grip on its edge. They slipped into the tub on either side of her and swirled the water sulkily.

My tub was large and deep—one of my few indulgences. I had only filled it halfway, but the water level nearly reached her collarbone.

"Should I drain some water so it is not so deep?" I asked.

She glared at me. "Don't you dare."

I kept a stack of washcloths and bars of soap on the window ledge. But before I could offer to help wash her, she leaned back against the side of the tub, her head on one of my tentacles as a pillow, and let out a long sigh. "Thanks, Vos," she murmured.

A comfortable silence settled over us. I did not want to interrupt it, or disturb Calla by staring at her again, so I turned my attention to the large windows and skylight around the tub. Thanks to the steaming water, condensation obscured our view of the sky and yard and the swamp beyond the wall. The morning drizzle had turned once more to a downpour that ran over the slanted skylight and down the windows.

After nearly five years on Iosa, I scarcely noticed the rain anymore, but whenever Calla was near, I noted everything, as if my mind subconsciously wanted to capture every detail of every moment I spent with her.

As a component of an economical and efficient capsule home designed to withstand Iosa's weather, my bathroom had originally been much smaller. I had doubled the size of this room using part of an old home that had been damaged in a storm and sold for parts. What the resulting space lacked in aesthetics it more than made up for by allowing me to have this enormous tub and an overhead shower. On days when I could not make the journey to the sea, the tub provided the peace and tranquility I craved of submerging in water.

Calla settled in more comfortably, her hand resting on her abdomen. I had learned that gesture meant she was hurting but did not want to show it.

A coo rose in my throat. Recalling her angry response the

last time I had made the sound, I suppressed it. A sharp pain in my chest made me jerk.

She raised her head, her eyes searching my face. "What's wrong?"

I opened my mouth to tell her it was nothing but a muscle twinge, but I could not bring myself to lie.

"I instinctively make a sound when you are hurt," I said. "It appears that if I hold it back, it causes discomfort."

She flinched again—but this time I did not think it was a reaction to her own pain. "Then don't hold it in. I don't want you hurting because of me." Her expression fell. She had probably realized her departure would do exactly that. "I mean… shit."

"It is all right," I said, though that was not entirely true. I simply wanted her to relax again.

She smacked the water with her hand, startling me. "No, it's *not* all right. Stop saying you're fine when you aren't."

"I might say the same to you," I said mildly.

Despite her fit of pique, her mouth twitched. "Okay, that's fair." She rested her head against my tentacle again. "Let's make a deal, then. We don't tell each other we're okay if we're not."

"I accept." I risked allowing the end of one of my unoccupied tentacles to wrap around her right ankle. When she snuggled against my hold and did not protest, I decided to take another risk. "Will you tell me of your past, Calla? I would very much like to know where you are from and why you chose to be a fighter pilot." And why she trusted no one, though I did not add that part.

She did not become tense or angry, but she said nothing for a very long time. I stayed quiet and let her think.

"I could tell you it's a long story, but it really isn't," she said finally, her tone as dry as the deserts of Solan. "Really, I can tell it in five words: I was born on Ganai."

My breath caught in my chest, and despite the steamy heat in the room, horror turned me cold all the way to my core.

CHAPTER 9

CALLA

Vos hadn't fooled me with his cool and distant façade. He probably knew he hadn't. We both knew he was trying to fool himself.

The real depth of his feelings showed plainly in the way his body seemed to turn to stone in the wake of my words, and how his tentacles that weren't holding me swirled around, sending a wave of bathwater over the side of the tub.

"So you can fill in the rest for yourself, probably," I continued, my voice calm, as if I hadn't noticed what was a simple statement of fact for me caused Vos to transform from reluctant bathtub lifeguard back to sea monster—as if the villains of the story weren't light-years away from this place.

As if I couldn't still smell the bloody dirt of the arena, or feel the cold metal of my child-sized but very deadly weapons in my hands.

A low, dangerous sound rumbled in his chest.

I kept talking because my voice might calm him. I didn't fear Vos anymore, but I also didn't want him enraged on my behalf.

We were having a relaxing bath—or trying to—and no amount of anger could change the past anyway.

"I'm the one Ganaian child gladiator in fifty who survived to sixteen and earned her freedom," I said. "I bartered my way off Ganai, put on an Alliance Defense uniform, and busted my ass to earn myself a flight suit." And a fighter, which now lay scattered in a million pieces across the ocean floor.

Strangely, that mental image didn't hurt as much as I'd expected. Part of me still wanted to reenlist and get that big bonus that would enable me to chase my dream of traveling the galaxy in relative freedom…but that goal had lost some of its luster. I'd spent the last several days lying in bed thinking about the fact getting that bonus would require me to serve two more years in the Defense, dodging death at every turn, either in battle or the kind of mishap that had caused my crash on Iosa. The odds of surviving long enough to see those credits show up in my savings account were slim.

Meanwhile, Vos's silence felt heavier and thicker than the steam that filled the bathroom. I lifted my head from where it rested so comfortably on his tentacle and looked up.

His expression had gone so cold, so deadly, and so utterly ferocious that it sent a chill through my entire body from the top of my head to the tips of my toes. But it wasn't fear that caused it.

It was desire.

His warmth…the hard muscles of his body…his selflessness…the way he held me as if I was the most precious thing in the world, even when he wanted to convince himself that he could crush his need for me under the weight of his will alone. It all made me wonder: was I wrong to have shot him down so quickly?

When we'd first met and he'd said I smelled like his true mate, I hadn't been remotely clear-headed at the time. I'd barely given him a moment's consideration before telling him thanks but no thanks.

Was I more clear-headed now, or simply grateful for his kindness and flattered that he looked ready to rend anything and anyone to pieces that posed a danger to me, while his tentacle around my ankle remained as gentle as ever? I wasn't sure.

His eyes turned that silvery-blue that had so terrified me on the raiders' boat. Now all I could think was how beautifully they glowed.

I couldn't help it; I reached up and cupped his face with my hand. His bioluminescence pulsed faster, moving along his skin toward my touch.

"It was a long time ago," I reminded him, stroking his jaw with my thumb. "I'm alive, and most of the people responsible for what happened to us are dead. Ganai is still a shithole, but it's a shithole without arenas where rich bastards from across the galaxy watch children fight to the death anymore. No need to be angry at a memory."

Vos held my hand against his face as if my touch comforted him. Maybe it did.

"I am always angry at memories." His voice was rough. "Mine, and now yours as well."

"My past isn't a burden you need to carry," I said, because I didn't want to cause him any more anguish than I already had. "That's not why I told you where I came from. I wanted you to understand why I don't trust easily—well, why I *usually* don't trust easily."

Vos's hand closed around mine and lowered it back to my lap. "I am not someone you should trust." His tone had gone cold again. "I am a monster."

He'd probably said it to shock and scare me because we'd had a moment of tenderness and that wasn't part of his plan to keep me at arm's length. But it didn't shock *or* scare me, for a lot of reasons.

I'd met monsters—real ones. Monsters who looked like monsters, and monsters who didn't. I had learned very early in my life that nothing about monstrosity was ever simple. In this case, I doubted Vos thought he was a monster because he was genetically engineered or had these beautiful deadly tentacles. His shame seemed to come from somewhere much deeper than that.

He'd asked me about my past. I was curious about him too—most especially why he considered himself a monster.

Vos had always been so candid when we spoke. I actually found that refreshing. I preferred forthrightness myself. Evasiveness and diplomacy, even about difficult or contentious topics, had never suited me. Really, that was a major reason I couldn't get along with the literally and metaphorically slimy Squad Captain Proos, who talked in circles and whose opinions always mirrored those above him in the chain of command whose favor served him best.

"Why do you call yourself a monster?" I asked.

Rather than appear offended by my bluntness, Vos tilted his head. "It would be difficult to find someone in all the galaxy who would not automatically consider a member of the Silent Guard a monster."

My heart twinged. The child gladiators of Ganai were certainly pitied, but many called us monsters too. We'd been trained to kill from an early age. Those who survived the arena often became mercenaries or worse in adulthood. Some of us *were* monsters, but most of us weren't. Most of us were just survivors.

"Well, you found someone who doesn't automatically think you're a monster," I said, and he blinked at me. "And I didn't ask what others thought of you; I asked why you call *yourself* a monster. Do you think being a killer makes you a monster?"

"Yes," he said, his voice quiet.

"Would you consider me a monster?"

His brow furrowed. "You are no kind of monster."

I snorted, then flinched because it hurt my abdomen. "You know me so well that you can make that assessment? Maybe you see what you want to see when you look at me, then. I'm a killer too, many times over. If that's all it takes to be a monster, then that's what I am."

Vos didn't like that at all, judging by his deepening scowl and the uneasy way his tentacles swirled in the water.

"You had no choice in the arena," he said. "Or in your fighter."

"You had no choice in the Guard," I countered. "And I didn't just kill in the arena and in my fighter. I took the scenic route from Ganai to the Alliance Defense. Traveled from planet to outpost to colony to more planets, doing what I had to in order to survive until I got to the Defense recruitment outpost on Havel Prime." I rested my head on his tentacle again. "There are bodies behind me, Vos. A lot of them, same as you. So you don't have a monopoly on that monster thing."

He studied me for a long time, clearly trying to figure out a way to justify his assessment of himself without condemning me too.

I understood him fairly well for having only known him a few days. Part of that was due to his candor, but I couldn't shake the feeling the resonance of the true mate physiology had something to do with this level of comfort between us. He certainly had an uncanny ability to understand my needs, both physical and emotional.

Maybe that was why every morning when I woke and Vos wasn't next to me in his bed that I felt like someone was missing, when I'd never felt that way before. Not ever.

And maybe that was why I'd told him the truth about my past. I'd certainly never felt compelled to tell anyone else I had survived Ganai's arenas. I usually made up a story of growing up in a frontier colony and being orphaned in a plague or raider attack. Before this, I'd found it much easier to deal with sympathy over a lie than real care about the awful truth.

More than anything, though, I let Vos into my secrets because he was the first person I'd ever met whose eyes reflected the same darkness I saw when I looked in the mirror. Plus, he deserved to know I might have fallen from the sky, but I was no gift from the heavens.

I didn't know what he might say next, and I certainly didn't anticipate what he did: he cooed.

Maybe it wasn't all that unexpected. I probably radiated anger, pain, grief, guilt, and more, so of course he'd instinctively wanted to help. All my tension slipped away, leaving me warm and relaxed. Even my aches and pains faded.

He instinctively made a sound that was just meant for me, designed to heal my hurts, whatever they were. That was a treasure in itself and not something I should just throw away for a reenlistment bonus or a nebulous dream of traveling the galaxy, as if I might somehow find happiness on some starship or distant world without finding it in myself first.

"Have I destroyed your vision of me?" I asked.

"Destroyed my vision of you? Never." He cupped my face then, so gently I could have fallen asleep with my head on his tentacles. It wouldn't be the first time that had happened, and hopefully it wouldn't be the last. "Calla, the more fully I see you, the more I know my soul fits to yours."

Those sweet words gave me the courage to murmur, "I would like to start over again, if you'd be willing to consider it."

His breath hitched and his tentacles vibrated.

"I understand if you don't want to," I continued. "I know I hurt you when I said I didn't want to stay here. At the time I did intend to leave as soon as I was able, but I've realized over the

past few days that I didn't give the situation as much consideration as you deserved. I'm sorry for that."

"Please do not apologize." Vos inhaled deeply. I could only
imagine how conflicted he must feel. "I have also come to
understand that it was unfair of me to reveal so much to you
only minutes after you awakened in a stranger's home following
such a traumatic incident. I was so lost in my own emotions
that I did not consider the reality of the situation as logically as
I should have. From my hearts, I apologize for placing you in
that position."

"Apology accepted." I waited a beat, then asked, "So starting
over…good idea? Bad idea? Need to sleep on it? Maybe drink on
it?" Was there even booze on this moon?

His eyes blazed with silvery-blue fire. "I would cut my way
through the entire raider camp for the chance to start again."

His ferocity stirred something in my belly: a kind of longing,
mixed with gratitude and hope. "You don't have to go through
any more raiders, Vos. I'm right here."

"I am more grateful for that fact than you will ever know."
He rested his head against mine and made a low, rumbly sound
deep in his chest. "Has the bath helped your pain?"

"Yes—with the aches, anyway." I sighed. "I'm sorry to ask, but
could you wash my hair? Trying to raise my arms over my head
hurts so badly."

"I am happy to help." One of his tentacles coiled around a bar
of soap that smelled sweet. "This will cleanse and soften your
hair. I made it myself, for my own hair."

I feigned indignation. "Are you saying my hair isn't soft?"

"It is wonderfully soft," he said quickly. "I wanted to assure
you it would remain so." After a hesitation, he asked, "Were you
teasing me?"

"I was," I admitted. "I'm sorry."

"I am not offended." His tentacles lowered the back of my

head into the water. "I am glad to hear you joke, even if it is at my expense."

A few minutes later, as he gently lathered my hair and massaged my scalp with his fingertips, I murmured with my eyes closed, "Will you start sleeping next to me in your own bed again?"

"I will," he said, equally quietly. "If that is what you want."

The hot water, steamy room, and Vos's gentle touch had me nearly asleep sitting up. "Thank you. I hate sleeping alone in your great big bed."

"These past few days have been difficult for both of us."

He lowered my upper body into the water to rinse my hair. Gods, his fingers were so incredibly gentle and soothing as he untangled my hair. And the smell of the hair soap was so pleasant and natural—a far cry from the chemically based cleansers aboard the outpost.

"This change of heart is not because you believe you owe me for caring for you?" Vos asked.

My eyes were closed because I didn't want to get soap in them, so I couldn't see his face, but his voice sounded guarded. And I couldn't blame him for wondering.

"Not at all," I promised. "Your kindness is a factor, but far from the only one."

"I will take you at your word. And now your lovely hair is clean." Vos raised my upper body and wiped water from my eyes with a towel. "Shall I wash the rest of you?"

"Yes, please." I opened my eyes to find him watching me intently. "What?" I asked, frowning.

"You flinched several times." His concern was palpable. "I am worried. And I wish I could ease your pain."

"It will be a long road to recovery. We both know that." I took his hand in mine. "But I'll take it over the alternative, okay? The fact I'm here at all is a miracle."

"Several miracles, in fact." He hesitated, then kissed my forehead. "I will finish washing you, and then we will lie down together in the bed, if that is all right with you."

I pictured myself curling up under the blankets, still warm from the bath, with Vos's tentacles around me. Heavenly. "Yes, please, Vos. Thank you." After a beat, I added, "Poe will be happy her scheme to get you in here with me worked."

The corners of his mouth turned up for the first time in days. "She is a good friend," he said, and picked up a washcloth and another bar of soap, this one green. "Perhaps later, if there is a break in the rain, I can take you outside to see the garden."

"Even if it's raining, I'd still like to go," I said. "I won't melt in the rain, you know. I haven't actually *felt* rain in years, other than on the raider boat. I lived on an outpost in orbit around the planet Solan."

Lived, not *live*.

Whether Vos noticed my choice of words, I couldn't tell. He lathered up the washcloth and began to wash me, starting with my face and shoulders.

When the cloth moved below my collarbone, though, he paused, his gaze on mine.

"It's all right," I said.

Carefully and extremely gently because they were covered in bruises and still healing from the injuries that had mangled my insides, he washed my chest, my breasts, my stomach, and my back with light swirling motions. And then he soaped my legs, lifting each out of the water one at a time, and then my feet and toes.

There was nothing overtly sexual about this bathing, and I thought he was being oh so careful *not* to make it feel romantic, but it was deeply sensual. My skin tingled wherever he touched. And the closer his hand and the cloth came to my inner thighs, the faster I breathed. My stomach fluttered in anticipation.

With his glowing gaze fixed on my face, he nudged my legs apart. His touch was so soft, so caring, and so intimate. My chest heaved with ragged breaths as the cloth brushed my most delicate skin.

"Calla," he said, his voice rough.

I couldn't help it—I made a desperate little sound and grabbed his arm before he could move away. "It's all right," I said again, though it was far more than all right to be touched with so much care and reverence. I'd never experienced that kind of touch before.

He kissed my hair, withdrew his arm gently from my grip, and squeezed the soapy water from the cloth before draping it neatly over the side of the tub. "We are done."

I took a shaky breath and tried for a smile. "I hope I smell better now."

"You have never smelled anything but good to me." Vos sat on the edge of the tub, draped a thick towel over his thighs, and lifted me from the water to sit crossways on his lap.

His tentacles held me upright as he meticulously dried me with another towel, even drying between my toes very carefully so he didn't tickle me. Then he towel-dried my hair, worked out the snarls with his own comb, and braided it.

By the time he finished, I was drowsy and my stomach hurt from sitting up for so long. I tried not to show I was in pain, but he knew anyway. Maybe he saw it in my eyes, or he could smell it somehow. Or both. I'd probably never be able to hide much from him. Strangely, that was more comforting than I thought it would be.

Cooing, he carried me back to the bed, wrapped me in blankets, and settled me under the covers before taking my little collection of cooking pots back to the kitchen. I didn't protest. Even I knew I wouldn't be doing any more weight-lifting today.

What would it be like to be with someone with whom I could be authentically myself, and know they were themselves too? To know I would receive an honest answer to any question

I asked, and feel comfortable answering questions honestly too? The Calla of a week ago would have scoffed at the idea.

When Vos slipped under the covers beside me and his tentacles wrapped around my blanket nest, an overwhelming sense of peace swept over me. He sighed in unmistakable contentment. Even his tentacles relaxed.

I might be achy and tired, and nothing at all about our future was settled, but this moment was something close to bliss. The fact he so clearly felt the same warmed me as much as the hot water and blankets.

Before I closed my eyes, I leaned over and kissed his jaw. He smelled like the same soaps he'd just used on me. I liked that very much. "Thank you for the bath."

He touched his forehead to mine. "It was my pleasure, my— Calla."

Even though he'd stopped himself from calling me *my mate*, or maybe *my Calla*, my name sounded like a coo again. It almost made me forget how much my arms ached from lifting those damn pots.

Ugh. *Almost.*

CHAPTER 10

VOS

As Calla slept beside me, wrapped in my tentacles and smelling of my homemade soap and contentment, I found myself caught between happiness at having a second chance to win her trust and heart, and nagging worry that I might fail.

When she had proposed starting over, I had hesitated, but only for a moment. I had so longed for this chance that, despite my reservations, to decline it seemed nearly incomprehensible —especially given how hopefully and sincerely she had asked.

The wonder of it sent me careening into a storm of yearning and uncertainty. My tiny flame of hope grew once more. I had not succeeded in extinguishing it—not even close. I had merely hidden it, and not very well at that.

If I fanned the flame, I might cause myself great pain. Starting over did not mean she would stay, or that we would find happiness, much less love, with one another. Calla had not offered any promises and I had no right to ask for one. But she *had* asked to start over, and that meant I could not dismiss what we had out of hand.

If I declined, I might feel less pain if she left me, but I would also deny myself a chance for joy.

The chance was slim—even lost in this euphoria, I knew that.

The Vos who had served the Guard would not have been put off by slim chances or long odds, or the prospect of pain. And even long after my retirement, I was still that man, as much as I preferred to think of him as a separate creature I had left light-years behind me. Vos Turek would not let anything come between him and his true mate—least of all his own fear.

Nothing about the future was certain except that if I did not allow myself this chance, I would regret it all my days.

I sensed a profound change in how Calla looked at me and my home. I was no longer a stranger to her, and my home was not merely shelter. My bed was not just a comfortable place to sleep, but a comfort, and she wanted to share it with me.

She had trusted me with the truth about her past and met my candor with her own. None of this meant she would stay once she had healed, but my instincts told me she now truly thought she might, and not just because she did not want to return to the Alliance Defense. I had become *important* to her.

Longing stirred when I recalled how she had trembled when I touched her during her bath. Today's bath had been nothing like the first time I had washed her, when she lay unconscious and barely alive in my tentacles. Today, we had shared something beautiful and intimate that put a song in my hearts.

Fear had not caused her to shiver and I had not imagined her reaction to my touches. I had tasted and smelled her desire. I had yearned to join her in the tub, to caress her and hold her and perhaps kiss her, but resisted the urge. She had only just asked to begin again, to see where this might lead, and she was still healing. I must wait and focus all my energy on winning her heart.

One of my tentacles slipped into her blankets and wrapped

around her lower leg. I closed my eyes to drink in her taste and scent.

What could I do to make her want to stay? What could I offer besides myself?

I could offer her a home.

With that goal in mind, I studied my bedroom with different eyes. I had always considered my capsule house ideal for my simple needs, and Poe was certainly very content, but I must do better for Calla. I should make our surroundings more pleasant, especially while her mobility was limited.

She had expressed an interest in my garden, so she might love growing things. And if she had lived on an outpost for years and not even seen rain during that time, she had been starved for connection with nature. Iosa would offer Calla wondrous opportunities to immerse herself in natural beauty.

Several plants grew in pots in my kitchen and living area and in the bathroom. Perhaps she would like a few in this room. I could move my vinefruit tree from the front room in here. Its fruit and blooms smelled very nice. And I could collect some of the crimson moss from the trees in the swamp and put it in a basket. Its scent was mild, but the color might make this room less bland.

Colorful stones from the seashore? I had little experience with such things, but Poe might have ideas for improving the appearance of these modest rooms.

Perhaps I could find some handmade trinkets in the village that would lift Calla's spirits. Her rare smiles warmed my soul like little else. I yearned to see her smile more.

Once Calla began to heal, she might want to decorate our home in ways that pleased her. My hearts swelled at the thought.

Suddenly, Calla whimpered in her sleep. The scent of her fear and pain swirled in the air. She trembled, curling up almost into a fetal position, her arms in front of her chest as if to protect it.

Tension rippled through my body and tentacles and made my stomach lurch and hearts ache. All daydreams of making a home with Calla evaporated.

I had not suffered a single nightmare since Calla's arrival, as if her mere presence had banished the ghosts of my past. Even the ambassador's child had not visited my dreams, which was nothing less than miraculous.

But sweet, fiery Calla had yet to pass a night, or even a nap, without signs of bad dreams or nightmares. Though I had resolved to keep my emotional and physical distance, I always cooed for her from the bedroom doorway and that seemed to soothe her. I did not think she knew I had done this.

Now, with our agreement to start again, I could do more.

Gently, so I did not wake her, I drew her close with my tentacles and tucked her head under my chin so my body heat and scent might offer comfort and strength. I cooed very softly, the sound thrumming in my chest. Perhaps that sensation would comfort her as well.

Did she dream of her time in the arena? Battles in her fighter? Some other torment from her past she had not yet revealed to me? Or did her deeper fears come to her in her dreams, as mine had done so frequently until recently?

In the bath, Calla had spoken so flatly, so dispassionately, about her time as a gladiator on Ganai. I recognized that tone and method of coping because I used it myself on the very rare occasions I discussed my past with Poe.

However my mate's presence had banished my nightmares, I longed to do the same for her. But how? If she accepted me as her mate, would that offer her the same peace? Would my contentment increase as well? I did not know.

For the first time, I was angry at myself for knowing so little about true mate physiology. And with no computer terminal in my home, I could not discover more unless I traveled to a town large enough to have one with access to the information I needed.

My desire to know more battled with my reluctance to leave Calla's side—especially now that she had asked to start again. My soul and all my hearts were fixed on persuading her to stay.

"Keela," Calla rasped, and let out a single sob.

A shudder of grief and guilt ran through me. Had asking about her past kindled this nightmare?

Cooing, I pressed my lips to her forehead. Her skin felt clammy despite the warmth of my body and the blankets. A single tear leaked from under one of her eyelids.

As much as she might need her sleep to recover from exercising and her bath, I could not bear to witness her pain any longer.

"Calla," I murmured, stroking her hair. "Calla, I am here. You are safe."

Her eyes flew open. She cried out, her hands clenching into fists.

"Calla," I repeated. "You are safe." Her chest heaved against mine. I cooed and stroked her hair until she took a ragged breath.

"Damn it," she rasped. "I'm sorry."

"You have no reason to be sorry," I said, gently but firmly. "You did nothing wrong. You only had a bad dream."

"Yeah, well." Her mouth twisted. "My bunkmates weren't very understanding when I woke up screaming. I think the rest of my squad fought over who had to share quarters with me."

Dark humor, like the detachment with which Calla had described her time on Ganai, belied the real depth of her hurt.

"You do not need to hide your pain from me," I said. "Your squad may not have understood what haunts your dreams, but I do." I cupped her less-injured left cheek, careful to avoid touching her bruises. "Tell me about your dream."

"Why?" Her voice had a sharp edge. "What good would it do either of us?"

If I told her the truth about how different my dreams had become since her arrival, I feared she might think I wanted her to stay for selfish reasons. But perhaps she would find it easier to open her heart if I did the same.

"Our burdens are lighter when we share them," I said quietly. "I have had nightmares all my life. Many days and nights I have lain awake, haunted by memories. But since you arrived, I have not had any. If you will trust me, I would like to do what I can to ease your hurt as you have eased mine."

Rather than react with anger or suspicion, her eyes widened in surprise and wonder. "Because I'm your true mate?" she asked, wiping her eyes with her shaking hand.

"I am not sure," I admitted. "I do not know much about the physiology of Fortusian true mates. But my hearts tell me it is so."

Calla leaned against my hand on her cheek and closed her eyes. Whether she realized it or not, she would not close her eyes if she did not trust me.

"Your true mate brings you peace, even in your dreams?" she murmured. "That's really lovely. It's almost like magic...except it's science."

Calla's mind was very practical and pragmatic. She had been raised as a gladiator in the arena, where analyzing opponents and preparing strategy was a matter of life and death, and then trained by the Defense as a fighter pilot. Science and analysis offered her a firm foundation—something she found safer than emotion.

I understood because I too had always found comfort in practicalities, but my life had become full of wonders since Calla came. I wished for her to feel some of the same awe.

"It is science, but that does not mean it is not also magic." I rested my forehead on hers. "Tell me about Keela, please. I would like to know."

Instead, she snuggled into my chest. I cooed and held her. She relaxed against me with a sigh, but still she said nothing.

What other comfort could I offer? What might make her feel she could unburden herself to me? Perhaps a story of my own.

Everything about my training and service in the Silent Guard was strictly confidential, under penalty of death. Decades of indoctrination made my stomach twist and hearts race at even the idea of sharing one of those secrets. Not for the first time, and likely not for the last, my need to comfort and care for Calla clashed with my Guard conditioning.

As I had done on the night Calla's fighter crashed in the ocean, I followed my hearts because that way lay joy and the potential to comfort my mate. What were the Guard's threats against that?

"I have told you I was made to serve in the Silent Guard," I said, my lips against her hair. "And that is true, in the same way you telling me you were born on Ganai is true. They are simple ways to say big, terrible truths. The reality is much worse and more complex than that."

She nestled her nose against my chest over my primary heart. Already her breathing had slowed and she no longer smelled like pain and unshed tears.

"I do not remember the woman who carried me, gave birth to me, and cared for me until I reached two standard years of age," I told her. "I have tried throughout my life to recall a single memory—a scent, a voice, even an impression—and I have none. My trainers and handlers at the Guard told me she was no one of importance and I should not spare her a thought. But I wanted so much to remember her, because to me she was my mother, my only family. The only person who had ever cared about me in any way. To everyone I knew, I was nothing more than as an investment or asset who could be easily replaced."

She took a shaky breath. "I can relate to that."

"I know." I kissed her hair and continued my tale. "I quickly learned never to speak of this to anyone. Guard trainees are encouraged to inform on members of their cohorts as a way of weeding out those who are…unsuitable."

Even so many years later, my throat closed on that word and my stomach clenched. To be deemed *unsuitable* was to disappear from the Guard training facility during the night without a trace, all belongings gone, empty bunk neatly made with clean bedding awaiting its next occupant. No one knew what befell these vanished trainees, but death was the unspoken assumption.

Calla slipped her much-smaller hand into mine. I did not squeeze because it was her right hand, not yet healed after being so badly broken by a raider's boot. Just holding her hand chased away the sickness in my gut created by these memories.

"When I was young, I imagined my mother would come to the training facility sometimes to observe me," I said. "Outside visitors were rare, but sometimes we would see unfamiliar people watching us train or sitting in classes. I did not know if she also had cephalopod characteristics, so to me, any of these female visitors might be her. I imagined what career she might have, if she might have a mate, if she had given birth to any other children. She lived a robust and full life in my imagination. I kept it all very secret, of course. You are the only person to ever hear of it."

She squeezed my hand then, just a little—all she could manage to do without causing herself pain. And she pressed her lips to my chest over my primary heart. It was not quite a kiss, but I lost my ability to breathe.

Finally, I found my voice again. "For Fortusians created to serve in the Guard, primary training begins between the ages of two and four standard years and continues until age fifteen. Those who survive primary training are then divided based on their inherent abilities and strengths and ranking within the cohort and begin a four-year intensive, specialized training regimen. Upon completion, the Guard decides who will be designated as elite Silent Guard assassins, and who to sell at auction as bodyguards, private operatives, and such."

Calla let out a little unhappy sound. Had she faced the prospect of being sold once her training was complete? The thought chilled me.

"Obviously, the Guard elected to keep me," I said. "When they did, I was given access to my official file. The purpose of this is to demonstrate the level of scrutiny I had lived under and should expect for the entirety of my twenty years of service. Every tiny detail of my life was in the file, from birth onward."

She raised her head, her eyes shimmering with unshed tears. "Her information was in the file?"

"Yes." For twenty-five years I had held this secret locked away. I took a deep breath through my nose and gills to fortify myself. "Her name was Deia, and she was an employee of the Silent Guard. During her prime childbearing years, she was a surrogate mother for six children. She cared for these children until the age of two standard years, when they began Guard training. I was the fourth of these six children."

She flinched, but I did not think physical pain caused it. "Go on," she said, her hand squeezing mine so gently it felt like a flutter.

"I did not have a mother," I said, my voice tight with grief that only now, so many years later, I allowed to surface. "A woman carried me to term, gave birth to me, and worked as my caregiver for my first two years of life, and then handed me over. It was her job to do so. She did not visit me during my training. She did not love me or care for me as a mother. My 'mother' was a figment of my imagination." I focused on Calla's scent and warmth until I could continue. "And as I read my file in front of my superiors, I had to take in that information without showing any emotions at all. If I had reacted, I likely would have been either sold at auction or killed outright."

"Oh, Vos." Calla withdrew her other hand from her blankets and clasped mine in both of hers. Her tears spilled over and ran down her face. "Gods, I am sorry."

My stomach churned because I had caused her grief by sharing this story. She likely would feel the same about sharing her own stories with me, and terribly vulnerable as well. Such vulnerability required as much courage as facing opponents in the arena or enemies in battle.

I ached because I had reopened this wound. It had festered for a very long time. Perhaps now it could heal.

And perhaps my Calla—yes, *my Calla*—and I could find a way to heal together, one story at a time.

CHAPTER 11

CALLA

When Vos had started telling his story, I'd prepared myself to hear about a mission during his service to the Silent Guard, or something that had taken place since he finished his twenty years of service.

I'd seen a lot of suffering in my life, and experienced more than my fair share, but nothing at all could have prepared me for this kind of hurt. The pain in Vos's eyes and the way his voice tightened with grief gutted me. He was so powerful, so deadly, and so fierce, but he'd yearned for a mother.

He didn't want to cause me anguish of any kind—I knew that as surely as I knew I didn't want to hurt him. He wanted me to know my hurts and memories would be safe with him. What better way to demonstrate that than sharing what must be one of his deepest, most carefully guarded secrets?

Even so, part of me wanted to pull away, close my eyes, and try to go back to sleep. Just because Vos had revealed something intensely private about himself didn't mean I had to do the same. And he wouldn't push. I could stay safely behind my walls if I wanted.

I'd asked him for a second opportunity to see where this might lead, though. He'd taken a chance by accepting, and then an even bigger one by telling me a story so painful that even now his hand trembled in mine. He had to be as full of fear as me, though he might be better at hiding it. I hadn't promised to stay. He was gambling that I might. It was an enormous risk—more so than I could probably comprehend.

And deep down I knew walls offered protection, but they could be a prison too.

Vos waited quietly while I thought, his chest rising and falling and hearts beating with that soothing rhythm I'd missed so much.

I wanted to wipe the tears off my face, but I didn't want to let go of his hand. He surprised me by using his free hand and the bedsheet to gently dab the wetness from my cheeks without hurting me by touching my bruises or cuts. That simple and thoughtful kindness meant more to me than I could have explained.

My stomach growled embarrassingly loudly.

"You are hungry," Vos said, nuzzling my hair. "I am glad your appetite is improving. It is well past midday. Should I prepare a meal?"

"If you don't mind. I wish I could help with the cooking." I hesitated. "Well, I've never really cooked, but I could help *you* cook. Hand you things."

He chuckled. "When you can stand unaided, I would be happy to teach you. In the meantime, I enjoy cooking and I must eat as well. It is not any extra work to cook for two." He started to rise.

"Can you take me to the sofa?" I asked. "I'd love to sit by the fire, and I like to watch you cook."

Vos blinked. "You like to watch me cook?"

My cheeks heated. "Yes."

"Then it is my privilege to take you to the sofa." He kissed my forehead and rose from the bed. Carefully, he adjusted my blankets and scooped me up with his tentacles.

As he straightened and I got close enough, I raised my head and kissed him. Which of us was more startled, I wasn't sure.

The kiss was quick, soft, and very sweet. His lips were hot and tasted a bit like the sea. He returned the kiss as gently as he held me.

I couldn't hold my head up very long before pain lanced through my neck. When my head fell back to rest on his tentacle, Vos smiled down at me.

"You surprised an assassin," he murmured. "Quite a feat, my Calla." His smile vanished, and his expression turned grave. "Calla, I apologize. I misspoke."

"It's all right. I don't mind." I touched his face. "Soup and toasted bread?"

"Whatever you would like." He carried me to the front room and arranged me so I lay in pillows on the sofa. "Is this comfortable?"

"Yes." I grimaced and settled in. "Not as comfortable as your tentacles, but comfortable enough."

He kissed the top of my head, turned up the fire in the fireplace, and hurried to the kitchen.

Toasty warm in my blankets, I basked in the heat from the fire as he selected frozen kaory meat and homegrown vegetables from the food storage unit. I hadn't said so, but I enjoyed watching his tentacles roam about the kitchen, picking up utensils and doing small tasks like straightening things as he prepped the food with his human hands. He hummed as he cooked—simple melodies that had become familiar though I didn't know them. And his tentacles swayed in rhythm.

The truth was, I simply enjoyed watching Vos do anything at all. He was beautiful. His skin shimmered and glowed and his tentacles were a wonder. How would he react if I confessed that to him? Would he laugh? Tease me? Remind me he enjoyed watching over me too?

Everything about this quiet home life was utterly new to me. From the incessant rain to the sounds and smells of cooking to the heavy purple fruit growing on the tree beside the sofa, I might as well have fallen through a rift in space and ended up in a different universe altogether from the one I'd inhabited. Did Vos feel the same?

Through the window, I spotted Poe in the garden contentedly nibbling on a leafy plant as she searched the grass for tiny, slow-moving creatures with shells Vos called *enni*.

"Why Iosa?" I asked as Vos meticulously sliced the meat and vegetables. "There are lots of other planets and moons that are sparsely populated and have beautiful oceans. Why live here?"

"The answer is not as profound as you might expect." He smiled over his shoulder, then went back to dicing. "I visited Jakora several times during my time with the Guard. The transports often flew past Iosa on their way to the planet. I believe I was the only passenger who found Iosa beautiful, or even paid it any attention. Long before I thought about where I might go if I survived my years of service, I felt drawn to this moon. And so when I left the Guard, I came here and purchased this home with the thought that I would live here for one year, and if I did not find it to my liking, I would leave."

"So obviously you like it." I gazed out the window. "I wish I'd gotten to see Iosa from space the way you did. I might have thought it was beautiful if I hadn't seen it as my probable grave."

The rhythm of his chopping missed a beat and his tentacles quivered. I winced. I might have been a little *too* blunt.

"What about Poe?" I asked, hoping to distract him. "How did you meet Poe?"

He finished cutting up the soup ingredients and began adding them to the pot. "A few weeks after I settled into this home, I started work on the wall. I was rushing to finish both the wall and the bathroom expansion before the arrival of the rainy season. One morning, as I was laying bricks, Poe emerged from the swamp and approached, limping. One of her legs was fractured, I believe from a fall. She asked for help."

"Oh, poor Poe," I said, grimacing. My right leg twinged, as if in sympathy.

Vos seasoned the soup, covered the pot, and left it to simmer while he took out a loaf of bread. "I put a cast on her leg so the bone could heal," he said, slicing the bread. "And I built her a nest in my home so she did not have to fear predators. In return, she helped me with my wall, and then with my bathroom and other construction. I told her she was welcome to stay once she had healed, and so she did."

I pictured Vos only weeks or months after leaving the Guard, making his home on an utterly unfamiliar moon he'd only seen in passing. An assassin building a wall one brick at a time, adding onto the little bathroom so he could have an enormous bathtub, crafting a nest for an injured creature with deadly claws and welcoming her into his house.

Making soup from scratch with vegetables he'd grown himself and meat taken from animals he'd hunted. Baking bread and watching Poe in the garden through the kitchen window.

Could this be a life I would want? Would it soothe my hurts like it soothed Vos? Could I grow to love the quiet and even the never-ending rain?

Despite my hunger, the fire's warmth and Vos's humming had made me drowsy by the time he brought the tray of food. He set the tray aside, scooped me up, sat on the sofa, and settled me on his lap before he picked up the tray again, resting it on his tentacle.

"Soup and toasted bread, as requested," he said, kissing the top of my head. "And fresh vinefruit for dessert."

We ate in companionable silence. The soup was much richer than earlier versions, and more seasoned. Even the kaory meat had a more savory taste. I couldn't tell if he'd changed how he made the soup or if I felt less pain and that made everything seem better.

The real treat was the vinefruit, which I'd never tried. He'd taken it from the tree next to the sofa, removed the rind, and sliced it neatly onto a plate. The fruit's flesh was purple and its seeds were plump and white.

"Are the seeds okay to eat?" I asked.

"Yes." He picked up a slice of fruit. "The fruit is very sweet and the seeds are tart."

He watched me take a bite, smiling as my eyes widened. "This is delicious," I said before I chewed. When I bit into the seed, though, its tartness made me grimace.

"I did warn you." He chuckled. "I suppose it is an acquired taste."

I ended up eating more of the vinefruit than he did, seeds and all. He rested his chin on top of my head as I ate the last piece. With a towel, he wiped the juice off my hands and his, set the tray aside, and rewrapped my blankets before tucking me against his chest.

I slipped my hand out of the blankets and rested it on my lap. He covered my hand with his much-larger one. Gods, I looked forward to the day I'd healed enough that simply eating and talking didn't leave me exhausted.

A few quiet minutes later, with a full stomach, warm and secure, I decided to take a chance.

I didn't really know how to start telling this story, so I said the hardest part first. "Keela was my sister," I said.

Vos didn't coo, which surprised me a little, and he didn't flinch as if he'd had to suppress the urge to do so. Maybe his instincts told him to let me tell my tale how I wanted to tell it, with all the emotions involved.

"I was three and a half when our mother sold us," I continued. Even with Vos's tentacles around me, every word felt as difficult to say as climbing up a steep hill. Had Vos felt the same while telling his story? "Keela was a year older than me. We went into different *tarjas*—training groups—because of our ages. Our *tarjas* trained in facilities twenty kilometers from each other. I didn't see her, or have any contact with her, for almost seven years."

I didn't need to tell Vos about my training; his was probably not all that different from mine. I was taught to kill. So was he. What else was there to say?

"I fought in the arena for the first time when I was five." This part wasn't as bad as talking about Keela. "From ages five to seven, our bouts were not to the death. Winners were declared based on points. You might know that."

"I do." His voice was kind. "I know some things about the arenas and fights. Some who completed Guard training became scouts and buying agents for keepers, before the arenas closed. We had access to the information."

That made it easier to talk about my years in the arena. I wouldn't have to explain what took place there, or who benefited from our suffering, or what my life had been like.

But talking about Keela wasn't easy, or anything close to it.

"I didn't tell anyone I had a sister," I said. "And I never tried to get a message to her because it would have been intercepted. Some of the highest-grossing bouts and *enaras*, or fights to the death, were between siblings or combatants who had emotional ties to one another. *Enaras* between girls who were related drew the biggest crowds and made the most money of all fights, except for the team fights."

"I did not know that." Vos's tentacles caressed me over my

blanket cocoon. "You did not want to have to face your sister in the arena."

"No. And I sure as hells didn't want all those rich assholes betting and making money on it." I heard and smelled the arena floor so clearly even now, so many years later. "Every time I saw my name posted on the schedule, I lived in terror that I might see Keela's name listed as my opponent. And like you, I couldn't show that fear—not to anyone. The gladiators were encouraged to rat on each other. And the more bouts you won, the more enemies you had, so you had to be *very* careful at all times. We lived in bunkhouses."

"So you had no privacy." He found an uninjured part of my hand and stroked it with his thumb. "Not even at night."

"No." I cleared my throat. "I sometimes lay awake wondering what I would do if I were to face Keela in the arena. I couldn't forfeit and neither could she because that meant a painful public execution. Would I fight to win? Fight to lose? What would *she* do? And she might not even recognize me. So many questions, so much fear, and I had to hide it."

He let me stay quiet for a while, stroking my hair as I rested. Talking was tiring, or maybe it was the subject matter that left me feeling so drained.

"By some miracle or twist of fate, we were never opponents or on the same fighting team," I said softly. My chest ached, but not because of my injuries. "But I saw her twice in the hall before fights—once when I was ten, and again when I was fourteen. And then I never saw her again."

Vos's tentacle slipped into my blankets to wrap around my ankle, as if trying to anchor me to the present. He smelled so good, and he was so warm.

"I never saw her name listed as having been killed in the arena," I added. "It's very possible I missed it. But it's also very possible she survived to age sixteen the year before I did, got her collar taken off, and found a way off Ganai."

"I hope that is what happened," Vos said, still stroking the side of my hand with his thumb. "There is no way to know?"

"None at all. The arenas burned. All the records went with them. And it's impossible to find out who took a transport off the planet." I took a ragged breath. "You know how you said you used to imagine your mother visiting the training facility and watching you?"

He kissed my hair. "Yes."

"After her sixteenth birthday passed, I used to imagine Keela was in the crowd watching me fight. I knew she wouldn't be, because no gladiator *ever* wanted to watch fights, but I still imagined it. Sometimes I'd look over the crowd to see if she was there, but all the faces were blurry to me." Bitterness made my stomach churn and my voice harsh. "I hated everyone who came to the fights. I would have burned down the arena with all of them trapped inside if I could have."

"I do not blame you for that. I imagine many felt the same."

I swallowed hard. "The day I heard the Alliance and the Barons Guild had forced the arenas to close, I sat in my rented room on Havel Prime and stared out the window, imagining Ganai burning. That was my fantasy, Vos. Not just our keepers and the arena owners dead and the training facilities and arenas burned—a *whole planet* laid waste. They all let the arenas stay open for so long just because a few people made so much money off them and convinced the people the arenas offered more benefit than harm. I hated everyone for that. I would have lit the fires myself."

"Your rage is more than understandable." He rested his cheek on top of my head. "Calla, I am sorry these atrocities happened to you and your sister, and doubly sorry you cannot hold those responsible accountable for their cruelty."

"Wait—I'm not done," I said, and now I began to tremble. "When I turned sixteen, after I was free but before I left Ganai, I went back to the town where I was born. I went looking for my mother. I wanted to know why she sold us. I felt so cold and quiet inside when I stepped off the transport. I had never felt so *cold* in my life. I had a dagger with me and I went looking for answers."

Vos's tentacles caressed me again. "I understand."

"Do you? I don't know if I do." My chuckle was dry and humorless. "At the time, I didn't know what I would do if I found her, or if whatever she said would matter. Nothing would justify what she'd done. But she was gone. When I got to my hometown, I discovered she'd died years earlier in a transport crash. So I never got to find out what I would have done if I'd found her. I just get to wonder. And I don't know if that dagger would have stayed in its sheath or not."

"I had a moment not so different from this, during my final mission for the Guard." He took a deep breath and exhaled. "I too cannot say what I would have done had the choice not been taken out of my hands. I find myself standing at that crossroads again and again in my dreams and in my imagination. Sometimes I make one choice, sometimes another. I believe I know which was the correct choice, the one I should have made, but then I reconsider and wonder if my fear of the repercussions would have won out. Like you, I do not know."

"What does it say about us that we don't know?" I asked. "Shouldn't we know what's right and what's wrong?"

"I am not sure." Vos moved so he could look into my eyes. His expression was thoughtful. "I do not know if it says anything definitive about us at all that we are unsure. But I think we yearn to have been able to make that choice rather than have it taken away from us. Perhaps we are haunted by the fact we did not get to choose."

I found myself unable to get a breath.

We did not get to choose.

All my life, until the day I took off my collar, I had not gotten to choose. I had traveled to my hometown wanting to know why I'd deserved that fate, only to discover that once again fate, or the gods, or happenstance, had taken away my ability to choose. I'd wanted control over *one thing* that day and been denied. I'd returned to the port consumed by anger and helplessness.

Right behind that realization was another: When my fighter was falling toward Iosa's surface, I'd had a moment of helplessness before I coached myself back to defiance and remembered I had the choice to fight. I'd probably survived only because I'd fought to the last to control my landing.

I might not have ended up on Iosa by choice, and be hurting and not much use while I healed, but I had the ability to choose what I did or didn't do. I also believed my ability to make choices for myself was every bit as important to Vos as it was to me. The thought was deeply empowering, and deeply comforting.

"Calla," Vos said, tipping my chin up so gently. "Tell me what you are thinking."

I was thinking about his lips, only centimeters from my own, and the way his eyes glowed like starlight.

"I think you're right," I said instead. "About not getting to decide haunting us. I think that makes more sense to me than just about anything else I've ever heard."

"So you do not regret sharing this story with me?" His gaze searched my face. "Or that I shared mine with you?"

I'd expected to feel more vulnerable now that he knew one of my most closely guarded secrets, but I didn't. He'd listened to every word—really *listened* and not just heard. I'd never felt like he'd judged me for my thoughts or actions. Empathy without pity was wonderfully comforting.

Was this kindness and comfort a result of him believing I was his true mate, or was this simply who Vos was? Was there a difference?

No, wait—he'd taken Poe in without a hesitation, healed her

injury, and treasured her as a companion and friend. That had nothing at all to do with true mate physiology and everything to do with kindness and empathy.

"Calla?" Vos prompted, jolting me out of my thoughts.

"No, I don't regret this conversation," I assured him. "As much as it hurt, I'm grateful for it."

"I am grateful too, and humbled by your trust in me." He frowned. "Does your stomach hurt?"

I'd wrapped both arms across my abdomen without realizing it. "It aches all the time," I admitted. "It's worse than usual right now because I've been sitting up for a while. But I want to stay out here instead of going back to bed."

He rearranged the pillows on the sofa so he could recline and then moved me very carefully so I was lying against his chest. The discomfort in my stomach began to ease.

"Thank you," I said with a sigh. "That's lovely. But don't let me keep you from doing things you need to take care of."

"Nothing needs my immediate attention but you," he promised, his lips against my forehead. "We can rest…my Calla."

He said it tentatively, though I'd told him I didn't mind being called his Calla. No fear rose when he said it, and I didn't resent it like I'd thought I would. But why?

Maybe because I'd begun to accept that behind the possessive *my* was a man who believed deeply in the importance of having choices. His tentacle around my ankle was gentle and never tight. He held me, but he would let me go if I asked.

Maybe no one valued body autonomy and choice like those who'd had neither for a very long time, and would never take those privileges for granted as long as they lived.

"May I have a kiss?" I asked.

Vos's breathing hitched. "Yes. Thank you for asking, but from now on, you do not need to ask." He drew me higher on his chest, bent his head, and kissed me.

This kiss was a little less gentle and a little hungrier than the first, but no less sweet. And the kiss lingered for several long moments before he raised his head.

"I love your eyes," I murmured, my fingertips brushing his lower lip. "They're like starlight."

"And to me, you are the sun." He settled me back in his arms and tentacles and tucked my head under his chin. "Rest now, my Calla." Softly, he cooed.

All my aches faded away, and I slept.

CHAPTER 12

VOS

The next week passed in a comforting routine.

My Calla began her days with breakfast and light exercise, then rested. She still could not stand without me taking most of her weight, and the pain in her legs and abdomen remained of great concern to me, but her appetite improved significantly and her pallor gave way to a much healthier color.

Perhaps best of all, she smiled frequently—at me, at the food I prepared for her, at Poe, and most especially upon waking to find I had moved a half-dozen potted plants into our bedroom, including a vinefruit sapling that would begin bearing fruit within a year.

I buried my worry that she might not still be here to see the fruit and focused on my happiness at the way her eyes lit up when she saw the little tree. She had indeed been starved for the comfort of growing things. What a wonder Iosa would be to her once the rainy season ended and the sun and rich soil turned my walled yard into a lush garden full of vegetables, fruits, and flowers.

Most of all I wanted to take her to my beloved ocean, but I could not risk it until she could not only walk but protect herself from predators during the journey and in the water. I expected to pine for the sea intensely in the meantime, but it seemed my body had forgotten its yearning if I could not bring Calla with me. I missed the ocean, but with my Calla near, I did not ache for its depths.

That she had given me permission to call her *my Calla* filled me with joy and deep contentment beyond words, despite twinges of unease that came with thoughts of Calla deciding to leave Iosa. Whenever I had such thoughts, rather than dwell on them, I busied myself around my home, transforming it as best I could from a stark and utilitarian space to a place of comfort and pleasant sights and smells. I could not make the choice for her, but I could do whatever was in my power to persuade her to stay.

Every morning when Calla opened her eyes, yawned, stretched gingerly, and smiled at me, it chipped away at my fears.

And each time she asked me to help her bathe, or kissed me, or requested to sit on the sofa to watch me cook, the song in my hearts grew.

"You're cheerful today," Calla said on the eighth morning since our agreement to start again. She had foregone her usual mid-morning nap and asked instead to sit on the sofa near the fire wrapped in blankets. The day was unseasonably chilly and high winds shook the house. A *nuoia* was rolling through along the coast. Even Poe had come inside and was dozing in her nest. We doubted anything would venture out of its shelter to invade our garden in this weather.

"You keep smiling like you know a secret," Calla added, her voice light with mirth. "Come on, Vos. Tell me what's got you looking so happy on such a cold and windy day."

"There is no secret." I set a clean cooking pot on a shelf and turned to find her smiling. My tentacles quivered with happiness at the sight. "It is you who makes me so happy. I have told you this. Do you doubt me?"

Her smile turned wry. "It's not that I doubt your word. I might doubt your judgment. Maybe you've lived here by yourself with Poe too long and I'm a fraction as smile-worthy as you think."

"I highly doubt it, but if it is so, then I am happily misguided." I poured a cup of water and brought it to the sofa. "Are you thirsty, my beautiful fantasy?"

Her laugh made my hearts soar. "I am. Don't tell me you could smell that I'm dehydrated."

"No, but I noticed you have not consumed any water yet today." I scooped her up, settled myself on the sofa, and arranged her on my lap so she was sitting up enough to drink from the cup. "I will make us tea once I have a chance to rest from making breakfast and cleaning the kitchen."

Her eyes narrowed at me over the rim of the cup. "Vos Turek, don't tell me you need to *rest* after cooking and tidying the kitchen. That is bullshit if I've ever heard it."

I chuckled and kissed the top of her head. "You have caught me in a lie. I missed holding you."

"You were holding me less than two hours ago," she pointed out, but she did not ask me to get up. She sipped her water, her gaze on the window. "It's pouring out there, even by Iosa standards. We're not in danger of flooding, are we?"

"No. At least, I do not think so," I amended. "I have lived here during storms like this and hurricanes and never seen flooding. Even if this area *did* become flooded, our home is very secure and watertight, even where I have added on to its original form."

If she noted my slip of *our home*, I hoped she assumed I had referred to Poe and myself.

"That's a relief. I don't think I'd be much help in an evacuation, even if you owned a boat." She settled in against my chest, the cup wrapped in her hands, and looked around. "I especially don't want anything to spoil all the work you've been doing. This looks like a different house now with all these plants and that pretty red moss. It's like living in a garden." She craned her neck and kissed my jaw. "Thank you."

"Your smiles are all the thanks I need." I covered one of her hands with mine. "Are you sleepy? Achy from the exercise?"

"Surprisingly, no. And believe it or not, my stomach doesn't hurt as much as usual either." Her smile returned. "We haven't used the medical scanner to check me over lately, but maybe some of the worst injuries are healing."

"We will check," I promised. I wanted nothing more than to see fewer orange and red notations on its screen and more blue. "Though you feel much improved, we must remain careful and not exceed your limitations. We have both been injured enough to know impatience and over-exertion during healing leads to significant setbacks."

"I know." Calla sighed. "I used to compete with my squadron mates to see who could do the most pull-ups or high-G jumps. Now I'm just happy to sit up for any length of time without it hurting. And yes, I know it's temporary," she added before I could speak. "I'll get there. I damn near took a step today, didn't I?"

"Yes, you did." I kissed her hair again, drinking in its silky softness and the lingering scent of my hair soap. "Have you slept better these last few days?"

"I have." She looked up at me. "Maybe that's why I'm not as tired during the day today. Have you seen me acting like I'm having a nightmare?"

"No, I have not." I smiled. "Nor have I needed to coo for you during the night. I hoped that meant your dreams have been more pleasant."

"Not all of them, but some." She squeezed my hand a little

tighter than before. She was getting stronger. "I had one last night that you and I were in the garden surrounded by plants and it wasn't raining. It seemed so real, but I knew it was a dream because it's never not raining."

The thought of sitting in the garden with my Calla made my hearts sing. "It will not always rain. The rainy season is drawing to an end."

"I wonder if I'll miss the sound of rain," she mused. "Assuming you're right and it *does* stop raining. Which I will believe only when I see it."

How wonderful to be comfortably teased like this. My mood, already light, became almost effervescent.

Quiet minutes passed as Calla drank her water and we watched and listened to heavy, windblown raindrops pummeling the window above the sofa. Poe had withdrawn into her shell to sleep, and eventually I found myself almost dozing.

"Vos," Calla murmured.

I pressed my lips to her hair. "Yes?"

"Tell me about the ocean."

I had not expected that question, but if she wanted to know more about our surroundings, I was happy to oblige.

"The oceans of Iosa are very beautiful," I said. "From my home, it is a two-kilometer journey across marsh and swamp to a small inlet where I like to enter the ocean. The walk is not entirely safe, but if you walk quickly and quietly, most trips are uneventful."

"I remember what you said about the kaory and the snakes." She wrinkled her nose. "So why that inlet?"

"I prefer not to be noticed in my comings and goings, especially by anyone from the raider camp. The inlet is secluded. I have never known anyone else to go there. I enter the water unseen and swim in the deep before returning the same way."

"That sounds so peaceful." She rested her head on my tentacle. "I can see why you like it here. As long as some gigantic sea creature doesn't swallow you whole, it seems perfect."

I chuckled softly. "The largest creatures of the deep do not come too near the coast. As for the rest, I smell like a predator to most sea life, so they tend to keep their distance."

Despite the heat from the fire, she shivered. I drew her blankets around her more snugly.

"The waters of the deep are purple, and the sea floor is covered with beautiful plants and marine life," I continued. "My favorite way to visit the sea is to drift with the deep current along the shore and then swim back to the inlet. Drifting is very restful, and the return is good exercise."

My Calla frowned. "Letting the current take you wherever it wants doesn't sound so restful, but I suppose you're safe enough."

After all she had suffered, naturally the thought of giving up control to an unpredictable outside force would unnerve her.

"It took many months for me to enjoy drifting," I admitted. "And even more until it became peaceful and meditative. I had to discover new depths within myself before I could find peace in surrendering myself to the currents."

"I can't imagine being able to do that." She shook her head. "Was that what you were doing the night I crashed? Drifting?"

"Yes." I drew her closer, in case memories of that night upset her. "I had just reached the farthest point I could go without getting too close to the raider camp and started to turn around when your fighter hit the water nearby."

"I'm sorry I almost landed on you." She smiled up at me, though the expression was fleeting. "I was trying to land in the water and not hit the lights I saw from above as I fell. I guess that was their camp."

"Yes, probably."

"Soulless bastards." She scowled. "The lot of them."

How I adored her ferocity. I kissed her gently. For all her

fierceness, her lips were so sweet and perfectly soft, and she returned my kiss.

Every little intimate touch sizzled on my skin and stirred longing in my hearts and tentacles. I carefully rationed my kisses and tried to keep my hands and tentacles on her blankets rather than her bare skin, other than the tentacle that habitually coiled around her ankle.

Despite my determination to not rush into physical intimacy, I yearned for her more with every passing day, and at night I dreamed of her body on mine. Just touching my lips to hers caused blood to rush to my cock.

I struggled to rein in my arousal before she noticed. I treasured this tenderness between us and did not want to jeopardize the connection we had built. Still, my desire burned like the fires of a forge.

"I am very grateful you almost landed on me, my Calla," I said. "I would have given anything to have made that night less terrible for you."

"We've made the best of it, though, haven't we?" This time her smile did not immediately fade. "Speaking of which, would you be willing to bathe me? It's raining too hard for you to do anything outside, and I worked up a good sweat exercising earlier. I'd like to feel clean and soak in hot water for a while."

If bathing was among her most favorite things about my home, I would not say no.

"I will fill the tub," I said, and started to rise.

"Thank you. Please throw in some of those pretty orange leaves that make the water smell so good." She caught my hand. "Will you bathe with me?"

All my longing for the ocean crested in a sudden wave of desire to do what I had not dared to do since Calla's first night in my home: cradle her in the water. I wanted that joy and pleasure so much that my hearts ached and my tentacles quivered. My fear of taking a wrong step warred with my need for her.

The way she held my gaze let me know she knew what being in the water with her meant to me. This was a step *she* wanted to take, and I yearned to take it with her. As long as I followed her lead and listened to my instincts, we could find something even more beautiful together. And I would forever be grateful for the privilege.

Calla squeezed my hand. "Vos, it's all right if you don't want to. I understand." She smiled ruefully. "I still need a lifeguard, though."

Once again she had offered me a choice, and once again I must follow my hearts.

"I would be happy to join you," I said, caressing her cheek very gently as she looked at me with those beautiful green eyes. "I will fill the tub."

She kissed my fingertips. "I'm not going anywhere, but don't take too long getting ready. I'm stinky and achy. I want to be in the water."

She did not *stink*, but I did not argue.

I rose, settled her on the sofa, and hurried to the bathroom to draw the bath, my tentacles dancing in happiness and anticipation.

CHAPTER 13

I'D FIBBED—I WASN'T REALLY IN ANY PAIN. I JUST WANTED TO BE in the water with Vos.

I wanted him to cradle me with nothing between us—no blankets, no clothing, no distance. I wanted to see more of the raw desire I'd glimpsed in unguarded moments when he thought I wasn't watching.

When I woke this morning, I hadn't necessarily planned to ask him to join me in the tub today. He'd been so obviously cautious not to push me in any way. But when he'd told me he smelled like a predator to most sea life, I couldn't hold back a shiver of desire.

He was a beautiful predator who'd been nothing but kind and gentle to me, and I wanted him. I ached with need—so much so that I had to fight the impulse to slip my hand under the blankets and between my legs, where wetness already dripped.

My healing body had limitations, but we'd find ways around that. Maybe his reminder that I had to be careful not to over-exert myself was about more than just my morning exercise routine. And maybe he was reminding himself too.

When he emerged from the bathroom, he had already removed his shirt, and his loose-fitting pants rested low on his hips. I let myself devour the sight of his broad chest and shoulders, the lines of his muscles, and his gills that fluttered as he breathed. Oh, to be able to swim with him in the sea and see him in his element. For now, the wonderfully enormous bathtub would have to do.

I'd gotten enough deep breaths to relax again, but that didn't mean my scent didn't give me away. I didn't mind, though. I liked that Vos would be able to tell how aroused I was. He didn't have to wonder, and I didn't have to say.

Vos scooped me up as carefully as ever, his eyes glowing. "Ready, my Calla?"

"Yes." I lay my head against his chest to listen to his hearts beat. "Very ready."

As he carried me to the bathroom, I spotted Poe's eyestalks peeping out from her shell. When she saw me looking at her, they darted back into hiding. She'd clasped her claws in front of her massive shell, which I'd learned was a sign of tranquility. Because she was warm, safe, and comfortable in Vos's house instead of outside in the nasty weather, or because Vos and I had decided to take another step toward the kind of relationship she so clearly wanted us to have? Either way, her contentment made me smile.

Vos kissed my temple. That spot had only recently stopped hurting from the crash and then being burned by the barrel of the Atolani raider's plasma gun.

"You probably think it is silly of me," he said, "but I will never tire of your smiles."

An unexpected pang in my heart made my smile fade. "I don't think I've smiled as many times in my life as I've smiled in the past week."

"I am sorry." He rested his forehead against mine. "But also I am glad."

"Me too," I said softly.

He closed the bathroom door to keep in the heat, slid his pants down and off, and sat on the side of the tub. Not only had he put in the leaves I'd requested, he'd added something that smelled sweet and made the water froth and bubble.

"My Calla," he said, his gaze on mine.

He unwrapped my blankets slowly. He was always careful not to touch any of my healing cuts or bruises, but he seemed to want to take his time. Maybe he wanted to savor this, or maybe he wanted to give me time to change my mind.

I was impatient to be out of my coverings and into the water with him, but I also wanted us to go slowly so I could watch him watching me. That candor I'd come to rely on was evident even now in the way he didn't seem embarrassed or self-conscious or shy about baring me in a very different way than ever before, and that kept my own self-consciousness at bay.

When the last of the blanket fell away, he let it slip to the floor, leaving me naked and cradled in his tentacles rather than sitting on his lap. His gaze devoured me so intensely I shivered.

Vos's hand caressed my shoulder, moved down my arm, and captured my hand to bring it to his lips. "Beautiful," he said, his mouth on my fingers. His sharp teeth pressed into my skin, a thrill of danger, as if he knew what his predatory side did to me. "Mercilessly beautiful, like a star."

I opened my mouth to say something self-deprecating, only for him to silence me by lowering his mouth to my right breast to catch my nipple between his lips. He flicked it with his tongue and sucked gently.

Oh, gods. I tried to arch my back, but Vos held me still.

"No, my Calla," he murmured, his softly glowing gaze locked on my face. "You must not injure yourself. I will give you pleasure, but I would die before I would hurt you."

He was right, but desperation and desire made it difficult to care. "Vos, *please.*"

In an inhumanly fluid movement far more reminiscent of a cephalopod than a man, he slipped us into the tub. The water was the perfect temperature—hot to the point of not quite scalding—and whatever made the water bubbly made my skin slick and soft.

But the moment I rested my head on his chest, the sensation of his hot, bare skin against mine and memories I'd kept buried since that night stole my breath right out of my lungs. Everything good about this moment evaporated.

Pain. Blood. Falling toward dark water. Broken bones and burns and fear.

Lying in this tub, in and out of consciousness, unsure if I would live or die, with only this hot skin and these heartbeats to cling to.

I let out a ragged sound and buried my face against his chest.

Vos's tentacles quivered. "My sweet Calla," he murmured into my hair, and cooed.

I lost myself in that wonderful comforting sound and the security of his arms and tentacles around me. Vos's coo didn't banish those memories, but they cut less deeply. One breath at a time, one gentle caress of Vos's tentacles at a time, the bitterness of terror faded.

I was safe now. I had survived. The raiders who'd been so cruel were dead. Vos had killed them all for what they'd done and they'd never hurt anyone else again.

And more than that, I was happy here. I was cared for and desired. I *smiled.*

Vos cupped the back of my head and held me close. "I am sorry these memories surfaced. I feared they might."

"I have to face the memories," I said, my voice not quite steady despite how much I meant those words. "I can't pretend it didn't happen. That really only makes it worse."

"Yes." He covered my hand with his where it lay on my stomach. "I too must make peace with my past, so I may see my future more clearly."

"What do you see in your future?" I asked. We'd talked about our pasts, but not about days to come. Maybe it was a dangerous topic because I had yet to decide what I would do once my injuries healed, but I wanted to know what he envisioned for himself. "If it's okay for me to ask," I amended.

"You may ask me anything. I will find the courage to answer." He rested his chin on the top of my head. "I am sure it will not surprise you to hear my dreams are of you."

No, it wasn't a surprise. His admission was very sweet, and far less anxiety-inducing than I'd thought it would be. Maybe that was because he'd cooed, or maybe because the prospect grew more pleasant by the day.

I managed a small smile. "I don't think anyone's ever dreamed of me like that."

He cooed softly.

Was he sorry that was true, or secretly happy that he was the first to think of me in that way? The answer might be that he felt both.

Two of Vos's tentacles stirred the water around us while another wrapped around my ankle. "What are your dreams, my Calla? You said you wanted to earn a bonus from the Defense and use it to travel."

How terrified he must be to ask that question—to bring up what I'd told him about what my plans were before the crash. To remind me of the choices that lay before me. But he'd answered me honestly, so I owed him the same.

"I've seen so many dark things," I said. "My time on Ganai was a nightmare. A lot of what I saw and did before I joined the Defense was too. As a pilot, I fought for Alliance ideals against the scum of the galaxy. My commanding officer wasn't all that much better than the scum I fought. Each day I put on my uniform and sat in a mission briefing with Captain Proos and told myself I could put up with anything if it meant getting that reenlistment bonus. Once I completed my service, it would help me finance travel to places where I could see beauty and good things and meet kind people."

I moved my head and rested it on his tentacle so I could look up. His expression was so tender that a lump formed in my throat.

"I've been lying in your bed thinking about it all," I continued, my voice raw. "What I dream of is choosing where I go and where I stay, and healing all these hurts. That's my dream and the future I want for myself. I'm just not sure anymore if that's out there somewhere or right here."

He bent his head and brushed his lips on mine. "I understand."

He really did, and that stirred more than desire. It warmed my heart, and maybe my soul too. I pulled his head down to mine and kissed him fiercely. His chest rumbled and his tentacles quivered.

When he raised his head, he gazed into my eyes. "Do you think you might find healing with…me?"

Vos had been so honest with me that his obvious reluctance to say what he'd had on the tip of his tongue made me squeeze his hand. What had he been about to say before he changed his mind? *Do you think you might find healing with a monster?*

Well, I'd already accepted his monstrous side, along with the side of him that cradled me like a treasure he was afraid to harm or lose. Maybe he was a monster, but he could be *my* monster, if he didn't mind me being his.

"Yes," I said, my voice quiet but firm. "I don't think being a monster is bad. Doing monstrous things *is*. You have not done one monstrous thing since I met you, and my gut tells me you never will. I might not trust anyone or anything in the universe, but I trust my gut. And I trust you." I ran my hand through his hair and cupped the back of his head. "I wanted to find beautiful and good, and I found you."

His grave expression became a grin. Gods above and below, the sight of his mouthful of sharp, pointed teeth made my pussy wet and my nipples hard.

He inhaled deeply, first with his nose and then with his gills. They fluttered against my skin. And his tentacles swirled in the water again, but not in anger or agitation. All four of them traveled up my legs and arms, coiling around me and plucking at my skin, as if Vos was drinking in my taste and smell in every way he could.

Every little suck at my skin made my pussy clench and ache because he wasn't filling it. And when I thought about the ways he might use those suckers on my most sensitive places, I felt myself gush for him.

"I cannot go back to how we were before," he said, his voice rough. "I will not live under the same roof as if we were strangers. I will be yours. I will kill anything that poses a danger to you."

"I will do the same." I touched his lips with my fingertips. "Once I'm back on my feet. Until then, you'll have to rely on Poe."

He smiled at that—a sweet smile that had the same effect on my desire as his toothy one because it showed the goodness of his heart.

"Kiss me," I said roughly. "Wrap me up in your beautiful tentacles and kiss me, *please*."

He did as I asked without hesitation, his tentacles coiling around me everywhere: my arms, my torso, my legs, tasting and drinking me in. I had never felt so safe, so desired, so *needed*.

With another low rumble, he bent his head and pressed his lips to mine.

CHAPTER 14

VOS

My Calla's lips tasted like the rest of her, but even better —more concentrated, more enchanting, a symphony of flavors that ignited every cell in my body.

Then, to my absolute horror, she threw her head back, screamed, and collapsed on my chest, shuddering violently.

Fear and fury swept over me, turning my body cold and my vision dark around the edges as if my own life were under threat. Had my worst fears come true, and her internal injuries proven even less healed than we had thought? I cooed, but for the first time, it did not seem to help.

"Calla!" I shouted, holding her in my arms as my tentacles waved frantically, sending water cascading over the side of the tub. "*Calla!* What have I done?"

"Vos..." Her nails dug into my arms as she struggled to respond. Her chest heaved with deep, ragged breaths.

I had longed to hear her cry out my name, but not like this. "Tell me what is wrong," I urged, tipping her chin up so I could see her eyes, which appeared unfocused. "Did I injure you?"

"No," she gasped. "Just…I need…a minute."

I forced myself to be calmer and assess her more clinically. I did not smell blood, and she was not holding her stomach like she always did when she hurt there.

What I *did* smell was her arousal.

As it had before we had kissed, it filled my nose and thrummed in my blood, calling me to her. It had taken on a sharper, stronger tang now, one that made my cock as hard as a meteorite despite my all-consuming worry that she had been harmed.

"You didn't…hurt me," she said breathlessly. She ran her fingers through my hair again, holding on tightly in a way that hurt and felt very good. "Not at all."

"Please explain." I demanded, my body tense and full of anger, confusion, and fear. "I do not understand."

"Your tentacles…when you kissed me, something happened." Calla took a deep, shaky breath and rested her head against my chest. "They made me come, from all over my body, all at once."

Now I was even more bewildered. "I cannot…my tentacles have no such power."

She looked up at me through her lashes, a faint smile on her lips. "On the contrary, I assure you they *do*."

The scent of her arousal *had* changed. Her reaction very well could have been not pain at all, but the sort of powerful orgasm she had described.

"I am…sorry." I did not know what to say. I had bedded many lovers over many years, including human women, and never given any orgasms with just the touches of my lips and tentacles. This must be another effect of finding my true mate.

"Oh, please don't *ever* apologize for giving me an orgasm." She let out a sigh of contentment that swept away the last of my fear and anger and nestled herself against my chest. "Believe me, you have nothing to be sorry for. I was surprised, but it was good. Really…" She sighed again. "Really good."

"What about your stomach and chest?" I asked as my tentacles quivered. "You thrashed around quite a lot."

"I'm all right, really." She chuckled. "I honestly don't remember what I did. It's all a blur."

First I had made a sound that was only for her, and now I could give her orgasms simply with a kiss and my tentacles. It was as if my body was made to care for her and make her happy.

I looked at Calla in my arms with the same amount of wonder as the first time I had held her. She gave me that wry smile I adored.

She is mine, I thought. *I will have no other.*

My vision turned silver around the edges, meaning my eyes were glowing very brightly. My heartsbeats thundered in my ears.

Her smile went from wry to playful. She tugged on my hair again. She did not fear me. That too was a wonder.

The scent and taste of her arousal filled my every sense through my nose and tentacles. My cock throbbed. I ached to be inside her—so much so that my hips moved and its tip brushed her thigh. She did not shy away from me or my cock. Instead, her expression changed, became hungry. She dug her nails into the back of my neck. Gods above and below, I wanted her tight cunt around my cock.

My rational mind set off alarm bells. *I cannot fuck her. She is still healing. I will hurt her if I try.*

Just as worrisome was the chance, however remote, that she might become pregnant. I carried human genes as part of my genetic makeup. Humans had become pregnant by Fortusians before, and Fortusians of many genders and sexes had become pregnant by humans. We must speak openly and plainly about what she wished to do.

She shared my concerns; I saw it in the way the taste and scent of her hunger changed and became something softer, but no less full of want.

"Please, Vos," she said, her gaze locked on mine. "Kiss me."

"What if it happens again?" I asked.

"Then it does." She pulled me closer. "You wouldn't deny me, would you?"

Never in the lifetime of the universe would I deny her anything. My tentacles encircled her again, and I kissed her, much more gently this time.

She gasped and moaned, quivering in my arms with a soft orgasm. So perhaps I could control the intensity of what she felt by how earnestly I embraced and kissed her.

She relaxed against me and parted her lips under mine. My Calla tasted like the heavens, or how I imagined the heavens would taste if they were made for me alone. Her lips, like the rest of her, were soft but fierce, and her kiss heated me all the way through. Her tongue flicked at my sharp teeth. My mate was fearless and demanding. I nicked the tip of her tongue and sucked on the tang of her blood. She moaned into my mouth.

Her hand slipped under the water and wrapped around my cock. Her eyes widened as she stroked it gently from tip to base, her fingertips exploring its shape and details. Her small human hand could not encircle its girth.

My mind blanked.

All that I was narrowed to the sensations of her fingers and palm sliding up and down my cock. I shuddered hard and closed my eyes, fighting not to come simply from her touch.

When I had control of myself, I drew back, sucking her lower lip before releasing it.

"What has surprised you?" I teased, because she had teased me earlier. "You peeked at me without clothes on the day you first woke in my bed, did you not?"

She smiled. Not a wry twist of her lips or a smirk, but a real, affectionate smile. "Well, yes, but you were not aroused at the time. I could only guess at what your cock might look and feel like."

The fact even then she had imagined how I might look when aroused made my cock throb. I was helpless in her hands. I could do nothing but let her do what she wanted.

My cock provided its own lubrication, allowing her fingers to move freely. Up and down she stroked, turning and caressing and exploring, her fingertips and nails teasing the tip until I growled. We could not fuck, but I had never wanted anything so much as to come with my Calla in this tub.

"With your permission, I will hold you still so you do not injure yourself." My guttural voice hardly sounded like my own. I made my tone stern despite how her touch made me tremble. "I do not mind giving pain with pleasure someday if that is what you like, but not the kind that might injure you."

"I would like that very much, someday." She kissed my jaw. "Permission to hold me granted."

With my tentacles, I moved her very carefully, turning her so she lay with her back against my upper chest. Then I spread her legs with mine so they lay draped over my thighs and she could not close them.

I wanted to see her beautiful cunt, so with one of my tentacles I opened the drain to lower the water level enough to reveal the small patch of hair at the apex of her legs and the sweet pink lips below. My swollen cock jutted from the water between her thighs.

My Calla arched back against me. "Vos…"

"Shhh, my mate." I wrapped my human arms around her torso to hold her upper body still. And then I used my lower tentacles to immobilize her legs by pinning them to my own.

My mate was now fully in my care, and fully at my pleasure and mercy. Heaven could offer me nothing better, except perhaps her cunt squeezing my cock in its wet heat.

She began to tremble in my arms. "Are you afraid?" I asked, my lips against her hair.

"No," she murmured. "I've had to fear a lot of things in my life, but I don't fear you. I *want* you."

I slipped one of my tentacles between her thighs and let it taste her pussy with just the cells on its very tip. She gasped, her body tensing against me, as her sweet slickness coated my tentacle's tip.

At the same moment, my body went rigid, and then sagged against the side of the tub, almost boneless. My thoughts spun away into a kaleidoscope of pleasures.

Her taste. Her scent. My world—my universe—dwindled to only her.

I had never smelled or tasted anything so good. No other lover, no food, no drink. Not even the water of the deep ocean filled my soul like her sweet juices. She sucked in a breath and shuddered hard in my arms.

All the gods above and below, I would slaughter anything that tried to take this woman from me. Whether she accepted me or not, I would be hers from this moment on. There was no turning back for me.

My back arched as my cock sought the pleasure of her cunt. My need for her was equally pleasure and pain. But I could not have that pleasure until she had healed from her injuries enough to take me.

Instead, I wrapped the end of one tentacle tightly around my cock and stroked, sliding along its lubricated ridges as my smallest suckers plucked at my flesh.

"Oh, gods," Calla said, her eyes on the movement. "Vos, that…that is going to make me come just from watching."

"That is not going to be what makes you come," I whispered into her ear. "I promise you that."

I slipped the tip of my tentacle along her sweet pussy until I found the already-swollen pearl near its top. My smallest, most dextrous sucker latched onto this pearl with a rapid series of sucks and releases.

My mate cried out in ecstasy. Only my grip on her torso and legs prevented her from thrashing.

"I like your scream," I told her.

Her chest heaving, Calla looked up at me. "Then make me scream more," she rasped. "I think…you might be right about what's going to make me come."

I bared my sharp teeth at her. Her back arched and her pussy gushed, drenching my tentacle in juices and scent. My flesh drank every drop as if given water after wandering in the desert for days.

I held her still and let the suckers on that tentacle do as they pleased.

CHAPTER 15

CALLA

I'D ALREADY COME TWICE, BUT THE SIGHT OF VOS'S SHARP TEETH and the ministrations of his tentacle's delicate suckers sent me careening back toward bliss. He held me so tightly, I couldn't move a muscle except to roll my head back and forth across his chest and dig my nails into his thighs.

"Vos," I pleaded. "Please..."

"Please what, my Calla?" he asked, his lips against my ear. "Tell me what you want." His suckers released my clit and brushed against it instead. Teasing. Tormenting.

My building orgasm waned. I almost wept. "I want to come. Please."

His tentacle returned to my clit, sucked at it a few times, then released it. I whimpered.

"Say my name," he commanded. "Tell me you want me to make you come hard."

I struggled against his grip because feeling so helplessly restrained aroused me more. He seemed to understand, because he didn't budge at all, and even tightened his grip a little.

"I want you to make me come hard," I rasped. "Vos, *please*. Make me come."

He stroked himself more quickly. I watched every move, memorized every detail of his beautiful cock.

Its head was thick and curved, with a prehensile tip that moved and a collar of tiny frills that hadn't become visible until he was aroused. Undulating ridges ran down its length, also lined with tiny frills that I imagined would make every thrust so much more pleasurable for me. His bioluminescence pulsed under his skin, the patterns wild and racing along with his heartbeats. The slick lubrication that beaded from his skin smelled sweet.

Lavender precum began to drip and then trickle from the tip of his cock. It shone with the same soft glow as his bioluminescence.

Oh gods, I thought, nearly delirious with need. *Even his cum glows.*

His tentacle latched onto my clit and sucked.

Pleasure and heat swept over me. I screamed, bucking my hips uncontrollably, but his grip held me still. I wailed Vos's name over and over as I fought to get away from sensations that terrified me with their intensity. He kissed my hair and murmured words that in my haze I could not understand.

Gods. *Gods.*

Vos.

I shuddered. "Please, Vos. I can't take more."

"You can," he countered.

He had no mercy. His suckers plucked at my clit until I sobbed with pleasure and desperation. Only then did he release my swollen clit in favor of stroking my slit lightly with the tip of his tentacle.

Gasping for air, I tried to reach for his cock. "Let me."

"No." He nicked my earlobe with one of his sharp teeth. I

trembled in his arms, caught up in the pleasure and pain of that little wound. "Watch," he told me.

It was torture being unable to move as his tentacle did what I longed to do with my hands, my mouth, my pussy. I squirmed, too aroused to feel embarrassed by how many times I gushed as he stroked himself. My arousal continued to build, and he showed no signs of reaching his own release.

It took me way too damn long to realize he *knew* it was torture to watch, and he was doing this on purpose. I'd played with him earlier, goading and teasing. He must have decided turnabout was fair play.

Apparently Vos liked this kind of game. That didn't surprise me in the least. Too bad for him I was better at it than him.

"Do you like my pussy?" I asked, making my tone uncertain. I even bit my lip for extra effect.

"Yes," he said, his voice in my ear rough. And he continued to stroke himself.

"Does it feel good when you touch it?"

His free tentacle slid up my thigh, leaving little red marks as the suckers plucked at my skin. I couldn't move away, but I twitched with each little suck.

"It feels good," he said. More stroking, slow and even.

"Does it taste good?"

His tentacle slid farther up my inner thigh and flicked at my pussy, just grazing the delicate skin of my lips. His strokes sped up, then slowed again.

"It tastes very good," he said. I heard the smile in his voice that time. The rate of his stroking increased again, and this time he didn't slow down.

I expected him to return the tip of his tentacle to my clit, but instead it delved along my slit, sucking at that delicate skin. My slickness allowed it to move easily. I automatically tried to arch my back, but I still couldn't move. I had enjoyed light bondage before, but I had never wanted to experience real restraint.

Until now. Now I wanted Vos to keep me at his mercy because I had never come harder than I did while held helpless by him.

The tip of a long, cool tongue traveled along the contours of my ear. "Do you want me to fuck you with my tentacle while you watch, my Calla?" he asked, making me shiver with desire. "Ask me for what you want."

More wetness ran from my desperate, aching pussy. "Yes, I want you to fuck me with your tentacle."

"Where do you want to be fucked?" He stroked himself more quickly now, and the tentacle playing with my slit slipped lower until its tip flicked at my opening. I held back a moan, but only barely. "Here?" he asked. "In your beautiful cunt?"

"Yes. Please."

"Tell me."

"I want you to fuck me with your tentacle. In my cunt."

His tentacle tip slipped inside. I gasped at the intrusion and the sensation of the tiny suckers that plucked at my slick, delicate skin.

"As soon as you are healed enough to take me fully, I will fill you with my cock," he said, his voice rough. "But until then, I will give you everything you need in other ways. All you must do is ask for what you want."

My pussy clenched, but he wasn't inside me enough yet. "Deeper, please," I begged. "Please fuck me with your tentacle, Vos."

He slid his tentacle in a little farther. I tried to move my hips to grind on it, but he held me still. "I am not sure you take my tentacle in your cunt, my Calla," he murmured. "Can you?"

"Yes. Yes."

He slipped it in another few centimeters and undulated it, the tip stroking inside me, searching for that magical spot. I shuddered, my eyes closing. "Vos. More."

The tip stroked lightly over my G-spot, and I cried out. "Oh, gods. Yes. Right there."

"Look at your beautiful cunt stretch around my tentacle. You take me so well." He nibbled at my ear again as his tentacle stroked my G-spot so lightly that I wanted to scream. "You cannot come until I say so this time, my Calla. We will come together. Say it."

I had never submitted to anyone during sex, and I hadn't wanted to until now. The thought hadn't interested me, much less aroused me. I had never wanted to be told what to do either, and chafed mightily at every order I got after I escaped Ganai, even during my service in the Alliance Defense, when I knew taking orders was part of the deal.

So what had changed to make me want to obey him, and even beg for pleasure?

I felt safe with Vos, when no other partner had ever made me feel that way. And though Vos was giving me orders, I believed—I *knew*—that he did so with my pleasure in mind, and that I could say no at any time and he would immediately respect that.

But I had a rebellious streak a light-year wide, so I said, "I'll come when I please, Vos."

Chuckling, he stroked his cock, then used the tip of that tentacle to gather up the lavender liquid that dripped from the opening. He brought the tentacle close to my lips. The smell of his precum, sweet and savory, reminded me of a pastry I'd loved while stationed on Fortusia. And its beautiful glow was almost mesmerizing.

"You will come when I say," he murmured into my ear. "Beautiful Calla, you are mine and I am yours. Open your mouth."

I shook my head no. Not because I didn't want to taste him, but because I wanted to see what he would do.

He brushed his tentacle over my lips, coating them with his precum. When I didn't open my mouth, he gathered up more lavender liquid and returned, this time prodding my lips as he stroked my G-spot more vigorously.

I couldn't help it; I caught the tip of his tentacle in my mouth and sucked on it. His precum tasted so sweet and delicious, and the suckers plucked lightly at my lips and tongue. So many sensations, all of them exquisite. I groaned.

Trembling, Vos released my left leg to wrap that tentacle around his cock and stroke it fast and hard. At the same time, his tentacle in my pussy rubbed and vibrated against my G-spot. I wailed.

"Come for me, my Calla," he grated into my ear.

I went over the edge so quickly, so hard, and so desperately that I threw my head back against his chest and screamed with one tentacle still in my mouth partially muffling my cry. My pussy clenched around his other tentacle as its tip continued to rub, making me gush again and again.

He kept his other tentacle in my mouth, holding it open as his beautiful cock spurted hot, glowing cum high into the air in thick ropes that splattered my face and body and landed on my tongue.

"Calla," he groaned. He let go of me with one human arm and wrapped his hand around my throat ever so gently, holding me against him and still so he could aim his spurts of cum at my mouth. "Calla, fuck. Fuck. *Fuck.*"

The taste of his cum, the sensation of his hand on my throat, and his tentacle rubbing on my G-spot made my entire body tense and release in another soft orgasm that made my toes curl.

I could have moved now with his grip loosened, but I didn't. I didn't want to hurt myself and delay my healing process. I wanted to be well again so he could fuck me with that beautiful cock. And he'd told me to stay still, so I had to obey.

The last of his cum dribbled down his cock head as he withdrew his tentacle from my lips. I swallowed what had landed in my mouth, licking my lips to savor the taste of him. I longed to lick his cock clean too, but a heavy, satisfied kind of exhaustion swept over me.

He withdrew his tentacle gently from my pussy and dragged his long tongue around and over its tip.

"I do not want to waste a drop of anything you give me," Vos said, his gaze on mine. "Everything about you is a treasure."

I could do nothing but tremble in his arms.

He turned on the water spigots to re-fill the tub. "My beautiful Calla," he said, kissing my forehead. "I will wash us both, and then we will rest together."

Nothing had ever sounded as good as that plan. "After all, I *did* want to get clean." I was so tired now, but a good kind of tired. A satisfied, sated, treasured kind of tired.

He rested his chin on the top of my head as scalding water filled the tub. Heavenly. If he didn't like the water being so hot, he didn't let on.

"Calla," he said.

"Mmm?" I closed my eyes and snuggled against his chest. His gills fluttered as the water level reached them. I liked that strange sensation.

"Do you have any regrets?" His body remained relaxed, but his voice sounded guarded. "Please tell me the truth."

I kissed his chest. "Not a single regret, other than the obvious ones."

I sensed him frown. "What are the obvious regrets?"

"That I didn't get to suck your cock," I murmured, a little crossly because he should have been able to figure that one out. "And that I'm not healed enough to be fucked by it either."

His chest shook with what I realized was silent laughter. I smiled.

"Soon," he promised. His tentacles ran over my arms and legs, tasting and smelling me thoroughly, before embracing me once more. "I want that very much, but we must be careful and mindful of your recovery above all else." He kissed my hair, picked up a washcloth and a bar of homemade soap, and went to work getting me clean.

CHAPTER 16

VOS

My Calla fell asleep before I finished bathing her and washing her beautiful hair. And for the first time since arriving at my home, she did not squirm or whimper in pain and even smiled slightly as she slept.

She did not stir when I rose from the tub, dried us both, and took her to the bed. Once I settled her under the covers, I did two things I rarely did: I drew the curtain over the window and closed the door that separated the bedroom from the rest of the house. I wanted Calla to rest in dim light and quiet.

Before I covered the window, I glimpsed Poe outside keeping watch. The heavy rain had eased and become more of a mist. She would happily guard our home for the remainder of the day, eating small creatures that entered the yard, tending her garden, and humming to herself.

My companion would likely be quite satisfied with this turn of events. Not half as satisfied as I was, however—nor a tenth as happy. My hearts felt full to bursting, and not just because I had given my mate orgasms that made her shake and scream in ecstasy.

Calla wanted me in bed next to her. Wanted my arms and tentacles around her. Wanted my cum on her lips and my cock in her mouth and cunt. And not only could I ease her worry and pain with a sound I made only for her, I could bring her to release with my touches alone. She *was* my mate. The joy of that simple fact threatened to overwhelm me.

I had earned her trust. If I could earn her heart, I would want for nothing. Even now, a deep contentment filled me, healing aches and hollowness I had thought would pain me for all my days.

Moving quietly, I took a box from under the bed and settled in beside my sleeping mate with my back against the wall. Two of my tentacles immediately slipped under the covers to coil around her arm and lower leg. Another wave of perfect tranquility swept through me as they drank in her taste and scent. The other two settled around her blanket-wrapped form, cradling and guarding her.

I took the lid off the box and withdrew a sewing kit and Calla's flight suit, washed clean. I had not had much time to repair her only piece of clothing, but with a few hours' work, I believed I could have it ready to wear. The material was extremely durable. Once I sewed it back together and patched the holes, she would no longer be forced to wear sheets taken from the bed as clothing. A man who preferred to avoid going into the village as much as possible became handy in many skills, including thread-craft.

I could go into town and purchase attire for her, but the shopkeepers would want to know why I needed clothing to fit a human woman. The longer I kept her presence secret, the safer we would be.

As I mended the cuts I had made in her uniform to remove it

from her injured body the night I first brought her home, I watched Calla sleep and listened to the rain. Another few weeks and the rainy season would give way to drier months. My garden would fill with fruits and vegetables to replenish my stores of food. The ocean would warm, the *nuoias* and hurricanes would come less frequently, and life on Iosa would be close to paradise.

No, it would be paradise itself, because Calla was here.

Distracted by the thought, I stabbed the pad of my left index finger with my sewing needle. A bead of violet blood welled up.

Memories of Calla's first night in my home flooded my mind: her mangled arms and legs, her cuts and bruises, her fractured jaw and skull. The list of injuries on the scanner's screen that went on and on and ended with the prediction that she had less than one percent chance of survival.

My desperation had been a living thing that night, a monster of its own capable of nearly unspeakable things. It snapped its teeth and snarled at me, howling that if I failed to save Calla's life that my own life was not worth having. I had resorted to an utterly desperate measure: sharing my blood and willing it with all my might and existence to do what the contents of my medical kits could not. My rage had only been quelled when Calla began to heal before my eyes and then miraculously survived the night.

And yet that greatest miracle of my life seemed to pale in comparison to what we had shared today and the closeness that had developed between us.

Now I had a chance to make her the center of my universe. I could not waste it by doing any less than everything in my power to ensure she was as happy and content in my presence as I was in hers.

Rather than get up and force my tentacles to relinquish their hold on my mate, I wiped my bloody finger on my pants leg. As

I bent my head again over my task, I envisioned each stitch as another step toward my future with a fierce and tender woman who had called me a beautiful monster as if that was a very good thing to be.

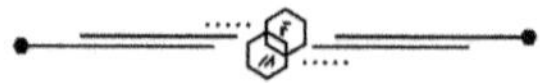

Much to my surprise, Calla slept soundly all day and through the night. She had not done so since her first days with me. She did not seem to be in distress, only tired. I stayed close, leaving her side only to eat a quick meal and tell Poe that we were lying down together. Poe was quite happy to stay on watch and leave us to our rest.

Just after midnight, I finished mending Calla's uniform and joined my mate under the covers, moving carefully so I did not wake her. She murmured and turned to face me in her sleep, snuggling close with her nose against my chest as if she wanted to breathe in my scent as much as I wanted hers.

I fell asleep not long after, almost drunk on the feeling of my mate in my arms and her warm breath on my skin. And I experienced no nightmares—only dreams of Calla.

Just after the sun's rise, I woke from the most rejuvenating sleep I had enjoyed in recent memory to find another miracle: my Calla wrapped in a sheet, standing next to the bed.

Standing. Unaided.

I rolled to my feet so quickly that I had no memory of actually moving. "Calla!" I gripped her upper arms, my tentacles plucking at her sheet in worry. "What are you doing?"

"This again?" She smiled up at me. "You need to get your vision examined. You keep asking me what I'm doing when the answer is obvious."

Yesterday, she had tried to stand but the pain was overwhelming. I did not understand how this was possible, but I could not deny the evidence of my own eyes.

"Standing does not hurt you?" I demanded.

"Well, it hurts a *little*," she admitted. "But not too badly. Just aches, really. No sharp pains at all."

Not only was she standing, her cuts and bruises that only yesterday had been easy to see were either gone or almost healed. Alarmed and confused in equal measures, I took my medical scanner from the windowsill and passed it over her. The results made no sense, so I scanned again. Same readout.

"Vos." Calla's sharp voice and frown drew my attention. "Basic medical care etiquette: don't scan me and then stare at the screen without speaking. It implies something very bad is going on and you don't know how to tell me."

"There is nothing bad," I said, almost in a daze. I showed her the scanner. "You are nearly healed."

"I suddenly healed while I was sleeping?" Her scowl deepened. "That makes no sense."

Startled, I took a step back. My tentacles quivered in agitation.

"What?" she demanded. "What does that mean to you?"

I struggled to put my suspicion into words. "Because of my genetic engineering, when I am badly injured, I sleep for a day or more as all my energy goes to recovery. And when I wake, I am usually fully healed."

"I don't understand." She sat on the side of the bed, still staring at me. "You didn't give me any blood since that first night, right? You wouldn't have done that without my permission."

"Of course not." I was glad she believed I would not do anything without her consent. "I did not even consider doing so."

"Then how did I heal suddenly? Is it something about being on Iosa? Was it something in the bathwater? Something—" Her eyes widened. "Oh gods, Vos."

The smell of her sudden fear sent me to my knees in front of her. My tentacles wrapped around her legs as I took her hands in mine. "Tell me what troubles you."

She swallowed. "You say your healing ability is in your blood. Is it possible it's also in other bodily fluids?"

"I have never—" I cut myself off before I finished the thought.

I had never healed anyone with my blood, but I had never tried.

I had never made that comforting cooing sound until Calla. I had never given orgasms with my tentacles and kiss until Calla. And I had certainly never healed any partner with my cum. Unlike my blood, there were instances in my past when that could have happened if it were possible.

The only answer that made sense was that I could heal my mate in more ways than with my blood. My Calla and I stared at each other in shared shock and disbelief.

A sudden terror gripped me: if she had reacted so strongly to the news that I had used my blood to heal her without asking permission, what would she think of me now?

"I did not know." If I were not already on my knees, I would have fallen to them in my earnestness. "I swear, I did not know."

She still smelled of fear, but now that scent was tinged with something else. Anger? Betrayal? No, hurt. Her expression looked bruised.

The thought she was in any kind of pain, emotional or physical, filled me with fear and rage. I did the only thing I knew to do: I cradled her and cooed. She buried her face against my chest, her shoulders hunched despite my attempt to comfort her.

I cupped the back of her head and kissed her hair. "Calla, please tell me what is wrong."

"I don't know why it hurts," she said, her voice rough. "It shouldn't, but it does." She said nothing more for a long time.

Rather than coo again, since it had done little to ease her

distress, I hummed a song from my homeworld, as I had done while bathing her the first night she had spent in my home. This lullaby was one of the few shreds of my childhood that had stayed in my memory despite every effort the Guard had made to eradicate such useless things.

Perhaps it was not so useless, though, because little by little Calla's shoulders relaxed and the smell of her fear and hurt began to wane.

When she spoke, her voice was so soft even with my enhanced hearing I had to strain to make out her words.

"I'd just barely survived a firefight with three raider vessels," she said. "I was on my way back to Outpost 60 in a half-working ship when I decided to stop at Jakora. I planned to bribe a mechanic to tell my commander my ship wasn't able to make the trip back without repairs that would take at least three or four days. I wanted to spend those days drinking, swimming in the ocean, and fucking someone I'd never see again once I left."

I rubbed my nose against her hair, fighting irrational anger at whatever hypothetical partner she might have found. Truly, I understood the urge to do all the things she had described. Her voice belied the emptiness she had felt and sought to fill on Jakora. Many who went there did so for the same reasons. I could not hold it against her.

I had done the same more than once on Jakora and similar worlds: endless drinks, recreation, sex with partners whose full names I had never asked. And I had left as lonely and unfulfilled as when I had arrived. Once glance at her grim expression confirmed she had fully expected the same outcome. We could lie to others about what we had found in such places, but never to ourselves.

"Then I hit some kind of debris in space," she continued, and now her voice sounded almost harsh. "It tore off one of my fighter's wings and sent me spiraling toward the surface of some moon I didn't even know existed. In a wild twist of fate that I can't begin to process, I ended up kidnapped by raiders and then rescued by a beautiful monster who can heal me and *only* me, comfort me and *only* me, and make *only* me come just with the right touch."

She looked up at me then, her eyes shimmering with unshed tears and pain that seemed to rip all my hearts right out of my chest. "And it fucking *hurts* because everything about you seems like it's made to take care of me, a scrap who fell out of the sky and deserves none of it at all."

A *scrap*. A Ganaian pejorative meaning worse than garbage. My rage and grief at hearing the word applied to my mate made me sick to my stomach. My tentacles quivered with the desire to slaughter whoever said such a thing.

With my hands, my tentacles, my teeth, I would tear to pieces anyone or anything who hurt my Calla or called her a scrap. But who could I kill when my Calla hurt herself? The people who had called her that word were not here—only their ghosts, whispering in her mind. Such ghosts could not be killed. I had spent a lifetime trying to kill my own.

All my life I had solved problems for others and myself by dealing death. Nothing had prepared me to face this moment, when I must try to heal wounds I could not see.

"You are no scrap," I said, my voice hoarse with the depth of my anger and sadness. "You are a treasure. A gift. Priceless beyond compare."

"To you, maybe." Her mouth twisted. "When I was born, I was a scrap. Once my mother sold me to my keepers on Ganai, I was a commodity who bled to make them lots of money. To the Alliance Defense, I'm a skilled but easily replaceable pilot they can use to protect colonies and travelers from raiders and invasions. But who am I?"

I too had asked this question throughout my life, especially during and immediately after my service in the Guard. Even now I struggled to answer, but at least I believed I had finally found the path to finding that answer.

"You must define yourself not as who or what you are to others, but to yourself," I said, tucking a strand of loose hair behind her ear. "Tell me who you are, Calla Wren."

She swallowed hard. "I don't know. Who are you, Vos Turek?"

I tilted my head and considered. "I am a former assassin now keeping a home on a quiet moon, living as peacefully and by my own rules as I can. I am haunted by nightmares and struggle to see what my future holds, but I have reason to hope for happiness—if not here, then somewhere."

My Calla thought about what I had said for a long time.

"I am a former child gladiator," she said finally. "Maybe now a former Defense pilot. I'm sharing a house with a big crab and a sexy cephalopod man and it rains here all the damn time. I have nightmares too and I don't know what my future holds, but I want happiness, either here or somewhere else."

Her expression turned fierce. "I like to protect people who can't protect themselves and I like to fight every once in a while to keep my skills up and because I'm good at it. I don't like being told what to do and I want to make my own rules for once." She glanced down at herself. "And I'm so very happy to be mostly healed because I'd love to be carried by you because I want to be, not because I *have* to be. So I guess all that is who I am. Am I too much?"

"Never." I stroked her cheek with my thumb for the first time without having to be careful not to touch a cut or bruise. What a wonderful simple joy. "I am so very glad to make your acquaintance, Calla Wren."

She smiled, and it felt as though the sun came out even though the rain continued outside unabated. "Likewise, Vos Turek." She ran her hand through my hair to cup the back of my head. "Have we just really met for the first time?"

"Perhaps." I returned her smile. "I have so much to learn about you still." I touched her face. "I cannot banish hurtful words and your terrible mistreatment from your mind any more than I can from my own, but while you are with me, I will dedicate my life to replacing those things with better days and better memories."

"As long as you let me do the same." Calla slipped her fingers between mine and held on. "I can't reciprocate your healing abilities, though, so our deal seems lopsided in my favor."

I kissed her forehead. "You may not mend my cuts and bruises, but you heal wounds you cannot see. Speaking of mending…" I withdrew the box from under the bed and slid it over to her. "I have a something for you."

She frowned. "A gift? I don't need a gift."

Perhaps she was not used to receiving gifts, or receiving gifts that did not come with strings attached.

"I respectfully disagree." I put the box in her lap. "Please."

With obvious reluctance, she lifted the lid and stared. "Vos, is this—my uniform?"

Now who was asking questions when the answer was obvious? I smiled. "Yes."

With almost childlike wonder, she let go of my hand to pick up her repaired flight suit. "It's all sewed back together." Her gaze swept over it and then moved to my face. "You did this?"

"Yes," I said again. "Bedsheets are not adequate clothing for you. Neither is a patched uniform, but until we can obtain something better, will this do? Your boots are in fine shape."

She ran her fingers over the uniform, inspecting my repairs and smiling. "This is incredible, Vos. Thank you so much." She started to pull my head closer, then hesitated. "Um, I guess a kiss isn't just a kiss if you're holding me with your tentacles."

"Perhaps not." I caressed her, then forced them to release her so she simply lay cradled in my human arms. "May I kiss you now?"

In answer, she grabbed me and kissed me so hard that my lips felt as though they would be bruised, and the feeling was the most delicious kind of joy and pain. When her mouth yielded under mine, I drew her closer, reveling in her taste and the way her little tongue teased mine and danced along the sharp edges and points of my teeth.

She drew back, smiling playfully. "I liked that kiss. How many tentacles does it take to turn a kiss into an orgasm, do you think?"

"Should we find out?" I trailed the tip of one tentacle along her bare arm before letting it coil around her wrist. "I for one am curious."

She shivered. "I like how that feels." Slowly, she kissed me, much more tenderly this time, and even a little tentatively.

When no release occurred, I wrapped another tentacle around her left wrist. Her kiss became more demanding, but still no orgasm. Gently, I encircled her right ankle. The scent of her desire grew, but she did not shudder or cry out.

I broke our kiss and raised my head to look into her eyes. "The answer may be four, my Calla," I said.

"Could be." She was breathing more heavily now, her lips swollen and desire shining in her eyes. "I'm willing to see if we're right, if you are."

Was I *willing* to feel her writhe in my arms and hear her call my name? It was as if she had asked me if I wanted to breathe.

"And if we are right, what else would you ask of me?" I brushed her lower lip with the pad of my thumb. "Tell me what you want."

She shivered again and held my gaze. "I want you to hold me down with your tentacles so I can't move at all."

I let the tip of my fourth tentacle brush her left leg. "What else, my mate?"

She whimpered. "I want your cock."

"You may have it." I dipped my head and nipped at her ear

with my sharp teeth. "What should I do once you are at my mercy?"

She took a deep, shaky breath. "Then I would like you to fuck me, Vos. Make me scream."

My brave Calla, asking her monster to make her scream.

But even as much as my desire made my hands and feet and tentacles tremble and my cock throb with need, two matters had to be settled first.

"My Calla," I said, very seriously, my hand cupping the back of her head so I could look into her eyes. "I must know that you are healed and I will not hurt you if I am…enthusiastic."

Her gentle smile melted me.

"You saw the scanner for yourself," she said. "A nearly clean bill of health from a reliable source. I think enthusiasm with reasonable care will keep me from needing medical intervention." Her smile faded. "I will tell you if something hurts in a bad way, I promise."

I had anticipated that response…but I had no idea how she might reply to my second question.

"What of pregnancy?" I asked. "There is a chance we could create a child."

A dozen emotions flashed in her eyes—more than I could process or understand.

"As you might imagine for someone with my background, I've taken steps to ensure there will not be any accidental pregnancies," she said, her voice matter-of-fact even as her eyes darkened with what I thought were bad memories. "Not permanent steps, yet, but very certain ones. So you don't need to worry about that."

I had no thoughts of my own about children, and certainly it was a matter for another day. For now, my world was Calla, and she had asked for my cock, and for me to make her scream.

Without warning, I wrapped my tentacle around her left ankle, and then I lifted her head to press my lips to hers.

My mate screamed in ecstasy, her body going rigid in the throes of an orgasm. She sobbed and wailed, thrashing against the iron grip of my tentacles and human arms. The sound of her cry ignited my senses and my body in entirely new ways.

And I knew as surely as I had known anything in my life that I would do anything—anything at all—to hear that scream again and again, for the rest of my days.

CHAPTER 17

CALLA

MY PUSSY CLENCHED AND GUSHED, AND OH, BY ALL THE GODS, DID I scream.

I came hard, helpless in his tentacles, and screamed into Vos's mouth. He devoured my cry, his eyes glowing with need.

He didn't bother to move to the bed. Instead, he lay me gently on the floor, my arms and legs outstretched with his tentacles, and pushed my sheet aside as he settled between my thighs, lifting me enough to bring my pussy to his lips and tongue.

He drew his long tongue along my soaked and sensitive pussy before my orgasm even began to wane, licking up every drop of my release before he slipped his tongue into my opening to lap at the slickness that dripped from it.

The sensations were too much. I fought to close my legs, but I couldn't move an centimeter. Not a millimeter. Just as I'd asked for.

My beautiful monster flicked my asshole with his tongue, then licked me slowly—maddeningly, infuriatingly, shriekinducingly slowly—all the way to my clit before he put his lips on my swollen pearl. He twirled my clit in his lips, sucking and releasing and teasing with the tip of his tongue.

My wails didn't even sound human. I came again, as hard as the first time, my body clenching from my fingers to my toes and everything in between. I couldn't see him through the haze, but I must have drenched his face with my release.

As I gasped for air, he crawled up my body, his tentacles still holding me immobilized by my wrists and ankles.

"I will eat your delicious cunt every day," Vos rasped into my ear. He was above me now, shirtless, pants low on his hips. His bioluminescence captivated me, even in my orgasmic haze. "I will drink your juices from your beautiful holes and sip and suck on your clit until you cry."

He moved behind me, raised my upper body, and cradled me with one arm so I could watch him slip his fingers into my pussy.

"Look at your greedy cunt," he murmured into my ear, pumping in and out slowly. "You want more. You want to scream for me again."

"Yes," I sobbed, almost as desperate to escape the waves of overwhelming pleasure as I was to come, though there was no freeing myself from those tentacles unless he let me go.

"Good." His searching fingertips found my G-spot and stroked just right. "Do not close your eyes. Watch yourself come on my hand, Calla, my mate."

His commanding voice. His fingertips stroking my G-spot. The sensation of his rock-hard cock against my lower back. The sight of his beautiful purple fingers, lit by bioluminescence and glistening with my slickness. A wave of delicious tension built inside me, threatening to sweep me away, but not quite reaching the peak I craved.

"Obey me," he growled into my ear, then bit my earlobe with his sharp, sharp teeth.

On that flash of pain, I came apart with a wail. I clenched around his fingers, and my wetness dripped from his hand.

He buried his face against the side of my neck as he stroked me without mercy. "Keep coming. Do not stop. I need every drop of honey you have to give."

I didn't stop coming. I couldn't. He needed my honey, and I wanted to obey.

When my head fell back against his chest, my chest heaving with shuddering gasps, he lay me gently on the floor and moved above me again.

Fabric tore, and then his pants were gone and his beautiful cock head pressed against my pussy, just millimeters from sliding inside. His skin pulsed with light and his eyes shone wild with a desire so fierce that it scared and thrilled me.

"Calla," he pleaded, his voice rough. "Please."

Vos looked on the verge of desperation. Not just desperate to fuck me, but desperate for something much more than that— a connection that went far deeper than his cock buried in me.

I didn't know what connection we had, or might have someday, but I'd wanted to feel that cock inside me from the moment I'd seen it. And though I appreciated that he'd asked permission, he sure as hells would not have to ask twice.

"Yes, Vos," I whispered. "Yes."

With a low rumble in his chest, he thrust his thick cock head into my pussy. Its girth made me gasp and arch my back to make it easier for him. He withdrew his cock and then pushed it in again, a little deeper this time. The ridges and frills that ran the length of his cock undulated and throbbed, and his cock head moved inside me, rubbing me in ways I had never felt before. I wanted him fully inside me, but these sensations made me quiver and moan.

He nestled his face into the crook of my neck, inhaled deeply, and thrust his cock into my pussy, all the way to his balls. Oh, gods. I screamed and pulled at his tentacles' grip on my wrists, but to no avail. I wanted to dig my nails into his back. I wanted to run my hands through his hair and hold him close. I wanted everything, and nothing at all except his cock filling me completely.

With one arm around my shoulder and cradling my head and his weight on the other so he didn't crush me, Vos stilled except for ragged breathing and what almost felt like shivers. His skin pulsed with light.

"Vos," I murmured. "Are you all right?"

Trembling, he raised his head. His glowing gaze had never looked so beautiful as it did now from above with his cock buried inside me.

"I am in heaven, my mate," he rasped. "Your cunt is a perfect fit for me. I knew it would be."

I pulled gently on his tentacle's grip on my right wrist. He released me immediately, obviously recognizing the difference between my playful and arousing attempts to free myself and this moment, when my desire to touch him meant more. And that was why I'd let him trap me—because I had the key to the trap and could free myself at any time.

I cupped his face with my hand. "Vos."

He leaned against my palm and closed his eyes, evidently savoring the moment. Then, without warning, he moved like lightning and caught my fingers gently in his sharp teeth before letting go.

"Be careful, my mate," he said, the corners of his mouth turning up. "Monsters bite."

"I know." I reached over his shoulder and dug my nails into his flesh. His back arched, and he made a delicious, deep rumbly sound that seemed to vibrate through his entire body, all the way to the tips of his tentacles. "But do they fuck their mates?"

Lightning fast, his tentacle lashed around my wrist and slapped it back in place on the floor.

Vos's lips hovered over mine. "They do," he rasped. He withdrew his cock from my pussy and drove it back in. I wailed. "Scream for me," he said.

With his tentacles, he placed my calves on his shoulders to raise my hips, and then he plunged his cock into me even deeper. And this time his cock head stroked over my G-spot at the perfect angle.

I screamed.

His cock pulsed with light as he fucked me, each stroke sending me closer and closer to another release.

"Ah, ah, ah," I wailed, my nails digging into my palms because I had nothing else to grab onto. "There—right there."

His cock undulated and stroked over my G-spot. A wave of heat and pleasure spread from my pussy to my entire body, to the tips of my fingers and toes. Moments later I came, my head thrown back as I screamed to all the gods above *and* below.

To my surprise, Vos withdrew his cock while I shuddered. With his tentacles still holding my legs raised and spread, he slid down and slipped his tongue into my pussy to lap at my wetness again. I cried out, grinding against his face so his tongue could find all the places that made me whimper and moan.

I'd wanted to know what it felt like to be fucked at his mercy, held captive by his tentacles, and it was *so fucking good.*

His lips closed on my clit as his fingers slipped into my pussy, stroking and plying me. Caught in pleasure almost too intense to bear, I tried to pull away just to catch my breath, but I couldn't. The tentacles around my ankles tightened. The feeling of being utterly at Vos's mercy made the pleasure even greater. I came again, softly this time and with a gasp instead of a scream.

Vos raised his head and licked his lips. "How many times have you come, my mate?"

"I don't know." My chest heaving, I reached for him. "Please..."

I didn't know exactly what I was asking for, but somehow he

understood what I needed. He moved above me and thrust his cock into me again.

Pleasure radiated through my body, rolling up my arms and legs from where his tentacles held me and straight to my pussy, where his cock stroked in and out so slowly and deliberately that I could not stop crying out.

Lost in a haze of ecstasy, I barely noticed when he pulled out of me and rubbed his cock's head against my slit, teasing me by slipping its tip inside and then withdrawing it. I thrashed in the iron grip of his tentacles, fighting to get him to go deeper, but he refused.

"Please." I raised my hips, but he evaded me. "Please…"

"Say my name," he ordered me. His body pulsed with patterns of bioluminescence that ran over his skin and down his cock, where its tip tormented me. "Say it."

"Vos," I panted.

The tip of his cock ran over my slit, stroking me without penetrating, and my pussy clenched desperately on its own emptiness.

"Louder," he commanded.

"*Vos!*" I screamed. This torment was simultaneously the worst and best thing I had ever felt. "Vos…*Vos.*"

His gaze traveled from my face and down my body to where his cock teased me. His beautiful glowing precum left marks on my skin everywhere he touched.

"What do you want?" he asked. "Tell me."

"Your cock. I want your cock."

He slipped its thick head inside me, then withdrew it. "Why do you want my cock?"

"Because it feels so good. Please…"

"Where do you want it?" Another teasing penetration. "In your beautiful cunt?"

"Yes." I pulled at his tentacles, to no avail. "In my cunt."

"In your mouth?" He dragged his cock head over my

abdomen and back down, painting me with his glowing precum. "Do you want to taste it?"

I would have agreed to anything, begged for everything, crawled on my hands and knees, and felt no shame.

"Yes! Let me suck your cock," I pleaded. "*Please*, let me suck your cock."

Now his cock slid over my pussy and farther down, where it pressed against my tight asshole. "In your ass?" he asked, smiling to show all of his sharp, sharp teeth. "Do you want my cock in your ass, Calla?"

I didn't even have to think about that. "Yes, I want it in my ass. Please—I want it in my ass."

He lowered his head and closed his lips on my right nipple, sucking and flicking it with his tongue. I moaned. I wanted to run my fingers through his hair and hold his head close, but I still couldn't move. And when he closed his sharp teeth on my delicate skin, just hard enough to leave marks but not quite enough to draw blood, I wailed.

He sucked my nipples until the combination of pain and arousal had me nearly sobbing, and all the time he teased my pussy and my ass with the tip of his cock. I screamed for him, begging and pleading and cursing, but he wouldn't give me what I wanted until I'd almost screamed myself hoarse. I couldn't even touch myself with my hands pinned.

Suddenly, he rolled onto his back in a single, inhumanly fluid movement, and lowered me to my knees beside him before releasing my hands. He kept his tentacles on my ankles. My wrists had red marks from the suckers. I loved how that looked, as if he'd branded me with his body, like with the glowing precum that now covered my pussy and stomach.

"Suck my cock, Calla," he said.

Finally, *finally*, I took his beautiful, slick cock in my hands. He groaned and trembled the moment my fingers wrapped around it, his back arching before I even stroked him. I licked my lips.

"Take me in your mouth," Vos said, his voice suddenly gentle instead of commanding. "Taste your mate."

I slipped my lips around his cock head. *Oh, gods.* He tasted so good, like sugar and musk with a hint of saltiness like the sea. He made a guttural sound.

I stroked him with my hand as I took his cock deep into my mouth, sucking as I ran my tongue along the frills and ridges and then over the tip, where precum dripped. His hips moved and then stilled, as if he were desperate to thrust into my mouth but held himself back and let me do what I wanted, at least for now.

I swallowed him as deeply as I could, then looked up at him through my lashes. He'd closed his eyes in bliss, his chest heaving and gills fluttering. He was at my mercy now. Vulnerable. Bared to my sight, his need for me unhidden.

As if he sensed my gaze, Vos opened his eyes. He ran his hand through my hair and gripped it gently but firmly. "You are the most magnificent woman I have ever known," he said. "Make me come, Calla. I am yours forever."

With my lips on his cock head and my tongue lapping at its opening, I stroked him with my hands, up and down the glowing length of his cock, finding the rhythm and pressure that made him groan and writhe. I discovered the places that made his cock head throb and bend and release pulses of precum that splattered my face and hands.

My explorations ended when he took control again, holding my head in place by my hair so he could fuck my mouth. He lifted my head so I could gasp for breath whenever my nails dug into his thighs. He seemed to like the feeling of my nails too, so each time I dug them in a little deeper, leaving marks everywhere I touched like his suckers made on me.

The tip of one of his tentacles slipped between my thighs,

sliding over the slickness that dripped from my pussy, and flicked at my clit. I nearly collapsed as that intense pleasure sent a shudder through my entire body. I wanted him to use his sucker there, but instead the tip of the tentacle moved farther down and slipped into my pussy, fucking me in time with my mouth on his cock. I moaned, the sound muffled.

He called my name and rasped words that were curses in Fortusian. The bioluminescent pulses moved faster along his skin too, racing with the beats of his hearts as his cock throbbed in my hands and between my lips.

"Calla…Calla," he groaned. "My mate."

I let go with my mouth and used my hands. His hips jerked in time to my strokes and his back arched away from the floor. He was losing control now, ceding possession of himself to me as he neared his release. The sight of him so lost in pleasure and sensation made me shiver with arousal and satisfaction.

Yesterday in the tub I had watched him come. I'd been desperate and aching to be the one to bring him to orgasm despite how arousing it was to see him stroking himself with his own tentacle.

And more than that, I wanted his cum all over me, to see and feel it splash my body and mouth and tongue—to drink him in the way he devoured my scent and taste every chance he got. I wanted to know what it would feel like to be the mate of this fierce man, to have him writhing and vulnerable for me.

"Come for me, Vos," I said, grinding on his tentacle in my pussy as I stroked his cock. "Mark me as your mate."

CHAPTER 18

VOS

Wracked with shudders, my tentacle buried in her cunt and my cock twitching in her hands, I obeyed my mate.

The first two thick ropes of my cum spurted across her beautiful face. She closed her eyes as they splashed over her mouth and tongue and cheeks. One by one, the rest painted lines of hot, glowing liquid across her breasts and stomach.

My orgasm in the tub yesterday had been the most powerful and pleasurable of my life up to that moment, but now I felt as though I left my body as I came from the heat and touch of her mouth and hands. And I had never seen anything as beautiful and captivating as my mate covered with my luminous, lavender cum.

My groans and growls turned primal, beastly, untamed. Uncaged and monstrous. I had never allowed myself to be so free with any other lover, and I reveled in it.

As my cum dripped from her face and body, my Calla did not seem afraid, nor smell of fear at the sound of my snarls—

only more aroused. As I watched, my chest heaving and muscles twitching with my release, she licked my cum from her lips.

"Delicious," she said, smiling. "Give me more, Vos."

I might be breathless, but I was energized, not spent, from this orgasm. I needed only a few minutes to be ready to fuck her again.

With my tentacles, I repositioned her on her hands and knees with her pussy and perfectly round ass facing me. I got to my knees behind her and dragged my tongue from her cunt to her asshole.

She collapsed forward, shaking, and only the grip of my tentacles on her arms and thighs kept her upright. "Oh," she gasped. "What are you doing?"

"Fucking my mate," I said. "Arch your back for me, my Calla. Show me your cunt."

Calla obeyed without protest. Gods above, the way she quivered in my hands, her beautiful holes enticing me with their slickness. I spread her ass with my hands so I could tongue her asshole. She shrieked and clung to the sheet she had used as clothing as my tongue explored her, forcing its way into the tight opening.

"Vos, gods above, more," she begged, grinding against my face. "Please, more."

To my last breath, I would give her everything she could want. I planned to make her come again and again until she lay breathless and too weak to move in my arms.

I slipped two of my fingers into her pussy, stroking as she fucked my fingers. "Spread your legs," I commanded.

She did as I told her. Two of my tentacles coiled around her breasts and teased her nipples. Her pleasure created more wetness in her pussy and helped her relax.

When I slipped my finger into her asshole, she convulsed. "Fuck, Vos, fuck…"

I stroked my cock with one hand as she ground against my

finger in her ass. I added a second finger, stretching her. Looking at her ass open for me and hearing her plead for me to fuck her made me hard again faster than I had ever managed before.

"Do you want my cock in your ass?" I asked, my fingers delving into her hot wetness. "Tell me what you want."

"Please, Vos," she wailed. "Please fuck my ass. Fuck me hard. I want to scream until I can't scream any more."

I wanted nothing more than to do exactly that. Her screams of ecstasy were gifts from the heavens.

Her asshole was still deliciously tight, but she could take me now. I wrapped my arm around her waist, held her in place with my tentacles, and pressed my cock against her asshole, where it leaked precum that dripped down her slit.

"Ready, my mate?" I asked.

In wordless answer, she ground back against me.

With my cock in my hand, I pushed its swollen head into her asshole. As it popped through the ring of muscle, she cried out, the sound guttural and full of both pain and pleasure. She writhed, her ass clenching around me. The sensation of her tight hole clamping onto my cock was almost enough to send me over the edge.

"Fuck," she groaned, shaking as she arched her back. "Fuck. Oh, my ass. Oh gods. That feels so good."

I slid my cock farther in. She cried out again. "Vos."

"Do you want me to stop?" I bent over to kiss her trembling back. "Tell me what you want, my Calla."

"No, I don't want you to stop." She let out a choked sound. "Gods, don't you dare stop."

"I promised I would fuck you until you could not scream any more." I slid my cock in another few centimeters. Moving slowly was delicious torture. My voice was ragged when I added, "I will always keep my promises to you."

Calla took a deep, shuddering breath. Her asshole relaxed

around me. "Then do it. Fuck my ass with your big, beautiful, glowing cock."

As she writhed and moaned, I slowly and steadily pushed my cock all the way into her ass until I was buried within her to the hilt, my balls resting against her cunt. And then I waited for her to speak.

"If I take you as my mate, will you fuck me this good forever?" she asked, her voice hoarse.

My hearts soared. "This and better," I vowed. "I will dedicate myself to pleasing you."

"Good." She wiggled against me. "My ass needs fucking, Vos."

I slapped her ass hard enough to leave a handprint. She shrieked, and her wetness dripped onto my balls. "Again," she said.

I slapped her ass again, pulled my cock almost all the way out, and drove it into her.

To my surprise, she came hard with a scream and sobs, her asshole clenching around me. Gods above.

"My cock belongs in your ass," I told her when I could speak. "Say it."

"Y-your c-cock belongs in m-my ass," she groaned.

"Good girl." I stroked in and out of her with slow, even thrusts because she shook with pleasure, and because every time I did, she moaned my name. "Where else does my cock belong?" I asked, my voice strained.

She whimpered. "M-my cunt."

As a reward, I rubbed her swollen clit. She wailed, and her slickness dripped onto my hand. "And where else, my mate?" I asked.

Her back arched as she tried to take my cock even deeper into her ass. "My mouth."

I moved my hand to her mouth, sliding my fingers between her lips so she could taste herself. She licked my fingers greedily and then bit them as I had bitten hers earlier. My cock twitched in her ass at the flash of pain.

"And what other cocks will go in your mouth, your pussy, or your asshole, my mate?" I asked, withdrawing my hand from her lips.

"None." She was fucking my cock now, her ass bouncing against my hips. "This is the only cock I want."

I slipped the tip of one of my tentacles back into her pussy and stroked her G-spot, and moments later she came with another ragged cry and a full-body shudder. Now my name fell from her lips over and over, like a song, as her ass fluttered around my cock. Her tightness and the sensations of her coming threatened to overwhelm me.

I wanted a better vantage point to watch her take my cock. Holding her in my tentacles so she did not move away, I rolled to my back, and then settled her in place facing away from me with her legs straddling my hips. Without being told, she fucked my cock with her ass, her hands braced on my thighs as she ground against me. I helped support her weight with my tentacles so she would not become tired.

This angle allowed me to watch every detail of how well she took my cock. Streaks of my glowing precum marked her lower back and dripped from her ass.

Mine, I thought with satisfaction. *My mate.*

I released her wrists so one tentacle could cup her breast and tease her nipple. The other slipped between her legs, seeking the sweetness of her cunt. She cried out as its tiny suckers plucked at her clit.

"How many times have you come, my mate?" I asked.

"I can't remember." She ground her ass on my cock. "Too many times."

My tentacle, hungry for the taste of her, stroked back and forth over her clit, and she nearly collapsed.

"Too many, or not enough?" I asked.

She groaned. "Not enough. I want…one more."

My sweet, greedy mate. I lifted her free of my cock with my tentacles. She made a protesting sound.

"I want your final orgasm to be on my tongue." I turned her onto her back and went to my knees. "Spread your legs and grant me this gift, my mate."

"Granted," she said, arms above her head, her smile lazy and eyes half-lidded. My cum still glowed on her face and body, and precum dripped from her holes. "Do you like the taste of my pussy, Vos?"

"I do, very much." I lay with my face between her legs and raised her hips to meet my lips. When my tentacles curled around her thighs and knees and spread her legs wide, she moaned, and her pussy gushed for me once again.

I teased her reddened and very sensitive asshole with my tongue so she would writhe. When my lips closed on her beautiful swollen clit, she cried out and ground against my face.

After so many orgasms, this time it took several minutes to make her come, but when she began to wail, "Ah, ah, ah," I knew I had brought her to the edge once more.

A few more moments of sucking and flicking her clit with my tongue, and she came for me, her fists twisted in the sheet as her juices flooded my mouth. I had never tasted anything as rich and honeyed, or heard anything so much like music as her calling my name.

As she shook and gasped, I stroked my cock until I came as well. This time I covered her cunt, thighs, and stomach with my glowing cum. I wanted to come inside her, but I would have other opportunities to do that. In our future together, I planned to see my cum drip from her cunt and her asshole and her mouth.

She was mine. My mate. My joy. My heart that beat outside my own body. My universe.

Trembling from my release, I lay on the floor beside her and drew her close so I could look into her eyes. "My mate, are you satisfied?"

Calla let out a sigh. "Gods above and below, of course I am."

With nothing but a sheet under us, the floor was not comfortable, but she seemed insensible to it and at the moment I did not care. I felt drunker than if I had drained a bottle of Bacorian wine.

I pressed my lips to her forehead and let my tentacles roam her body at will. She tasted of sweat and smelled like sex. Nothing in the galaxy could be better than this.

"This is strange," she said, her voice soft. Blinking slowly, she touched my lower lip. "Vos, I'm suddenly so sleepy."

I kissed her fingertips. "You are healing, my Calla." I gathered her in my tentacles and rose. "Sleep. I will bathe you and put you in bed."

"Thank—" A yawn interrupted her. "Thank you."

I carried her to the bathroom and sat on the edge of the tub. As it began to fill, she murmured, "I'm sorry."

I brushed hair back from her forehead and searched her face for some clue as to what weighed heavily on her mind. "For what could you possibly be sorry, my mate?"

"Lots of things." She nestled her head against my chest and closed her eyes before adding, "More than you could know." Moments later, she was fast asleep, her brow furrowed.

Now uneasy, I slipped into the hot bathwater with my Calla in my arms.

She had asked me if I would fuck her this thoroughly if she took me as her mate, and of course I had promised to do so. But she had not said anything more on the subject, and now she had apologized for reasons she did not want to disclose.

I did not believe our lovemaking had been only casual sex to her, but I feared what might happen after she slept and healed.

That she was my mate and I was hers, I knew in my hearts. Everything else I did not know for certain.

Despite how peacefully Calla slept in my arms, all that remained in the balance would keep me unsettled for the remainder of the day and well into the night.

CHAPTER 19

CALLA

ACCORDING TO VOS, IN THE LANGUAGE OF ITS FIRST SETTLERS from Jakora, *Iosa* meant "a new beginning."

But as I sat alone in Vos's garden the next morning with a cup of tea, watching Poe putter around and enjoying a rare hour without rain, I wondered what "new beginning" meant to me.

Could someone who'd enlisted in the Galactic Alliance Defense with such enthusiasm and felt most alive in the cockpit of a fighter somehow find happiness living on a sparsely populated moon of a non-Alliance planet on the edge of uncharted space, even if Vos really was everything he seemed to be?

I truly didn't know.

I couldn't think clearly around Vos because every time I looked at him I wanted to jump on his face or his cock, so I'd come outside by myself to consider my options. And as much as he clearly wanted to be by my side, he'd stayed in the house—after telling Poe that I must be safe at all costs.

No one had ever said that about me. The closest I'd ever come to that level of protection was my squadron mates, who'd always had my back in any battle just as I'd had theirs, and not just because of honor or duty. Even so, Vos's care was different. He didn't just want me safe. He wanted me to be happy, content, sheltered, and satisfied, in every sense of those words.

I expected his devotion to feel smothering. The fact it wasn't, and that I wanted more of it, left me confused and lost.

I'd had no parents to speak of, no family, and no sense of belonging until I joined the Alliance Defense and spent years living, working, fighting, and surviving with my squadron. Maybe it made sense that I wanted to be treasured and adored for a change, even if I'd never really entertained that possibility before. Treasured and adored simply weren't in my vocabulary —or hadn't been until after I'd crashed on Iosa.

Who are you, Calla Wren? Vos had asked me yesterday. I'd given him a reply, but the question had swirled in my mind ever since as if I hadn't found the right answer yet.

Who was I? I didn't really know. And if I couldn't answer that, how could I tell Vos whether I'd stay with him?

I sipped my tea and studied the trees beyond the wall as if the answer could be found in the scarlet moss that hung from their branches or the wings of the carrion birds perched near the tree tops, waiting to feast on whatever bits the predators left behind.

I didn't love Vos, and I was certain he didn't love me—not yet. He wanted me like he wanted air to breathe because something about me had activated some primal part of him that desired me as his true mate. I didn't know how or why it had happened, but it had. That fact was as inescapable as this moon's gravity or that my fighter was nothing but chunks of twisted metal strewn across the ocean floor. There was simply too much evidence for me to reach any other conclusion.

On the other hand, humans didn't have true mates; that was a fact too. The science was clear. So I couldn't blame or credit my feelings or desires, or even how Vos's worshipful care didn't smother me as I thought it should, on some innate biological drive. And I knew myself well enough to know it wasn't his cock either that made me want to stay. He was good at what he did, but I'd had other partners with as much skill. The universe was vast and full of beings who wanted to give and enjoy pleasure.

I was healed now, or very nearly so. The scanner had confirmed it when I woke this morning, and more than that, I felt good. I felt *better* than good. I felt whole. I knew why I was healed, or at least we were pretty damn sure we knew. But why I felt whole was a different story entirely. I had no explanation for that.

Or maybe I did, but I wasn't ready to accept it. Or maybe I didn't want to, because deep down I knew I *was* a scrap born in a shack on Ganai, and scraps didn't get treasured, adored, or sheltered in the storm. They stood cold and alone in the rain.

I thought of Vos then, how he'd stayed outside in torrential wind and downpours while I lay in his bed too injured to move. Yes, he'd been guarding the house, but that wasn't why he'd gone outside. He'd tried to put some distance between us and protect himself because I'd shot him down that first day, and he'd ended up standing alone and cold in the rain.

My gut contracted. I let out a little mewl of grief.

I jumped when our Anomuran companion touched my arm.

"Poe?" she asked anxiously, tapping her claws together.

Two of her eyes watched our surroundings while one leaned close as if trying to see the cause of my sorrow. Her antennae waved too, stirring the air between us. How much she could discern from scent, I wasn't sure, but she bobbed her eyestalks in what I'd learned meant she was troubled.

"Poe?" she asked again, her voice quavering.

"I'm all right," I assured her, though it wasn't true and she didn't need any special senses to tell I was lying. "I was just thinking about something that made me sad."

"Poe," she murmured and caressed my arm very gently with her razor-edged claw.

I held perfectly still. I didn't fear that she'd hurt me on purpose, but I didn't want to startle her. I'd seen her snap tree limbs thicker than my arm with that same claw without much effort.

When I smiled at her, she trundled off back to her garden, stopping to pick up and eat *enni* on the way.

"Calla?"

I turned my head at the sound of Vos's voice and grimaced at a sharp twinge in my upper back.

He was at my side in a heartbeat, and without spilling a drop from the teapot in his hand. "Pain?" he asked, his tentacles caressing my back and shoulders and plucking at my uniform in worry.

"Just a little. I'm okay." I rolled my shoulders and neck and the ache faded. "Probably just from sitting and staring into space for too long." I held up my mug. "Thank you for bringing more tea."

He filled my cup, set the pot on a little table beside my chair, and crouched so he didn't tower over me. His tentacles wrapped around me gently. "My pleasure. You like it?"

"Very much." I was not a habitual tea drinker, but this blend Vos had made himself was wonderful. "Do you need help with anything?"

"Not at the moment." He touched my cheek, his eyes glowing softly. "I am enjoying this break from the rain. I am very happy to look out the window and see you sitting in the garden for the first time. Soon the rainy season will pass. We will have many more days like this, and sunshine as well."

I glanced up at the lavender-gray sky. "Again, I'll believe it when I see it, Vos."

His mouth turned up at the corners. "I speak only truth to you, my mate. Even on matters as simple as the weather."

He was teasing me, but the earnestness in his tone and the way his gaze locked on mine told me he truly wanted me to believe I could trust him and that my trust meant everything to him. Maybe more than anything else, including my body, which came alive at the sensation of his thumb on my cheek and his tentacles wrapping gently around my lower legs.

Giving him my trust would mean everything to me too, if I could allow myself to take a chance on someone besides myself.

"Should I go back inside?" Vos asked. "I do not want you to feel alone."

"I don't feel alone," I assured him. "Poe's right there, and you're close by. But yes, I do need more thinking time."

"All right." His tentacles released me. I missed their touch immediately. He kissed my forehead gently as he rose. "I will leave the teapot."

"Thank you." I touched his hand. "For everything."

"You are most welcome, my Calla."

I listened to his footsteps return to the house, but didn't hear the door close. A glance over my shoulder confirmed he'd left the windows open as well to let the breeze blow through. The sky remained overcast, but no thunder rumbled. The lack of rain was almost unnerving after hearing nothing else for weeks.

I folded my hands around my mug as Poe hummed to herself and tended her garden. Unlike Vos's planned fruit and vegetable garden, which remained covered and unused until the rainy season ended, Poe's welcomed the daily deluges. Her garden plants were both her food and attractive to the *enni* and other small animals she ate.

After the severity of my injuries, my time lying in bed, and the expectation that my recovery would take weeks or months, not days, I'd fully expected to wake today restless and itching for adventure. Instead, I found myself enjoying my first pain-free day sitting in Vos's single outdoor chair with a cup of tea, lost in thought.

Despite all its dangers, I wanted to explore the swamp, and go with Vos to the ocean. He'd scarcely been there since he'd brought me home. The wistful way he described swimming in its depths told me he missed it, but his worry about my safety overrode even what must be his most innate desires.

Thinking about the swamp and ocean was a way of distracting myself from the real decision I needed to make: whether to journey to the regional capital to relay a message to Outpost 60, where I was now weeks overdue and likely presumed dead.

My squadron—and Epsilon Squad Captain Proos, with the so-punchable face—would know I'd gone missing somewhere between my patrol assignment and the outpost. Proos I didn't care about, but I didn't want my squadron mates to think I was marooned somewhere, or captive, or dead. I didn't want them to grieve for me.

I'd had no comms after the raider attack and hadn't been able to activate any kind of emergency beacon, so they would have no way of knowing where I'd ended up—or whether my ship and I were now merely atoms drifting through space. Parts of my ship were presumably still up there, but eventually they'd get demolished by large passing ships or burn up in the atmosphere. As long as no one knew about the remains of my fighter on the ocean floor, no one would know I'd ended up here.

I really could make this a new beginning and let the Alliance Defense go on without me, but was that what I wanted? Or would I soon grow tired of Vos and this simple home on Iosa, leaving me restless and yearning for my days as a pilot?

If I didn't contact Outpost 60 right away, I'd have to explain why I'd waited. Vos's cock and tentacles were pretty great, but I doubted Proos or his superiors would consider them a good reason to go AWOL for however long it took for me to get rest-less. That meant either a dishonorable discharge or prison, or both. Certainly no bonus to fund my relocation to a planet where I could live and work until I'd saved enough to travel the galaxy. That had been what I wanted most when I'd enlisted, besides a roof over my head, food in my tummy, and the promise of someday sitting in the cockpit of a long-range fighter.

I had a third option, too. If I did stay here for a while, I could always leave later and do something else. Plenty of opportunities in the cosmos for an experienced pilot. I'd be up for whatever job paid well, as long as it didn't involve becoming a mercenary raider. I did have principles, after all. Even being a cargo ship pilot didn't sound too bad, only lonely.

If I contacted Proos, he'd immediately arrange for my rescue and I'd likely never step foot on Iosa again until I finished my enlistment. While on active duty, I had very limited free time.

I had a measure of camaraderie with my squadron. I wanted to help defend the Alliance. I loved the adventure, danger, and prestige of piloting a fighter, and the gig paid well. But very few pilots retired out of the Defense. Most left after their first enlistment to do other things, and many died before they had that chance.

Vos had assured me I could find work here, or we could live comfortably on his savings. I had good savings too, which I was sure I could get my hands on thanks to shady friends who'd transfer the funds and keep my secret for a percentage. And Vos seemed willing to consider leaving Iosa, if that was what we wanted to do. Whether Poe could come with us, I wasn't sure, but maybe we could keep this home and visit often.

As I thought about leaving my squadron and the Alliance Defense behind, I expected to feel grief and regret. Instead, I found myself looking forward rather than back. Even my flight suit, painstakingly cleaned and mended by Vos, felt less like my identity now and more like a utilitarian piece of clothing.

As much as I still yearned to put my fist in the middle of

Proos's face, when I thought about sending a distress call to Outpost 60, my stomach twisted with nausea.

But when I pictured myself with Vos, I felt…peaceful. And when I thought about him wrapping me in his tentacles and kissing the back of my neck as I slept beside him, warmth and happiness spread from my heart all the way down to my toes.

The more I sat and thought and sipped my tea, the more clear the answer seemed. I had so little to gain if I made that call, and so much to lose. I didn't want to stand alone in the rain anymore. And I didn't want Vos out there either. I wanted to be his shelter every bit as much as he was mine, and wherever we were and whatever we were doing, that would make me happy.

"I'm Calla Wren," I murmured, holding my mug in both hands as I drained the last of the tea. "Nothing special. Just… Calla."

That didn't sound like quite the right answer either, but it felt closer to the truth than what I'd said yesterday.

I set my empty cup on the little handmade table next to my chair. "Vos?"

A moment later, his human arms wrapped around my shoulders as his tentacles coiled once more around my legs and the chair. He must have waited at the window, listening for my voice. Of course I hadn't heard him come up behind me. My beautiful monster. My lover.

Maybe someday, my…mate. Whatever that might mean to someone like me.

"Yes, Calla?" Vos rested his chin on my shoulder. "You have been thinking a long time."

He'd clearly tried to keep his tone neutral, but I caught the note of hope in his voice. I didn't have much experience being anyone's cause for hope. The thought made my stomach flutter as if I'd swallowed Ngaran moths.

"I had a lot to think about." And still did, but I didn't make him wait for me to tell him what I'd decided, since he'd already waited several hours. Or a lifetime, depending on how I looked at his situation. "I think I'd like to stay with you. No, I don't *think* I want to stay," I amended. "I *want* to stay."

Vos came around the chair and knelt in front of me, his tentacles around my lower legs as he took my hands. His expression was very serious. "My Calla, I will not cage you, and I do not demand any promises you do not want to give."

"I know you don't." I took his face in my hands so I could look into his beautiful glowing eyes. "And I don't make any promises I don't intend to keep, so that works out just fine."

He did something entirely unexpected then: he straightened and bowed his head. That pose must hurt like crazy with all his weight on his knees on the stone terrace.

Something like panic bubbled up inside me. "What are you doing?" I demanded.

"Showing my respect," he said, his gaze on my feet. "Fortusians show their respect to their mates during courtship by kneeling."

Damn it, I couldn't tell him not to honor the customs of his homeworld. Even so…

I leaned over and raised his chin so he could see me smiling. "On my homeworld, my people show their respect to their mates during courtship by cooking and eating a good meal together, sharing secrets or gossip, maybe watching some form of entertainment, and then having lots of sex—not necessarily in that order."

"This is true?" His gaze searched my face, as if he thought I wasn't being serious. "You do these things rather than kneel?"

I could think of several things I could enjoy that involved him kneeling at my feet, and vice versa. "Well, we can respect both cultures," I said.

He smiled. "Excellent."

Suddenly, I found myself wrapped in his tentacles and we were heading for the open door of his house.

"Hey!" I protested. "Why go inside? It's not raining."

"You said on your homeworld your people show their mates respect with lots of sex," Vos reminded me, hurrying through his front room and heading for his bed—*our* bed.

"I did say that, didn't I?" I trailed my fingertips over one of his tentacles. It quivered in excitement. "I suppose we can spend a few hours being respectful to one another, then, if that sounds good to you."

"It most certainly does." He placed me on the bed as carefully as ever, though my injuries had all but healed. His tentacles ran over my body, tugging at my uniform's fastenings. "My Calla, what do you want?"

"Your beautiful cock, of course." I entwined my fingers through his and drew him onto the bed so his body was above mine. "Then rain or not, I want you to take me to the ocean."

CHAPTER 20

VOS

I MADE LOVE TO MY MATE UNTIL SHE LAY EXHAUSTED AND SATED in my arms, gasping for air and trembling as I kissed her all over, drinking in the scents and tastes of her body and our lovemaking.

When the rain returned, she murmured protests when I rose to close the windows and door, then nestled into my tentacles again when I returned to the bed, her head against my chest. Though she dozed, she did not lapse into a healing sleep.

My Calla was well again, and for the first time I did not feel fear in addition to relief at the thought.

She wants to stay. She wants to visit the ocean with me.

In my hearts, disbelief warred with joy and profound contentment.

"An Alliance credit for your thoughts," she murmured, startling me from my reverie. Her eyelashes fluttered open, revealing her lovely green eyes. "So quiet, my Vos."

My Vos. Such simple syllables, but they filled me with warmth.

"I am thinking of you, of course," I said, brushing damp, sweaty hair from her forehead. "What else could I have on my mind?"

Her wry smile made me smile in return. "You don't really have to flatter me so much, you know. You got your way. I want to stay. Now you can just be yourself."

At first I thought she was teasing me, but some shadow lurked in her eyes, making me think her thoughts had taken an unexpectedly serious turn.

"My Calla, I have never been anything but myself with you," I said. "In fact, I do not think I have ever been *more* myself."

"I was afraid of that." She cupped my face with her hand and brushed my lower lip with her thumb. "Do you think you would have been half as interested in me if I wasn't your true mate? If I'd just been a human female pilot whose fighter crashed nearby, would we be lying in this bed right now?"

Unease began to replace my contentment. "Why do you ask me this?"

"How could I not wonder?" My Calla laced our fingers together with her free hand. "You said you'd never sought companionship until you smelled me, and then finding, healing, and making love to me suddenly became everything to you—so much so that you've hardly been to the ocean or left my side since you brought me home. Doesn't that bother you?" Her eyes had that bruised look again that worried and disturbed me so much. "I feel like I've bewitched you and you're not doing this of your own choice."

I did not need to read her mind to know these questions arose more from her belief that she was not worthy of my care and worship than any fear of having actually magically enchanted me.

"I promise I have made many choices that led to this moment." I kissed her forehead. "I do not say my biological drive has not been a factor, because most assuredly it *has*. But that is far from the only reason I call you my Calla. And you have made choices as well. Many more lie before us. We will make our own future."

"But would you have wanted *me?*" Her voice was quiet now. "Imagine you'd found me in the boat with the raiders but I *wasn't* your true mate—just myself, Calla Wren. What would you have done?"

I thought back to that night on the storm-tossed ocean, when I had witnessed her, bloody and battered but with fiery eyes, bite the Atolani raider's arm and stare me down with defiance and determination. Her fire had captivated me and stirred feelings and emotions I had not known I possessed, or even dreamed of having, only minutes earlier.

Try as I might, I could not separate my feelings of desire and admiration from the siren call of my mate, but perhaps there was no need to. Perhaps those feelings were one and the same.

She might want to hear that nothing would be different if she had not been my true mate, but I had no way of knowing. Above all, I must be honest with my Calla.

"I did not have a chance to meet you without knowing you were my mate," I said. "I understand why you ask me this, but I will not lie and say I would certainly have done the same regardless of circumstances. The truth is, I chose to take a chance on happiness with you when I did not have to. In fact, it was far from an easy choice, because my own past persists in telling me I am unworthy of you. With time and effort, I hope to make myself worthy."

She lay her head on my chest again and said nothing for a long time, keeping our fingers entwined.

"So we're both sure we don't deserve each other?" she asked finally, her tone wry. "What a pair we are."

I rested my chin on top of her head. "You are my Calla and I am your Vos. If that is true, what else matters?"

"I can't argue with that logic." Her warm chuckle eased some of my tension. "Will you promise to tell me if ever you feel I have in fact bewitched you?"

She was teasing me now, but still with an undercurrent of disquiet that I would give anything to banish.

"I promise," I said, very solemnly. "As long as you promise to tell me if you ever feel that you no longer want to bewitch me."

"Deal." She kissed my chest. "I'm ready to get cleaned up and do something outside. But before we walk to the ocean, would you spar with me? I feel like I'm healed, but I have to make sure I'm up for a fight if something happens. First blood wins."

"Of course I will spar." The thought of practicing combat with my mate sent shivers of anticipation, joy, and excitement through my body, all the way to the tips of my tentacles. "Unarmed? Armed?"

"Armed, if you don't mind." She raised her head so she could see my face. "I'm assuming you have at least a few weapons here?"

"A few," I said, my voice bland. The past was never so far past that a retired assassin shunned weapons. "Shall we wash and dress, and then choose our weapons?"

"That is probably the sexiest thing anyone has ever said to me." She kissed my chest again, and this time she rubbed her nose on my skin as I liked to do with her. "There you go with the perfect answers again. What can I do with someone who always knows the right thing to say?"

"Spar with him," I said, tucking a loose strand of hair behind her ear. "Then go with him to visit his ocean home."

"Then let's go," she said, and now her eyes sparkled with happiness and even eagerness. "I'm ready to have blades in my hands again. But do you think we can bathe together without getting distracted?"

I looked over my lovely Calla, at the way her perspiration glimmered on her skin, and the marks I had left with my teeth and suckers, and the streaks of glowing lavender cum that criss-crossed her body, and felt myself growing hard once more.

"I do not," I said.

With a lazy chuckle, she pushed on my chest. "Then you go wash up first. I want to lie here and feel good for a while."

Even for a man who had completed many seemingly impossible tasks over a long career as an assassin, it took no small amount of determination to leave her naked on the bed with the sheets tangled around her legs. Only the promise of sparring and going to the ocean afterward kept me from simply giving in to the desire to make love to her again.

Rather than linger in a tub full of water, I used the overhead shower to clean myself quickly. My tentacles quivered in displeasure at both my choice not to bathe and the ache of my Calla's most personal scents washing away.

Truly, though, her smell and taste had soaked into my skin deeply enough that no amount of soap and water could take those away. Even under the spray of hot water, with the air filled with the scent of the plants that lived in the bathroom and released oils into the air when the room filled with steam, I still smelled her. That did not make my tentacles any less unhappy, but it allowed me to smile despite the fact she was not in my arms.

When I emerged from the bathroom fully dressed, Calla rose from the bed. "I'll be quick," she said, standing on her toes to kiss my jaw. "I can't wait to see what weapons you have."

"Do not rush on my account," I caught her hand and held on so I could drink in her scent for a moment. "Enjoy your shower. The ocean will not boil away in the meantime."

She squeezed my hand and went into the bathroom, closing the door behind her.

Unsurprisingly, despite my admonishment not to hurry, she soon rejoined me, dressed in her Alliance Defense-issued flight suit and boots, with her hair styled in a long braid she had wrapped with a strip of cloth and tied at the end.

She found me waiting by the bed with my hands clasped behind my back. Nearly two dozen different weapons from across the galaxy, all very lethal, lay in rows atop the bed. I had changed the bedding while she washed.

Hands on her hips, she looked over my offerings. "These are my choices?"

I blinked. "Yes."

Did she find the contents of my armory insufficient? Lacking in quality? I had long taken pride in my collection, but suddenly I felt as though she had judged my cache and found it wanting.

Humming under her breath, she picked up a pair of Hardanian scythe-knives and spun one in each hand, testing their weight and balance. Perhaps she did not like how they felt, because she returned them to their place and hefted the weapon to their right: a set of heavy Tocanian spiked bolos. Impressive to look at and a showpiece of my collection, but impractical for hand-to-hand sparring. Apparently she felt the same, and put them down. With a glance, she assessed and quickly dismissed my priceless Fylorian sword without even touching it, then moved on to a pair of Fortusian daggers.

My Calla did not look at me, and her expression remained inscrutable, but I knew instantly she would choose to wield them to spar with me because they were the sole weapon on the bed native to my homeworld. I hid my smile. Naturally my mischievous mate would want to show me how well she could use them against me.

She spun the daggers in each hand the same way she had tested the Hardanian scythe-knives. Then she browsed the remainder of my offerings, testing all her options and demonstrating ability and skill with each. My approval and appreciation of my warrior Calla grew.

And every movement, every glint of a blade, every spin and *snick* of metal on metal or wood made my cock twitch and harden that much more. She must have noted my reaction, but she did not acknowledge it in any way.

In the end, she did indeed select the Fortusian daggers. She spun them forward and backward, switched grip styles lightning fast, and then turned to face me, a blade in each hand.

"You should have chosen first," she said, with a smile.

In answer, I picked up the heavy plasma-edged Ganaian broadsword that she had swung in a few arcs before dropping it back on the bed. No doubt she had wielded one of these notoriously deadly weapons many times throughout her life.

With my gaze on hers, I turned my wrist, swinging the sword in a circle, followed by a series of fast lunges with right-to-left and left-to-right slashes that blurred. The point of the sword whizzed past the end of her nose and stirred the loose hairs around her face, but my Calla did not so much as flinch. In fact, her smile grew.

"Oh, Vos." She chuckled. "You want to play? Then by all means, let's play."

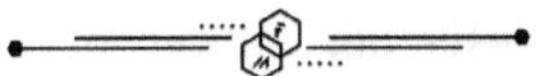

I HAD HOPED THE RAIN WOULD EASE TO A DRIZZLE BY THE TIME WE went outside, but if anything the downpour had increased in volume. If the deluge bothered Calla, she did not say so. Poe moved out of our way, trundling in a perimeter around the inside of the wall, monitoring our surroundings with two eyes while the third watched us.

"I am used to heavy rain, but it puts you at a disadvantage," I said as my Calla and I faced each other in the garden. "We can postpone this match until it eases, if you want."

She smiled as if she knew I was provoking her. "It's just rain, Vos. I won't melt."

"I will not use my tentacles, then." I tucked them behind my back and made my expression sympathetic. "I am already much faster and larger than you. We are only sparring, but even so, the fight must not be so lopsided in my favor."

"I'd be more susceptible to your goading if I hadn't spent so many years taking shit from the rest of my squad. They're much, *much* better at it than you." She raised an eyebrow. "Unless you want to forfeit because you're scared to hurt your sweet little mate? I'm disappointed in you, Vos. You didn't have any trouble giving me pain an hour ago when I asked you for it."

I went for her before she finished speaking, moving at about three-quarters of my true speed, with the crackling edge of my sword facing away from her chest so only the sharp metal would touch her skin. We had agreed we would draw blood, but the plasma would cause an excruciating wound.

When my blade reached where she had been standing, though, she was no longer there.

The point of a dagger prodded my lower back, directly above one of my kidneys.

"Missed me," she said, laughing.

My tentacles darted to grab her as I spun, blade raised. I turned just in time to see her roll out of their reach and flip to her feet. I felt the sting where her dagger had poked me, but my back was not bleeding.

"I took pity on you," my Calla said, smirking as she braced herself with blades at the ready. "That was too easy. I think you might be out of practice. I'll have to move slower to give you a chance."

"There is more to you than meets the eye, Calla Wren." I studied her stance. A modified J'noran close-combat position, ideal for someone her height and weight. She had adapted it to account for wielding mid-sized daggers rather than the longer curved blades of J'noran *intanas*. Perfection.

How was it possible that each time I thought I could not

desire her more, she found a new way to be utterly captivating? Perhaps she *had* bewitched me, but not with magic—with the many facets of her wonderful, glorious, complex self.

"Are you going to stare at me all day, or come at me like you actually want to win?" she taunted. "Come on, Vos. Stop looking at me like you want to fuck me and come play with me."

Come play with me.

I would, forever, if she gave me the chance.

With a grin, I went for her, sword raised. She met me with her daggers and a laugh before spinning out of my grasp and the reach of my blade once again.

We traded parries, thrusts, and light blows around the garden. And gods above, she was good. Better than good— exquisite, fast, and light on her feet, more like a dancer than any opponent I had faced in a very long time.

True to her word about wanting to find her limits after her injuries and recovery, my Calla came after me with all her skill and ability. She pushed herself hard, and once she found her confidence, she drove herself harder, until she dripped with sweat in addition to rain.

Her blades sliced through the fabric of my tunic and my pants three times, never quite drawing blood, while she avoided the edge and point of my sword altogether.

My warrior Calla was truly magnificent, and my awe knew no bounds.

Even so, I could not forget that much of her skill had come at an unfathomable cost: eleven years in the arenas. I had not asked her age, but she seemed more than twenty-five standard years, if not closer to thirty. What had she done during the intervening years between leaving Ganai and enlisting in the Alliance Defense? She had only spoken of that time obliquely, alluding to its violence and peril, but given no specifics.

Someday I would ask, but not now. The fact she had not told me indicated she did not yet wish to say.

All too soon, I felt I must call a halt to the match. We had a long walk to the ocean. My Calla must have enough energy and strength not only to make the journey there and back and swim if she wanted, but to fight if necessary.

And so a few steps at a time I backed her up to the wall of the house, blocked her escape with my tentacles, and crushed my mouth to hers, hoping she could feel all my adoration and admiration in my kiss. If not, I was not above falling to my knees in the mud so she would know how in awe of her I was.

A sharp sting in my thigh and a trickle of heat from the wound made me gasp.

"First blood, but we can call it a draw if you want," she murmured against my lips, her eyes twinkling. "Now, my Vos, take me to the sea."

CHAPTER 21

CALLA

The glimpses I'd caught of the swamp outside Vos's garden wall and his warnings about its dangers had not prepared me for how breathtaking it was.

I wore a small pack on my back that contained drinking water, fruits, and other items Vos deemed necessary for our walk. My borrowed daggers rested in sheaths on my thighs. I'd slipped a third, smaller blade into a sheath in my right boot. Vos carried the Ganaian sword on his back. He'd told me he rarely went into the swamp armed with anything more than his tentacles. I suspected despite his clear confidence in my fighting ability, having me along increased his concern about possible dangers.

Every tree and branch drooped under the weight of thick, sweet-smelling pink and crimson moss. Tall grasses and reeds swayed in the wind and light rain. The competing odors of wet earth, plants, brackish water, and decay filled my nose. I had to stifle several sneezes.

Despite outweighing me significantly, Vos tread silently as

we followed a trail worn through the grasses and over spongy marshes. This wasn't just Vos's path to the sea; I spotted a dozen footprints of varying sizes. Most had claws that dug deeply into the muck.

We relied primarily on hand signals on the rare occasions we needed to communicate. Vos had warned me most predators in the area were drawn to the sound of voices. In particular I didn't want to meet a kaory today, given Vos's description of their venomous spines and razor-sharp teeth. No doubt Vos and I could kill one, but I preferred a nice, quiet, uneventful walk.

Vos had said a kaory's venom was cytotoxic, just like the deno'lia on Fortusia that had very nearly killed me. Even now, almost two years later, the memories of excruciating pain and my rapidly rotting flesh haunted me. Only swift medical intervention had saved me from an utterly hellish death.

Still, kaory and all the other creatures lurking in the trees and water be damned. I didn't fear crossing this swamp because I had weapons and training and Vos.

When we paused to rest and drink water about two-thirds of the way to Vos's favorite inlet, I pointed wordlessly at some of the scarlet moss and raised my eyebrows, asking if it was safe to touch. Vos smiled, freed some of the moss from a branch, and handed it to me.

As he watched for potential threats, I drank water and sat on a rock to rest, listening to water lapping at the marshes around us and the calls of birds. The swamp really was lovely. Even the smell of decay wasn't bad once I got used to it.

The curly, tangled moss was as soft and silky as it appeared. When I rubbed it between my fingers, it gave off a sweet scent and turned my fingertips pink.

With a quiet chuckle, Vos tugged me to my feet, kissed my forehead, and led me on toward the ocean.

Two kilometers on most terrains wasn't very far, but two kilometers through a swamp where I had to be mindful of every step seemed to take an eternity and a half. My impatience to reach the ocean and the ache in my legs from slogging through muck added to my perception that the journey took half the day when it was probably closer to a little more than an hour.

And with every step, twinge of pain, and ragged breath, in the back of my mind I pictured Vos running the other direction up this path in the dark of night with my broken body cradled in his tentacles, racing to get me home for even a chance to keep me alive. And that was after he'd fought and killed a boat full of raiders to get to me, only for me to threaten to kill him if he didn't let me go.

I'd known all of that, but it wasn't until I'd made this trek myself—albeit in much better circumstances—that the enormity of what he'd done that night really sank in. He hadn't been my Vos then, but he'd believed I was his Calla. That belief had given him the strength not only to make the journey but to save my life. I'd never been worth that much to anyone. Even my keepers on Ganai, who'd made a fortune on my success in the arena, wouldn't have lifted a finger to get me away from a dozen raiders, much less swim and then run to get me home. As for giving me their own blood to save me…ha. Not in a million years.

For that matter, Squad Captain Proos wouldn't spit on me if I were on fire. The feeling was mutual, though, so I supposed I couldn't fault him too much for it. Why I'd wasted so much time thinking I wanted to go back to that, I didn't know.

Just as the ache in my right calf reached the point that I considered asking Vos for a short break, I heard something that swept away all my pain and fatigue: the telltale sound of waves and wind. About fifty meters ahead, through the trees and swaying moss, I glimpsed a treeless lavender-gray sky and purple ocean.

With my attention on that sight instead of the path in front of me, my foot caught in something, and down I went. With one of those uncanny, lightning-fast moves, Vos caught me before I ended up in the muck.

My face heated and I scowled. Oh, well done. I'd shown him some of my skills with blades and then promptly fell on my face simply trying to walk.

A flash of movement to my right.

Instinctively, I pulled my dagger and drove it hilt-deep through the skull of an enormous crimson serpent, pinning it to the trunk of a tree covered with lichen almost exactly the same color as the snake.

The snake's body thrashed wildly and fell from the branches where it had been concealed. The gods-damned thing had to be nearly six meters long.

I'd put a blade all the way through its brain, but the serpent hissed. Both of its long, triple-forked black tongues shot out toward my arm.

In a single fluid movement, Vos yanked me out of the path of those tongues, pulled his broadsword, and sliced through the snake's thick body and the tree with the sizzling, plasma-edged blade.

As the tree fell, both parts of the snake's body—the section pinned to the tree stump and the other, much longer part—thrashed wildly until Vos hacked them into small pieces. And even then, they continued to twitch.

"My Calla," Vos rasped, returning his sword to its scabbard on his back. "You are not bitten?"

I shook my head no.

He pulled my dagger out of the snake's head, cleaned the blade on the wet grass, and handed it to me. Then he wrapped me in his tentacles and bolted from the scene, up the path toward the ocean. The noise and blood would draw predators and scavengers alike.

So much for a quiet walk to the sea.

Before we reached the shore, Vos startled me by veering off

the path onto a narrow trail that cut through thick marsh grasses.

He slowed to a walk, but didn't stop until we reached a small, secluded, hook-shaped inlet with a steep, grassy bank out of sight of the open sea. This must be his place to enter the water and slip unnoticed into its depths.

My gaze swept the inlet. This part of the bank was grassy and muddy, while the rest was lined with craggy rocks worn sharp by eons of rising and falling tides. Only the slightest breeze stirred the trees. The only sound was water lapping at the shore. And unlike the swamp we'd crossed, the salty air here smelled fresh and clean.

I looked at Vos and found him staring at me, his eyes glowing softly.

"Vos?" I whispered. "Are you all right?"

"My Calla." His voice was barely audible. He kissed my temple, then rested his forehead on mine, his eyes closed despite the dangers around us. Given I'd just narrowly avoided getting envenomated by a serpent, I couldn't quite allow myself to do the same, but I relished the moment anyway.

If he trusted me to keep watch over us both, he trusted me with all his hearts, and that was truly an enormous gift.

Vos opened his eyes and pressed his lips to my ear. "When I climbed this bank with you in my arms that first night, I dreamed of returning here with you as my mate. I knew it was a dream, and as much as I willed it to be, I do not think I truly *believed* until this moment. Even now, I fear I am dreaming."

"It's not a dream, I promise." I kissed his jaw. "My legs ache too much for this to be a dream."

He chuckled softly. "May I ask you a favor, my mate?"

I raised my eyebrows. "Yes?"

"If you are willing…" His voice became rough with emotion. "I would like to carry you naked into my ocean home as my people do with their mates on my homeworld."

I had never envisioned myself wanting to swim naked in the ocean—not even in the beautiful water on Jakora, where nude swimming was permitted and even encouraged. Even with a dagger on my thigh, I would have felt too vulnerable. But here, with Vos, all I wanted was to swim with him in the way he'd dreamed.

I swallowed hard around the sudden lump in my throat. "Of course you may."

Vos set me on my feet and kept watch as I stripped off my uniform and boots, stacking them neatly on the grass with my daggers and small pack on top. Then we traded roles and I guarded us as he removed his own clothing and sword.

Gods, he was so gorgeous—even more so here, surrounded by the oranges and reds of the swamp and the lavender water. Suddenly I couldn't think of anything I wanted more in the world than to see him in the ocean.

When we were both naked, he scooped me up in his tentacles, kissed my forehead once more, and carried me down the steep bank into the water. The ocean was lovely and cool but not cold, lavender, and crystal clear.

When the water reached my chin, Vos paused and adjusted how he carried me so I was wrapped in his human arms. Now freed, his tentacles swirled in the water around us, as if dancing for joy to be in the ocean once more.

"Beautiful," I murmured. "You're so beautiful. Maybe this *is* a dream."

"If it is a dream, then let neither of us wake." He kissed my lips gently, his gaze searching my face. "Swim in the deep with me, my mate?"

"Yes, please." It was my turn to chuckle. "But don't get so carried away that you go *too* deep. And don't forget I need air."

"I will not forget." His tentacles danced again, this time in what might have been impatience. "Deep breath, my Calla."

My heart racing with anticipation, I took several deep

breaths to stretch my lungs, and then drew in one big breath and nodded.

With a grin, Vos dove us headlong under the water, then propelled us with his tentacles through the inlet and out to the sea.

CHAPTER 22

In the purple depths of the sea, my hearts and body sang.

My mate. My love. My world, in my arms, in the deep with me.

My joy made me feel buoyant, even as our bodies skimmed the sand along the ocean floor. I could not take her to the deepest places, as her body was not made to withstand the pressures there, but this…this was bliss.

My Calla's eyelids were closed. Human eyes experienced discomfort in very salty water, so I could not see her beautiful green eyes and she could not see our surroundings as my tentacles propelled us through the water, but her expression was rapturous nonetheless. I would happily buy her eye protection for swimming underwater at my first opportunity.

Mindful of her need for air, I used my tentacles to bring us slowly to the water's surface well before her fingers tightened on my arm. We surfaced near the shore, in an area well-hidden by long, low-hanging tree branches draped with red curtains of moss that concealed us. I did not want my Calla to be seen by anyone who might pass by, especially raider ships leaving or approaching their base.

Calla surprised me by wrapping her legs around my waist and kissing me deeply the moment she got a breath. I held her to my chest while my tentacles swirled, keeping us steady and afloat with our heads and shoulders above the water.

"This is even more wonderful than I'd imagined," she said, her head against my shoulder. Her long red hair floated around her like a fiery cape. "Thank you for bringing me here."

"The privilege is mine, my mate." I kissed her hair. "You are not afraid? You are not from the sea like me."

"The shore is right there if we need to get out," she reminded me. "The shallows are far less scary than open water. You said the big predators don't come this close to shore. And any small predators—well, they're more likely to be afraid of *you*."

"It is not so shallow here." I gestured past our feet at the inky purple darkness. "But yes, nothing large comes this close to shore. At least, I have never seen it."

"Good." She adjusted her position, settling in more comfortably and securely with her thighs on my hips and ankles crossed behind my back, and put her head back on my chest. "So we have the place to ourselves."

At the sensation of her legs squeezing my waist and her bare cunt against my lower abdomen, my cock stirred and began to harden. "Calla…"

"Hmm?" She let out a contented sigh. "I do want to swim more, but this is so nice. Can we just float for a while?"

Gods, even now she had no idea how much I craved her, body and soul. "Of course."

And I had fully intended to float peacefully for as long as she wanted, but as my senses filled with the scent of her body mixed with those of my ocean home, I suddenly felt displaced, as if transported back to the night I had first caught her scent on her fighter, mixed with the smells of rain and the sea—to the moment I knew fate, or the gods, or chance, had brought my true mate and I together.

And just as before, as those scents filled me, my mind blanked, and my world dwindled until all I knew was her. But this time, something changed.

Blood rushed to my cock so swiftly that a shiver rolled through my body, followed by a strange tightening sensation that traveled from my balls to the base of my cock. Not the same feeling as when I was about to come, but similar. My arousal became a sharper, more needful, more demanding urge. I shivered again, much more powerfully, from my toes to the tips of my tentacles.

Calla raised her head, her brow furrowed. "What's wrong?"

My mate. My everything.

"My Calla," I said, my voice rough and teeth bared. I felt monstrous, on the edge of madness, nearly wild with desperation. "I need you."

Despite my growing haze of desire, I worried my Calla might shy away from my teeth and sudden fierceness, but she did not.

"I need you too," she said.

She moved a little to the side and rubbed herself against my hip, her slickness evident even under the water. The sensory cells in my skin drank in the taste and smell of her. My body went almost as rigid as my cock. My tentacles stilled, and we started to slip under the water before they began swirling again.

Smiling, her eyes half-lidded with her own arousal, Calla held my gaze as her hand wrapped around my cock, stroking its length. "You're so hard for me already, my Vos." Her fingers explored the ridges and fringes, and I quaked at every sensation. "Do you want my pussy to squeeze your cock?"

At her words, my cock twitched in her hand and my balls

drew up. As much as I had previously enjoyed demanding that she tell me explicitly what she wanted of me, I found myself nearly shuddering with need as she commanded me the same way. For this pleasure, I would let her rule me to her heart's content.

"Yes," I rasped. "I want your sweet pussy, my love."

"You're so slick." She raised her hand from the water to show me the gleaming, glowing lubrication and precum on her fingers before she licked them one by one, her eyes locked on mine. "Delicious," she said.

I could have come right then, but I held myself back—if only barely.

"Are you sure you want my pussy?" She reached for me again, stroking my cock harder, faster, her nails skimming my tender flesh in an exquisite combination of pleasure and pain. "Tell me what else you want, my Vos."

Gods above, I wanted all of her, all at once. I wanted my mouth on her cunt to drink her juices when she came. I wanted my cock in her mouth, in her cunt, in her ass. I wanted my tentacles on her body to taste every part of her as she screamed my name.

But most of all, I wanted my cock inside her as she came, and to give her every drop of my cum as we floated in my ocean home.

I held her close with one arm as my trembling hand found her pussy, already so slick and quivering and needy that she impatiently impaled herself onto my fingers. My head fell back at the sensation and taste of her honeyed heat.

"Yes," she groaned, her hand sliding up and down my cock as she fucked my fingers. "Oh, gods, yes. Make me come, Vos. Make me come."

In a near-haze of desire, I used three of my tentacles to keep us afloat so the fourth could travel over her beautiful body, sucking on her nipples and clit in turns and making her shake and moan. I covered her mouth with mine to drink in her cries.

"Beautiful Calla," I murmured against her lips.

Her body tensed as her release neared. When her pussy began to flutter around my fingers, the tip of my roaming tentacle nudged and sucked at her asshole. With a wail, my Calla came, trembling and clinging to me, her warm juices flooding my hand.

"Yes," I rasped. "Come for me, my mate."

My skin drank her in as greedily as her cunt ground against my fingers, seeking pleasure from my touch. My cock felt ten times more sensitive than ever before, and the straining sensation at its base increased.

She ran her hand through my hair and pulled, and the pain made my cock throb. "I want to be fucked, Vos."

What could I do but obey? I grabbed her hips and drove my cock into her delicious, slick heat.

"Oh, gods," she gasped, her arms around my neck. "Oh, oh, yes."

Each time her cunt took my cock to the hilt, the straining sensation at its base became pleasure so intense that I could not breathe. And now I felt the frills and ridges on my cock swelling, forming wide, thick bumps that throbbed and sent pulses of pleasure through my body every time they entered or pulled out of my mate.

"Vos," my Calla gasped, her eyes wide and nails digging into my back. "Vos...what...oh, gods." She came hard, her cunt squeezing and fluttering around my cock as she wailed.

My body was changing shape, but I did not fear these changes. They were for my pleasure and that of my mate, and nothing about that could be bad or wrong.

As her orgasm continued, I lost myself in the pleasure of my Calla's slickness and heat, the sensations that rolled through my body, my own release building—

—and then Calla cried out, her arms tightening around my neck. That note of pain and the way she clung to me cut through my haze of pleasure like a blade.

I froze, my chest heaving. "I hurt you?"

Trembling, she lay her head on my shoulder. "Something's changed," she said breathlessly.

She did not deny that I had hurt her, which meant I had. My stomach filled with guilt and dread. "Calla, I am sorry."

"No, no, I'm okay. But…can you feel this?" Biting her lip, she moved gently up and down on my cock, sliding over the bumps that had formed. Then, slowly, carefully, she took in a much larger bump near the base, moaning and whimpering with every centimeter. Intense pleasure turned my vision gray around the edges. When I was fully inside her, she stilled and held onto me, shaking.

Thinking clearly had become difficult, but I realized my cock had swollen at its base, to the point that it had become difficult and even painful for her to take me.

Moments ago, I believed my body's changes were for her pleasure and mine. But how could I fuck my mate if I caused her pain she did not want? Had my body betrayed us both?

When I started to withdraw, though, she held me still. "Don't," she murmured, trembling against me, her face pressed to my chest. "I want to take you, my Vos. I want your knot. Please don't stop."

My…knot?

I did not have a knot. I had never had one. Even with Calla, whose arrival had changed my physiology and life so much, I had never felt even an inkling of a knot. I knew what one was, of course, and what its purposes were, but I did not know my genetic engineering had included one.

But then again, my creators had supposedly removed my need or ability to find a true mate, and yet here she was. Perhaps those who made me knew far less than I had credited them for. The proof was plain to see.

Now, in my ocean home, making love to my Calla had caused another physiological change—one that promised an even deeper connection to my mate. But hurting her was not acceptable to me. Why would my body change in a way that caused my mate harm? I would sooner die.

Utterly lost, I rested my forehead against hers. "What should I do?"

My Calla looked into my eyes and laced her fingers tenderly through mine. "I'm your Calla, and you're my Vos. You know how to take my pain away."

Understanding, warm and reassuring, rolled through me, taking away my worry and hurt. I *did* know. I had known from the moment I first held her in my arms.

"Let me feel this with you," she said, her voice thick with emotion. "Take me, Vos."

I kissed her forehead, wrapped my free arm around her, and cooed.

She relaxed into my embrace with a sigh that almost sounded like a sob, but I saw no grief on her face...only desire and trust.

With my tentacle around her waist to steady her, I withdrew my cock and then slid back inside her, much more gently than before. My knot fit her far easier now, and she did not wince.

Still, I did not move again until she lay her head on my chest. "Yes," she whispered. "Like that."

For all the frenzy and pleasure of my earlier thrusting, that was not what I wanted now that I understood what we were sharing. My desire built again, much more gradually, with every slow slide of my cock in and out of her.

A new kind of pleasure coursed through me—pure and powerful, rolling through my body in waves. My knot swelled slowly, but my mate took it perfectly. Each time it entered her and then withdrew, we trembled together.

"I am not hurting you?" I murmured, tipping her chin up so I could see her face. "Tell me if I am."

"No." Her shimmering gaze met mine. "Not at all."

My body was made for hers. All other wonders of the universe paled in comparison to this.

My release built with every thrust, but I could not come until I gave my Calla another release of her own. I needed to hear her cry out and feel her flutter around my cock again. Only then could I find my completion.

Gently, I turned her away from me, wrapped one arm around her waist, and thrust inside her from behind as my fingers found her swollen clit.

She gasped, her head falling back. "Yes. More. *More*, Vos. Harder now."

My cock head rubbed against her G-spot as my hand ministered to her clit. Her cries became more desperate, the pitch rising in a way I knew so well.

"My beautiful Calla," I said, my voice guttural. "Come for me."

She came undone with a desperate, warbling cry, her body going rigid and then boneless in my arms, her release a flood of honey. I held her tightly against my chest and thrust fully into her sweet heat. Every time she squeezed around my cock, I growled, the sound ripped from somewhere inside me that was purely monstrous.

As I slid my knot inside her once again to seat myself fully within her, my ears filled with a rushing sound that drowned out all else. My balls tightened, and my knot swelled, locking me inside my mate in a new sensation that grayed my vision completely.

Nothing in my life had ever felt so good as this.

With a helpless, plummeting sensation like hurtling over a

cliff, the wave of pure pleasure broke. I came hard, my body convulsing and hips jerking, my tentacles swirling in the water.

"Fill me, Vos," Calla said, the back of her head against my chest, her chest heaving and her nails digging into my thighs in a way I would feel in my dreams. "Fill me completely."

With my throbbing cock and knot buried inside her, I emptied myself into my mate in spurts that wracked my body one hot pulse at a time, until I had nothing left. I had never come like this, not even with my Calla.

I felt both hollow and full to bursting, utterly spent and more alive than ever before, torn apart and yet completely whole, buried to the hilt inside my mate and unable to withdraw from her, my cum filling her completely, as she had asked me to do.

"Calla," I murmured, my lips on her hair. "My Calla?"

"I'm all right." She released her grip on my thighs and held on to my arms with shaking hands. When she took a breath, the sound was ragged. "Gods, Vos. That was…I've never…I've never taken anyone's knot before. I never wanted to."

It was a selfish thought, and I would never have thought less of her nor held it against her if the situation had been different, but I was glad we had shared the wonder of this first time together. This new way to join our bodies was ours alone.

"You do not regret it?" I asked, because the silence had stretched out.

"No." Her voice was quiet, though, so even without seeing her face, I knew something weighed on her mind. "Do you?" she asked.

"Not in the least, as long as you do not." I rested my chin on her head. "Tell me what you are thinking."

She did not speak for a while. When she did, her voice was small. "Choices."

I let out a soft coo, and she sighed and settled in against me. "Which choices, my mate?" I asked.

"All the choices I made that led me here to you, and all the choices I didn't get to make that brought me here too."

"I understand." I pressed my lips to her hair. "I think of these things as well. How could we not, when we have each known such darkness and now find ourselves in the light?"

"Yes, exactly." She took a shaky breath. "Sometimes I think you can read my mind."

"I cannot," I assured her. "At least, not yet."

She chuckled softly, and the snarl of worry in my belly eased. "With everything else that's happened since we met, I suppose it wouldn't surprise me…but do please say something if you start picking up my thoughts. I'd like to know what you're overhearing."

I did not know whether such a thing was possible, but that was an easy promise to make. "Of course. Your thoughts, like everything else about you, is yours to share or not."

"You say that like it's a universal truth." Now her voice had a caustic edge. "But that would be news to a lot of people I've known."

"It *is* a universal truth, whether or not some people believe it." I kissed her hair. "We each have choices. What to ask for, what to give, and what to accept. Your body is your own. I am privileged to touch you, hold you, treasure you, even fill you, but only when you ask. All choices remain yours."

"I know." She squeezed my arm. "I wouldn't still be here if that weren't the case, and I won't be if it ever changes."

She did not mean it as a threat, and I did not take it as such, but the thought of her leaving made my tentacles quiver in distress.

"I don't ask for much, my Vos, but I must have that," she added quietly. "If I don't own myself, what do I have?"

Her hurts ran so deep. I would give anything, shred anything, suffer anything, to ease that pain.

"I too know what it is like to be owned," I said. "My service to the Guard was not the same as what you experienced, but close enough to understand why your autonomy means so much. I told you from the moment you decided to stay that I will not cage you, and that is the truth. No cages of any kind, ever."

She made a little sound that might have been stifled sob.

Another coo rose in my chest, but before it could pass my lips, she said, "Thank you." She laced her fingers through mine. "Being your Calla makes me happy because I *choose* to be your Calla, and that's the truth too. No, not just happy," she added, and I sensed her frown. "More than that. Content." A pause. "Whole."

My hearts soared. "I feel the same."

I was startled when, little by little, my knot began to ease. The sensation was strange. Perhaps I would become used to it in time, but at the moment, I found it...unsettling.

I was not alone in my disquiet, apparently. When my cock moved slightly, as if to slip from her, Calla made a little sound.

"Are you all right?" I asked.

"Yes." She gripped my arms. "Hold me, please, Vos. Just... don't let go."

As if I ever would.

I held her tightly, my tentacles swirling gently around us to keep us afloat, as my knot eased. We could not stay like this—I knew that—but I did not want to move. And my Calla seemed almost afraid. Her fingernails bit into my arms, but not in the way she had used them while I came. Now they seemed to be a kind of anchor. But what did she fear? Pain? Separation? Or something else that she could not bring herself to reveal?

Only moments remained of this first knotted coupling. I cooed and held her tightly as her body relaxed against me. When my cock slipped gently from her, a rush of my glowing cum followed, swirling away into the sea.

She sighed and turned to curl up in my arms, her head

against my chest and eyes closed. Why she closed them, and what I might have seen in them that she might have wished to hide from me, I did not know.

"That is enough time in the ocean today, my mate," I said softly, brushing wet hair back from her face and kissing her brow. "We will come back another day."

CHAPTER 23

CALLA

THAT NIGHT, FOR THE FIRST TIME SINCE MY ARRIVAL AT VOS'S home, sleep eluded me.

Exhausted from our outing to the sea, warm from a hot bath, and wrapped in Vos's arms and tentacles, I fell asleep easily enough, but woke only a few hours later in darkness with my heartbeat thundering in my ears and my stomach churning.

Had a sound woken me? I listened for well over a minute, but heard only the rain and Vos's steady, deep breathing against the back of my neck. I couldn't remember if I'd had a dream or nightmare, but my heart raced as if something had frightened me.

I didn't want to wake Vos because he would worry, so I lay still and quiet with my head resting on one of his tentacles. Another had coiled around my lower right leg. I'd grown so accustomed to that sensation that I barely noticed it anymore—but the moment I did, I felt guarded and needed and content.

How quickly I'd settled into Vos's tentacles, home, and bed. And hearts.

My love.

Today, in the ocean, he'd called me his love. *I want your sweet pussy, my love,* he'd said, his eyes glowing and cock rigid in my hand. He'd said it so easily, so simply, that lost in my arousal I'd scarcely given it a thought. Now those two words had ripped me from my sleep and echoed in my mind like a shout in a cavern.

My love.

Terror and nausea rose. I bit my own hand to hold back a choking sound and swallowed hard. Vos stirred, then relaxed again, his breathing deep and even.

How could he love me? He barely knew me.

A true mate, I understood. That was biological, physiological. There was *science* behind it, even the metaphysical elements. But love—love was make-believe. Love was illusory. Love was a lie and a trap. Wasn't it?

I thought about the way Vos looked at me, the way he softened when he held me, how he treated me like a treasure and called himself *privileged* to care for me and fill me. Was that love, or the mate bond? Was there a difference?

Of course there was. True mates were physical. Love came from something else. Science couldn't measure it, quantify it, examine it under a scanner, or dissect it into component parts.

My love, he'd said without a hesitation of any kind, as if loving me and saying so was the most natural thing in the world.

Vos's tentacles caressed me as if they sensed or smelled my distress. They probably did. How strange and wonderful to be treasured and cared for by Vos and his tentacles too.

If Vos were awake, he would coo, and all this confusion and fear and anger and doubt would melt away. I would feel safe and secure again, and maybe I could close my eyes and sleep. But he wasn't awake, and I felt as lost as when I woke in this bed the first time.

I doubted he would mind if I woke him, especially if it meant he could soothe my hurts. But if I didn't sort through these thoughts and feelings, I'd still be as adrift tomorrow as I was right now.

I had faced squadrons of raider ships and beasts in the arena and more terrors on more planets than I cared to think about, but none of those nightmares scared me as much as Vos's love.

Why? Because it didn't make sense. He'd given his hearts and more to a scrap from Ganai.

I closed my eyes to hold back my tears, but they leaked from under my lids.

I hadn't made a sound, but it didn't matter. I both heard and felt it when Vos inhaled deeply, and then he drew me closer with his arm around my middle until my back pressed against his chest.

"My Calla," he said, his voice fully awake though he'd been sound asleep a moment ago. "Do you weep?"

"No." It came out as a sob.

Ever so gently, his tentacles turned me to face him. His eyes shone in the dark, beautiful and silvery-blue and as gentle as the rest of him, full of worry and care and love.

How had I not seen it before? Maybe I hadn't wanted to.

"What hurts you, my mate?" His tentacles roamed my body, tasting and scenting my skin, maybe searching for injuries. "Why do you cry?"

How could I tell him that his greatest gift to me caused me pain? The words made little sense in my head, and they'd make even less out loud.

He cupped my face and used his thumbs to wipe away my tears. "Please, Calla. Let me help."

"Today, in the sea, you called me your love," I whispered, because if I didn't speak the words I felt like I'd choke on them instead. "Did you mean it?"

"Of course." He pressed a kiss to my forehead. "My Calla, did you not know?"

I opened my mouth to tell him I didn't know what love was, but that wasn't true. I'd recognized it, so I must know. So where did this terrible ache come from?

Maybe the part of my heart that was terribly—and I feared irrevocably—broken.

"I don't think I can love you, or anyone," I said, my voice rough. "I'm sorry."

I had no idea what he would say or do. I thought maybe he'd coo, or he'd argue with me, or he might be angry.

Instead, he held me against his chest. I burrowed my face against his skin. His scent had become a balm for me even when my hurts threatened to carry me away. His bioluminescence pulsed faintly along with his heartbeats, so strong and even. My stomach still churned, but I found my own heart slowing and my aches easing as I listened to that familiar, reassuring sound.

It was a long, long time before he spoke.

"Five standard years, three lunar cycles, and five days ago," he said softly, "I completed my final assignment for the Silent Guard."

My breath caught in my chest.

With his arms around me and his head resting against mine, Vos told me the story of the death of the Kurutan Ambassador N'Vors.

He tried to keep his tone even, but I heard the strain in his voice and felt the tension in his body as he described the impossible choice he'd faced about whether to fire his weapon and risk killing the ambassador's child, and then how terribly wrong his mission had gone thanks to an unknown killer or killers.

Why he had chosen to tell me this story now, I wasn't sure, but if I could take some of his hurt away by listening, I would. And I held him tightly until the story ended and he went quiet.

"N'Vors gave their life to save their child," I said quietly. "Or in the hope that they might save them."

"Yes." He kissed my hair. "I do not know what N'Vors's final thoughts were, but I imagine they were a prayer for their child —that if they did live, their life would be good."

Such incredible selflessness. I swallowed hard around the lump in my throat. "Did you know the child's name?"

"No. I do not speak Kurutan, and I did not inquire." He took a deep breath, his gills fluttering, and let it out. "I wished the past to be past."

Gods, if only it could. "Did you ever find out what *La ka na* means?" I asked.

"Yes." His tentacles caressed me, but I thought it more for their comfort than mine. "It means *Are you an angel*, or something similar to that. There is no direct translation to Alliance Standard. The people of Kuruta believe divine aspects of their gods walk among them, and intervene to save the lives of certain people when their lives have special meaning. If I had known at the time what it meant, I would not have answered in the affirmative."

"Oh." The lump in my throat grew into an ache. "You *were* that child's angel that day. They lived because of you *and* N'Vors."

"I am no angel." Now he sounded almost savage. "Not by any metric, my Calla."

"Who are you to say?" I countered, my voice soft to counter his harshness. "The universe is vast. We understand so little about our own existence. And maybe all that matters is that you were there and you saved that child's life, even though doing so put yours at risk. You had all those years of Guard indoctrination and training and brutality, but you couldn't leave a child to die. Your soul is good, Vos. It's so good."

When he didn't reply, I raised my head and put my palm on his chest above his hearts. His expression was grave, his eyes dark with memories. I imagined my own eyes often looked similar.

"Choices," I said.

He blinked twice. Whatever he'd expected me to say, that wasn't it.

"Fate, or the universe, or chance, may put us in a certain place at a certain time," I told him. "Exactly how our lives unfold, I don't know, but we make choices too. N'Vors made theirs. You made yours. And yours was good and kind. And… loving." My voice trailed off.

Oh. Now I understood why he'd wanted to tell me that story, besides the fact the events of that day haunted him, and he believed I could ease that pain by listening.

I knew as much or as little about the Silent Guard as anyone who'd served in the Alliance Defense, but it was common knowledge the details of their missions were confidential to the extreme. By revealing this to me, he had broken his vows to the Guard—and made himself subject to their deadly retribution if anyone ever found out.

He leaned his forehead against mine. "My Calla, N'Vors acted out of love. That is what I saw when I beheld their body and heard the cry of their child. I had never known love, but I recognized it, and it compelled me to carry the child to safety. N'Vors's loving sacrifice gave their child life, and gave me hope. And because I had hope, I followed your scent to the raiders' boat and brought you home."

And so, in a roundabout way, N'Vors's loving sacrifice had led to this moment, when I lay in Vos's arms asking myself if love was real and if my battered heart could be capable of it.

The enormity of that realization left me stunned into silence.

Vos cupped my cheek with his hand. "Do you fear loving and being loved, because love makes you vulnerable? As long as you are my Calla and I am your Vos, your love is safe with me." He studied me. "Or do you not believe you are worthy of love? Because if it is the latter, I will spend the rest of my life proving you are wrong, if that is what I must do."

I didn't have to admit it; he saw my answer in my expression, and in the way my tears spilled over again.

He tucked my head under his chin. "I know what I see when I look into your eyes," he murmured into my hair. "The word itself matters far less than that."

How did I look at him? What did he read in my eyes that revealed more to him than I saw in my own heart?

"You'd love me even if I didn't love you back?" I asked.

"My love for you has no conditions." He settled in, forming a nest for me with his tentacles as he'd done in our first days together, and cupped the back of my head with his hand. "My Calla, there is no need to search for reasons that I might not love you. There are none to find."

We lay together for a long time after that, awake but quiet. What he thought about, I didn't know, but my own thoughts were full of his story and the question of love—what it was, what it wasn't, and what a force it might be, even when we weren't aware of it.

I wanted him to rest, because both of us didn't need to be tired tomorrow, but he wouldn't sleep until I did. I had learned that early on. Even so, I couldn't sleep, couldn't even close my eyes…

…Until he began to sing.

It started as soft murmurs that turned into a melody I recognized. The Fortusian lullaby. The song he'd hummed for me during our first bath, the one that let me know I was safe and cared for and that I would live. He'd hummed it for me after we discovered he could heal me with more than just his blood and I'd questioned how such a miracle was possible. But now there were words as well as melody. His voice was wonderfully deep and sonorous.

I'd relied on translators while stationed on Fortusia and never learned Vos's language, so I understood only a few of the words of the song, but recognized enough to know it was about water and going home.

I thought about the way Vos had carried me into the ocean today: reverently, worshipfully...lovingly. His arms around me in the deep, holding me close, bringing me up to air and then giving me all of himself only when I'd asked him to. Only after his gentle coo had made it not only not painful, but pure pleasure to take him.

Yes, that was the physiology of being true mates, but it was certainly love too. But what did I have to give him in return?

Maybe something I was afraid to give, or maybe something I was afraid I'd be giving up.

Finally, Vos's loving lullaby and comforting heartbeats carried me away into sleep.

CHAPTER 24

VOS

Days passed, and then weeks, and my Calla bloomed like the plants in Poe's garden that opened their petals to celebrate the end of the rainy season and the arrival of sunshine. Paradise had come to our corner of Iosa.

And no matter how many times I woke at dawn to see my mate sleeping peacefully in our bed, or watched her sitting or working in the garden, or took her swimming in the sea, or felt her coming in my arms, each was more wondrous than the last.

Since the day of our first knotted coupling, the matter of love remained unspoken between us, but my Calla's love was as real and bright and warm as the sun that drenched us from morning to night. And mine grew with her every laugh, footstep, curse, flashing blade, teardrop, and cry of my name.

Even Poe trilled throughout the day, whether tending her own garden, resting in her nest, or guarding the wall. I had not known her to sing more than a handful of times in the three years she had lived with me. Our shared happiness was a paradise of its own.

"Vos."

Calla's exasperated voice startled me from my reverie. She was standing in front of my chair, hands on hips, with dirt on her face and mud on her knees. She wore a summery dress today, one of the items of clothing I had purchased during last week's trip to a nearby village for supplies. Her feet were bare because the day was sunny and warm.

"I am sorry," I said, marveling at the way her hair shimmered in the sunlight. "What did you ask?"

"I asked what you wanted to plant on the far end of the vegetable garden." She sighed. "Have I been talking to myself for the last ten minutes?"

I winced. "Perhaps."

She scowled.

With a chuckle, I gathered her in my tentacles and placed her sideways on my lap. She leaned her head against my shoulder and let out a long, much more contented sigh. "Thanks. I'm worn out and my back hurts." After a beat, she added, "I'm still mad at you, though. I was *talking* to you."

"I am sorry," I said again, my lips on her hair. She smelled of fresh-tilled earth, sunshine, and sweat. "May I make it up to you by taking you to the sea today?"

Calla scoffed. "Vos, I see right through you. We both know why you love going with me to the ocean."

"Do you not want to go?" I asked, feigning hurt.

"I didn't say that." She wiggled on my lap, and my cock very predictably stirred in response. "We've been so busy getting the garden ready. It's been almost a week, hasn't it? I have been missing…you."

"What have you been missing, my mate?" I slipped one of my tentacles under her dress to play with the edge of her underwear and she shivered. The scent of her arousal grew. "Have you missed my knot?"

"You know I have." She bit my shoulder just hard enough to make my cock twitch. "When can we go?"

"As soon as you have changed." As much as I loved the sight of them, bare legs were inadvisable in the swamp. "There is more to my invitation than you give me credit for, though, my Calla. The season has changed, and the area in and around our inlet has become home to something I am very much looking forward to showing you."

She sat up, her eyes sparkling with interest. "Really? What is it?"

Making sure at least one of my tentacles was not touching her, I kissed her. "Get dressed, put on your boots, and I will show you."

"You know, you're already on thin ice with me." Calla slid her dress up to show me the dagger she kept in a thigh sheath in case something got over the wall. And of course my cock began to harden at the peek of inner thigh and the blade. "Don't make me turn you into kaory bait."

"With that little knife?" I made a *tsk*ing sound. "That would only tickle me, my Calla. You must improve your threats."

"Improve my threats," she muttered, rising from my lap. "I promise you wouldn't want me to *really* threaten you."

"Truly, no, my warrior Calla." I caught her hand and kissed it. "I would not."

She smiled and went inside to change.

While I waited, I rose to admire the garden bed. Save for the far end, which had not yet been planted, within a week, I expected to see stems and leaves emerge. In two lunar cycles, we would begin harvesting. Iosa's rich soil supported fast, healthy growth.

Poe joined me. "Poe," she said, her claws waving at the neat rows of planted seeds.

"She is a natural gardener," I said, beaming with pride. "Impressive, for someone who has never gardened before."

"Poe," my Anomuran companion said agreeably. She touched my hand with her claw, then swiveled her eyestalks toward the swamp. "Poe?"

"Just for a few hours," I assured her. "I want to show Calla the shells."

"Poe." She waved her claws over her abdomen. "Poe?"

"I will bring some back," I promised. "The best and most delicious I can find."

Trilling happily, Poe trundled back to her garden, stopping to snack on a few enni along the way.

Not long after, Calla emerged from the house in her flight suit and boots with her small pack of provisions on her back. The suit was, we had agreed, the best clothing for her to wear during walks to the sea. The material was tougher than any for sale in the village, and her boots could withstand the bites of serpents and even small kaory. The soles were nearly impenetrable, in case she stepped on something sharp.

With my help, she had painstakingly removed the patches, insignias, name badge, and all other distinguishing characteristics. Its color and design might still be recognized as having been issued by the Alliance Defense, but we had done our best to eliminate anything that identified her. I looked forward to the day we could replace it with some other clothing and she could put away or destroy this last vestige of her service.

"Ready," she announced, patting her Fortusian daggers in their sheaths on her thighs.

Her body, including her lovely thighs, had thickened with both muscle and pleasant softness. She appeared healthy, happy, and content, and my hearts swelled with love and satisfaction.

We latched the gate behind us, left Poe on watch, and began our walk to the sea, hand in hand until the narrowness of the trail forced us to walk single file. And for the first time, my Calla took the lead for half the walk. She had memorized the path after only a few trips, and had tried to bet me she could walk it with her eyes closed. I had refused to accept the bet only because of the danger, and ruefully submitted to her teasing that I feared I would lose.

Also unlike our first trips to the sea, my Calla did not require stops to rest along the way or complain of soreness in her legs. She walked as quickly and silently as I, her eyes bright with anticipation of reaching our inlet. I found myself smiling when her attention was elsewhere, enjoying her excitement and confidence as she fearlessly crossed a swamp so many others would not step foot in for any amount of money.

When we reached the bank and she began to take off her boots, I put my hand on her arm. "Wait here."

"What?" She frowned. "Why?"

"Please," I said, kissing her forehead before I pulled my tunic off over my head. "I wish to surprise you."

She sighed. "This had better be worth it, whatever you're up to. I'm hot and that water looks very good right now." She eyed me and unfastened the collar of her suit. "As do you. Hurry up, Vos."

I left my clothing on the bank near the base of a tree and descended the steep bank into the water. I heard Calla make a quiet sound and turned back to see her biting her lip.

"What is wrong?" I asked.

She slid the top of her suit down off her shoulders, baring herself to the waist. At the sight of her lovely, full breasts and her rosy nipples pebbling in the air, I nearly bolted back up the bank.

"Oh, nothing," Calla said with a flash of a sad smile. "It's just…that's the first time you've gone into the water without carrying me."

"I will carry you," I promised. I would not miss doing that for the world. "I will only be gone a few minutes."

"Okay." She bent to remove her boots. "Go ahead."

I dove under the water and made my way quickly to the

deepest part of the inlet. Sure enough, there they were: dozens of brightly colored shells in clusters. The sea enni had arrived.

I found a half-dozen unoccupied shells abandoned by the creatures that had resided within them. They had likely left their shells to feed or mate and been eaten. Inlets like this one were safe havens during their mating season, or at least far safer than open water, but no place was truly without danger.

When I surfaced, I found my Calla waiting on the bank, undressed, sitting in the grass. "Well?" she asked as I climbed the bank with the shells hidden in my arms. "What did you bring me?"

Proudly, I held out my hands and presented her with the collection.

Her mouth fell open. "Oh, gods, Vos—these are beautiful!" Eyes wide as a child's, she looked up at me. "Can I hold one?"

I handed her the most lovely one, a deep purple shell with green whorls. "Of course. The enni that lived inside it is no longer there."

"These are enni shells?" She marveled at its beauty, turning it in her hands and peeking inside the curled, hidden parts. "These are *way* bigger than the enni in the garden. Poe would feast on these!"

"She *will* feast." I laughed. "I promised to bring some home for her. She looks forward to the arrival of the sea enni each year."

"Are they the same color as the enni in the garden?"

I shook my head. "They are the same color as their shells."

"Oh, I'd love to see that. The ones in our garden are so plain and gray. Hey, this one looks like you." She held up the purple shell so she could look from it to me and back again. "It's not as beautiful, though."

"Such flattery, my mate." I crouched and arranged the collection of shells on the grass in front of her. "Which do you like best?"

"Hmm." She picked up each one and looked it over. "Purple, blue, green…I think I love the purple one best because it reminds me of you. Such a pretty purple. The enni who lived in it must be pretty too—well, for an enni."

To be compared to a sea enni or its shell would not be a compliment from anyone but my lovely Calla. "And second best?" I asked.

She bit her lip again. "I don't suppose you saw any red ones down there?"

I tilted my head and thought. "I did not. They are much more rare. Should I look?"

"Could you?" Her eyes sparkled as she twirled her hair around her finger. "I would love a red one to go with the purple."

Now I understood. I smiled and cupped my Calla's face. "I will find a red one for you, my mate. I may be gone longer this time."

"That's all right. I'm comfortable. But don't take *too* long." She kissed my palm. "I still want you to carry me into the water properly, and then we can visit our grotto."

Our hidden place under the trees was not truly a grotto, as its walls were curtains of moss rather than a cave of stone, but she had dubbed it as such and I liked the name. The Fortusian word *gar'uto* meant *sea home*, and our grotto was very much that to me.

I returned to the water in search of red shells. I found a few, but rejected them as unworthy of my Calla. I wanted at least one or two in pristine condition, and as lustrously red as her hair.

At long last I found one, hidden behind rocks in a small cluster of shells on the far side of the inlet where it opened to the sea. This one was perfect in every way: the right color, without scratches or broken edges, and freshly abandoned because the inside was gleaming white. My Calla would beam at its beauty. My tentacles danced in anticipation and glee.

With my prize in hand, I made my way back across the inlet along the sandy bottom, seeking other shells that caught my eye with their color or shape. I found another purple and green one that rivaled my earlier offering for beauty and brought that too.

If my Calla wanted a collection of the most perfect sea enni shells, I would gather as many as she desired, or help her find them. I had brought a net bag to transport Poe's meal and a second in case Calla wanted to gather her own. Perhaps she would want to use them as decorations in our home or garden. I would love that as well.

I reached our shore and broke the surface of the water, holding up the shells in triumph.

My Calla was not there.

For a moment, I stood frozen, staring at the empty bank, as if she might appear from the grass or from behind a tree, laughing at my expression. But my Calla would not play this kind of trick on me.

In a heartsbeat I was out of the water and at the top of the bank with no memory of having traveled there. Calla's uniform, boots, backpack, and daggers remained in a neat pile next to my own clothes beside the tree, but the shells I had lovingly gathered were scattered across the grass, not in the neat row in which I had left them.

Then a scent reached me that sent me crashing to my knees: Calla's blood. A spray of crimson across the shells I had gathered for her.

My world went silent and cold, as if the sun had been blotted from the sky.

Darkness closed in until all I saw or smelled was that blood, spilled while I was only meters away, searching for shells when *I should have been here guarding her.*

The thought was a roar in my mind.

Deep in my soul, a great crashing black wave of rage rose. This was the monster I had held at bay for so very long, who had slept peacefully once my Calla came. But now someone had taken my Calla, and the monster had awakened.

I opened my mouth and bellowed, the sound rolling through the swamp like boulders down the slope of a mountain. Everything went silent, as if the predators of the water and land knew something much deadlier than they had emerged.

My vision sharpened, turned silvery and crystal clear. My tentacles lashed the air, quivering in rage, the claws on their tips flaring from the sheaths that kept them hidden.

Like a beast, on my hands, feet, and tentacles, I searched the bank. In moments I found the track: the lingering scent of Calla's blood and strange prints that led away into the marsh in the opposite direction of our home. A half-dozen or more sets of prints, none of them humanoid. Raiders? Perhaps. Or perhaps an enemy from my past had come looking for me and taken my Calla instead.

Whoever had done this, I would not stop until I found my mate. And then I would leave nothing of her attackers but their blood on my hands.

Growling, I stuffed our clothing and Calla's daggers into the pack, adjusted its straps so it fit on my back, and took off following the tracks and the scent of my mate's blood.

CHAPTER 25

CALLA

I woke naked and in agony, lying on my right side on a dirt floor. The air stank of body odor, chemical fire, and old fuel cells.

With a groan, I rolled to my back, looked up, and let out a strangled, pain-filled cry.

The creature looming over me was enormous, with a black segmented carapace, two bright blue multifaceted eyes on long stalks, two clawed hands on jointed arms, and four thick legs with wide, flipper-like feet planted on either side of my body. I didn't recognize the species by sight, but the gods-damned thing must weigh nearly two thousand kilograms. If they sat or fell on me, I would die instantly.

My chest heaving, I reached for my left shoulder, the source of so much pain. My fingers found a lot of blood and some kind of thick, round, metal bolt about four centimeters wide protruding from my flesh.

Son of Valodian batkeeper, I'd been shot—and with something much nastier than a standard plasma gun. The back of my neck stung too, like maybe I'd been darted with something that knocked me out.

The last thing I recalled was sitting on the grass at the inlet waiting for Vos to return with more shells. I had no memory of actually *being* shot, or hearing or seeing my attackers, or how I got to wherever the hells I was, but clearly I'd been kidnapped. I had no idea how long I'd been unconscious. Was I even still on Iosa?

My stomach churned and heaved with pain, fear, and anger. What about Vos? *Where was my Vos?*

I turned my head to look around what appeared to be some kind of small, filthy, poorly lit bunkhouse, but saw no one but this creature. A metal cuff on a thick chain bound my right ankle to a tipped-over double bunk bed. No sign of Vos anywhere. What did that mean? The possibilities terrified me more than the creature above me.

The creature bent their head and eyestalks until their blue eyeballs nearly touched my face. They studied me as if I were a test subject in a lab. I stared back, my jaw clenched to hold in my pain. I'd be gods-damned if I gave this being the satisfaction of hearing me whimper.

"Does it hurt?" my captor asked in Alliance Standard, each word accompanied by thick clicking sounds. Clearly the language was not natural for the shape and design of their mouth, but I understood the words well enough. And the tone was unmistakably vicious.

"Fuck you," I said, my voice strained. "Where's Vos?"

The creature made a strange grating sound I realized was a chortle or laugh. "I am sure he will find us soon," they said, their eyeballs roving above my face, maybe enjoying my pain. "We left many tracks in many directions, but an assassin of his calibre will not be fooled for long. I must make the most of what time I have with you, little plaything."

My pain and fear became anger. "At least tell me who the hells you are."

"Stalling, little one?" They made that grating sound again. "Buying time for Vos Turek to find you? I have told you he will come, but he will not like what he finds. I will leave him pieces of you. Perhaps he will try to put you back together."

This must be someone from Vos's past out for revenge. They looked at me as nothing more than a way to hurt him. I'd encountered this kind of cruelty before. It didn't bode well for me.

If I was an object to this being, they wouldn't see me as a person and would have no empathy for my suffering. That much was evident already in the utterly unnecessary bolt they'd shot through my shoulder. Maybe it kept me from running, or maybe it was a tracker. Or maybe an incendiary device. The creature had said they would leave me in pieces. A bomb would accomplish that.

A wash of cold and dizziness rolled through me, making me shiver uncontrollably. My ears rang, and my thoughts became fragmented in a growing fog. I'd experienced it enough to know this was shock and blood loss.

Every movement sent white-hot agony through my shoulder, even breathing, but I inhaled as deeply as I could and fought to stay awake. Passing out would doom me. If I was awake, I had a chance to find a way out of this. If I was awake, I could help fight when Vos came.

Because if this creature put one claw on my Vos, by all the gods above and below, I would rip their arms off or die trying.

Something nagged at me, fighting to rise to the surface in my muddled mind. Something about the possibility the bolt in my shoulder was explosive, but I couldn't quite make sense of what seemed significant about that.

I blinked up at the creature, fighting to focus as another wave of lightheadedness made everything go hazy. Their eyes bobbed in a way that reminded me of Poe, but they lacked her gentleness to go along with the deadly claws and menacing bulk.

"Before you kill me, I'd at least like to know why," I said. My voice didn't shake, which was a wonder in itself because the pain in my shoulder had me on the verge of throwing up. "If this is about Vos, and not because of something I've done, I think I deserve that much."

"If you know you are here because of Vos Turek, then you know enough," they said, clacking their jaw. Maybe speaking Alliance Standard was uncomfortable for them. "You are not innocent in this if you find him worthy of your body and love. Your soul must be as rotten as his."

Had they been watching us before they attacked? If so, for how long? Surely Vos or I would have noticed if we were under surveillance. Or had they seen something in my eyes when I asked about him that made them think I loved him? I didn't know the answer to that, and I wasn't likely to get an explanation.

I wished the past to be past, Vos had told me. But the lives we'd led before we'd come to Iosa were not the sort that made peace likely. Maybe it had only ever been a matter of time before our pasts caught up to us.

And with that thought, the word *bomb* and the physical characteristics of this creature finally found something in my memory to latch onto.

"N'Vors," I whispered.

With a nauseating grinding noise like bone on bone, the creature reared up on its back legs, and then came crashing down with most of its enormous weight on its front feet only centimeters from pulverizing my head. Their jaws snapped so close to my nose that they damn near tore off my face.

"Silence, you worthless thing," they ground out, the words so grating and full of clicking that I barely made them out. "If you insult my parent's name again by speaking of them, I will kill you where you lie, and I will do so slowly, with my own hands."

My breath caught. I was face-to-face with the full-grown offspring of the Kurutan Ambassador N'Vors.

"I know who you are," I said, my voice tight with grief, pain, anger, and a dozen other emotions. "Vos told me about you. You're the child he saved on Bordia."

They clamped their claw onto the head of the bolt in my shoulder and twisted it.

Oh, all the fucking great gods above and below, the pain.

A rush of hot blood ran down my chest from the wound. I rolled to my side and vomited.

"Vos Turek is a murderer," the Kurutan said, their face centimeters from my own, which was the only reason I could hear them over the ringing in my ears. "He did not save me. He *spared* me. There is a universe of difference."

The agony was damn near unbearable. With a choked sob, I dug my fingernails into the dirt, as if by hanging on to something—anything—I could keep from passing out. Hot tears of anger ran down my face.

"I have dedicated two standard years to tracking him down," they continued, "and I will avenge my parent's death even if it means the end of my own life. Vos Turek will find you dead and know what it is like to lose the one most precious to him."

Two years? I hurt so, so badly, but at least some of that pain came from the realization this Kurutan had spent two of their five years of life hunting Vos because they mistakenly thought he'd killed N'Vors.

They ran their claw over my bare right shoulder, leaving a bloody incision I barely felt over the rest of my pain.

"You fuck this murderer," they said. "You *love* this murderer. Who are you, worthless thing, who would find him worthy of either?"

"I'm not worthless," I said roughly. "And I'm not a *thing*. I am Calla Wren, survivor of the arenas of Ganai."

"Oh." The Kurutan clacked their jaw and rose to stand over me again. "So, a scrap. I see. No one else will have you but Vos Turek. I pity you, then, Calla Wren."

Every word hit me as hard as physical blows because some part of me believed the same. Still, I rolled to my back once more, holding in whimpers with sheer will alone.

"He did save you," I rasped. "He was sent to kill your parent, but he wasn't responsible for their death."

The Kurutan rested the tip of their claw on the bolt.

I raised my chin and didn't flinch at the clear threat. "He was hidden in an air duct with a dart gun loaded with poison gas. But when he saw you, he couldn't pull the trigger, because the poison would have killed you too."

"This is all lies." They pushed on the bolt, sending agony through me. I choked back a scream. "Lies he has fed you."

"Why would he lie?" My voice was ragged. "He would have no reason to lie to me. We had no idea you might come for him."

"Does he brag to you of his kills?" Another push on the bolt, and another gush of blood from the wound. My vision grew hazy. "This is bed talk for you?"

"No." I fought to keep unconsciousness at bay. "This is the only story of his past he's told me. He wanted to tell me how he knew what love was."

The Kurutan stilled. "What does this story have to do with love, Calla Wren?"

"When someone threw a bomb into the embassy, your parent covered your body with theirs," I said, and if my voice was edged with a sob I couldn't help it. "They loved you so much, they gave their life to ensure you lived. Vos saw that. And then as the building was collapsing around you, he carried you out and gave you to the Bordians. He even covered your eyes so you didn't see your parent, because he knew seeing their body might cause you to die."

I managed a deep, shaky breath. "You asked him '*La ka na?*' and he said yes without knowing what the question meant. But he *was* your angel, you see. He *was*."

"Lies," they repeated.

"Not lies." Gently, I put my hand on their claw where it rested on the bolt. "Not lies, I swear. He'd come to assassinate your parent with a dart gun. Why would he use a bomb, then, when it might have killed him? The Guard doesn't use bombs that take out whole groups of people anyway. You must know that. That's never been their practice. And it was his last mission for the Guard. He wouldn't have wanted to die. He wanted to live. He wanted *you* to live. He made sure you did."

"I survived," they grated. "That is not the same."

"I know that." I nearly shouted it, and the effort of doing so made everything go hazy again. "Gods, do I know. I told you I survived the Ganai arenas, didn't I? Vos survived a twenty-year service in the Guard. Do you think either of us signed up for that? How old were you when all you'd known was ripped away? They got him when he was two. I was three and a half. You must have been less than a year old."

"Not yet eight lunar cycles," they grated. And thank all the gods in the cosmos, they took their claw off the bolt. "You believe this story Vos Turek has told you, but I do not. You have every reason to lie, to save him and save yourself."

And yet, maybe they had a doubt now. That was a million times more of a chance than I'd had minutes ago.

"I do have reason to lie, but I'm not." Maybe it was the blood loss, or maybe I figured I didn't have much to lose, or maybe I just wanted N'Vors's child to believe the true version of events over the one they'd shaped their life around, so I added, "I don't know how to prove it to you, but if you're not in the business of killing people for no reason like whoever was responsible for the bombing on Bordia, maybe you should be sure before you blow me to pieces to punish Vos for a crime he didn't commit."

My captor said nothing. I couldn't decide if that was a good sign or a bad one.

"Please, tell me your name," I said. "I really want to know."

"I am N'Mora," they said as they rose to their full height.

I let out a breath. Gods, did I hurt. "And where are we, N'Mora?"

"What remains of a raider camp, a few kilometers from Vos Turek's home." They took a step back, so for the first time since I woke up I wasn't staring straight up at their claws, which was a welcome change. "Whoever lived here must have abandoned it after fighting among themselves. Most of the camp was burned and we found corpses in the debris. Only this building and one other remain standing. There are no ships here now and no sign they intend to return."

Neither Vos nor I had ventured anywhere close to the camp since the night I'd crashed. So maybe the surviving raiders, left without their leader, had squabbled, killed one another, and then packed up and left this moon. That was a shred of good news.

Belatedly, I realized N'Mora had said something unexpected. "Who's 'we'?" I asked. "Who's here besides you?"

"My bodyguards." N'Mora clacked their claws. "I did not come alone to face Vos Turek. I do not underestimate him. They await him outside."

I struggled to lift my head. "N'Mora, don't kill Vos until you've heard him tell you what happened on Bordia. Please."

"I do not think Vos Turek will want to speak to me when he comes." N'Mora moved between me and the door to the bunkhouse. "He found your blood where we took you. My people report he is enraged, gone bestial."

My stomach twisted and my eyes filled with tears. My poor Vos. I pictured him emerging from the sea and finding nothing but my blood on the grass. He must have blamed himself, and been gutted.

"You hurt him." I forced myself to sit up despite the pain and sickness it caused. "I understand why you did it, N'Mora, but it must have broken his heart when he found me gone."

N'Mora clicked. "Why did he leave you alone in such a place?"

"He was gathering pretty shells for me." I covered the bolt in my shoulder with my other hand, as if somehow it might hurt less and stop bleeding if I couldn't see it. "Instead of meeting him at the door, let me talk to him when he gets here. He'll listen."

"I do not think so, Calla Wren." N'Mora inclined their head. "My people say he is closing in and prepared for battle. He will try to kill me. Probably one or both of us will die. It is better this way."

"No, it's not." Gasping, gagging, staggering, I got to my feet. "Give me a chance. Tell your people to let him come here. You deserve to hear the truth, and Vos deserves to know why this happened."

"He smells your blood," N'Mora countered. "He will go through you to kill me. The beasts of Fortusia, they do not know reason when their rage is too great."

"Don't call him a beast," I snapped. "He's hurt and he's angry, but he's a man, not a beast. I'm his true mate. *He will listen to me.*"

N'Mora made that grinding sound again. "He has taken a true mate?"

"Yes!"

From outside the bunkhouse, I heard a bellow nearby, and the sound of something like the smashing of a wall, followed by a much louder crash. The ground trembled. Probably the other building that had survived the raiders' departure collapsing. Another bellow, this one only what sounded like meters away from the door to the bunkhouse.

I hobbled forward as far as the chain around my ankle would allow and reached for N'Mora's clawed hand. "Get behind me, N'Mora!"

With a chittering sound, N'Mora did as I asked, leaving me facing the door—

—Just as it, and the wall around it, exploded toward us.

CHAPTER 26

VOS

My Calla's captors had left many false trails, but finally I found the one that led me to the raider camp—or what remained of it.

My rage had claws and teeth, and my thoughts were jagged.

I smashed through the door of the raiders' hut and stood on the threshold, my tentacles ripping at the walls and my fists clenched. But it was not a group of raiders who greeted me.

Instead, I saw my mate, naked and covered in blood, pale, on her feet but her eyes unfocused, as though she might collapse at any moment. A chain bound her right ankle—the ankle my tentacles habitually cradled for their comfort and hers. A bolt-shaped J'Noran incendiary device was buried deep into my Calla's shoulder, as if plunged through her flesh and bones with brute force.

An enormous Kurutan stood behind my mate, using her as a shield against my wrath.

My Calla. *My Calla,* bloody and badly wounded and possibly

dying, with a *bomb* inside her. My fury seared me and wrenched a low growl from deep in my chest.

My tentacles flared around me, their tips facing my mate's tormentor with claws extended. They could not penetrate the Kurutan's carapace, but they had other vulnerable places on their body.

"Coward," I snarled. "Spineless coward, face me."

To my surprise, it was Calla who spoke.

"Vos." Her voice was strained and shaking. She reached for me with her bloodstained hand. The smell of her blood suffocated me. "Vos, take my hand," she said, and now she sounded as though she might weep. "Take my hand, my love."

My Calla did not call me her love. What kind of trap was this?

I snarled at the Kurutan. "Step out from behind my mate, scum who bloodies unarmed women and uses the weapons of a coward."

The Kurutan made a grating sound.

"Vos," Calla repeated. She stretched out her hand as far as she could, held back by that gods-damned wicked chain, and whimpered in pain. Her fingers trembled so badly that despite my rage, a coo rose in my chest. "Vos, listen to me. This is N'Mora, the child of Ambassador N'Vors."

My body went cold.

The child I had carried out of danger in my tentacles had come to Iosa and taken my Calla. They had brutally plunged a bomb into my Calla. Had used my Calla to bring me here, likely to witness her death. I had saved this Kurutan, and in return they intended to take from me the only good thing I had ever had.

I hissed at N'Mora through my teeth, envisioning tearing each limb from their body and forcing them to eat the pieces so they tasted their own flesh.

"I told you he would not listen," N'Mora said in Alliance Standard. "He is a beast, Calla Wren."

"Stop it. He is not a beast. He's listening." Calla swayed on her feet. "Vos, N'Mora thinks you killed their parent. I told them the truth, but they don't believe me. Please tell them what happened on Bordia the day N'Vors died. Tell them what you did and why."

"I do not believe her," N'Mora said, their voice harsh. "You are a murderer and a liar, Vos Turek. You do not deserve a true mate."

"Perhaps I do not." I took a step closer, calculating how quickly I could get to N'Mora. But I did not know where the detonator for the bomb was, and until I did, I could not risk an attack. "But my Calla *is* my true mate and I love her. If you wish to avenge your parent, I offer you my throat instead."

Despite her condition, Calla bristled, her eyes fiery. "No. The hells you will."

"It is not your throat I want." N'Mora raised one of their clawed hands behind Calla's head. Even at my fastest, they could snap her neck before I could reach them. "I want you to live with your pain the way I have lived with mine."

"Vos." Calla sagged and then fell to her knees, no longer able to stand. "My love, I told them to get behind me so you would talk to them. They deserve to hear the story of how their parent died."

Nothing had tasted as bitter and sweet as finally hearing the words *my love* from my Calla while my body was full of the scent of her blood and her life hung in the balance.

My Calla looked up at me, her gaze pleading. "N'Vors gave you hope. You can give their child peace."

N'Mora made a strange sound then—a kind of chittering song. The last time I had heard it, I was lying on my belly in an air duct on Bordia, and N'Vors was speaking to their child, not knowing only minutes later they would die shielding them. I thought perhaps this was a comforting sound, though who N'Mora wished to comfort, I did not know.

It was at least an opportunity to ask for the thing I wanted most.

I forced my tentacles to lower themselves and sheath their claws. "May I hold my mate? Please. She is hurting."

"You may." N'Mora raised their other clawed hand, revealing a small red disk. The detonator. "But do not attempt to take her and flee or remove the device, Vos Turek. I will give no further warning."

Moving slowly so N'Mora would not think I planned to attack, I went to my Calla and gathered her in my tentacles. Gods, she was so cold and pale, and she shivered violently. My rage threatened to consume me, but instead I focused on wrapping her in warmth and comfort. And I cooed.

With her head on my shoulder, she gave me a fleeting smile. "Thanks for listening to me this time, my Vos."

For a beat, I did not understand. Then I recalled our exchange in the garden earlier today—a lifetime ago, it seemed—when I had been lost in thought and not heard her talking.

I pressed a kiss to her hair. "My love, rest. I will protect you."

"I know." The words were barely audible. Her eyes drifted closed. When I pressed my fingertips against her wrist, I found her pulse weak but steady.

With my hand cupping my Calla's face, I looked up at N'Mora. "If she dies, so do you," I said.

N'Mora inclined their head. "I do not think she will, Vos Turek. Your mate's will is stronger than yours or mine." They settled onto the dirt floor, their legs bent beneath their bulk. "I am owed a story. Tell me of the day my parent died."

The monster within me wanted to rend N'Mora into the smallest pieces, but my Calla's life depended on me acquiescing to the Kurutan's demand. And so I put my monster back in its cage and told N'Mora every detail I could recall.

When I spoke of the moment N'Mora, as a child, had asked me "*La ka na?*" the Kurutan made the chittering song again.

"I remembered your eyes," N'Mora said after a very long silence. "They shone like starlight when you said yes. I recall thinking that you must be divine, because no eyes I had ever seen had shone like that."

My Calla had said my eyes reminded her of starlight as well. I had always considered their glow to be part of my monstrous self, but perhaps I had been mistaken.

"I am sorry for lying to you. I did not intend to do so." I adjusted my hold on Calla so her breath warmed my chest over my primary heart. The sensation reassured me. "Had I known what it was you asked, I would have said no."

"But perhaps *that* would have been a lie." N'Mora rose on all four legs and stretched, their joints popping. They dropped the detonation disk on the dirt beside us. "I believe your story, Vos Turek. You may remove the device from your mate."

Given my Calla's pallor, that statement did not offer me as much reassurance as it might. "She may bleed to death if I do. She has lost too much blood already."

"If she is your true mate, you can heal her with your blood, can you not?"

I stared at the Kurutan. How would they know such a thing? I had not known of this myself until recently.

"No," I said, feigning confusion. "That is not possible."

N'Mora made a low grating sound. "There is no need to lie to me, Vos Turek. I know much of your physiology. I made study of you my adult profession. I suppose now I must find another."

Would they seek their parent's true killer, or seek peace instead? Would one lead to the other? I did not know what I would do were I in N'Mora's place. The choice would certainly be a difficult one.

"I will leave you here to tend to your true mate," N'Mora

said. "Do we have an agreement that I will not seek you out again, and you will not seek me?"

"How can you demand that of me?" Fury swept over me. "Look what you have done to my Calla. She is innocent in this matter."

"That is true, and for her suffering I am sorry." N'Mora dipped their head. "But we all have survived this meeting. Perhaps someday we will do more than merely survive."

My monstrous self would have preferred to follow through on my intention to rend N'Mora limb from limb, but my hearts knew Calla would not want me to. She was wiser and more good, and so I would follow her counsel. She had yet to steer me wrong. And as much fury as I still felt toward N'Mora, I knew the quiet bitterness of mere survival.

"I wish you a good life, then," I said. And since I did not forgive as easily as my Calla would, I added, "And a swift departure."

With one last dip of their head, N'Mora left through the opening I had made in the doorway and disappeared into the night.

"My Calla." I cooed, holding her close and smoothing her hair back from her face. "My Calla, wake, please."

She stirred. Her lashes fluttered but her eyes did not open. "What is it?" she murmured, her lips against my chest. "Are we home?"

"Not yet, my love." I kissed her forehead. "I must remove this device. You are badly hurt. I need your permission to share my blood with you."

"Of course." She let out a sigh. "It's all right. It doesn't hurt anymore."

I could think of only one reason she no longer felt the agony of her injury, and terror like I had never experienced gripped me.

"It will hurt when I remove it," I said, my voice rough. "But I will make it quick, and then I will heal you as best I can and take you home."

"All right." She snuggled close. A flinch crossed her features, and then they smoothed. "Then can we go back for more shells?"

In that moment, I came the closest to weeping as I had in my life. "Yes, my love. We will collect every shell your heart desires. The most beautiful purples and reds to be found."

Before she could reply, my Calla lost consciousness again. Fury turned my vision dark around the edges. I breathed in her scent to calm myself. When I could think clearly again, I broke the cuff around her ankle into pieces and flung it and the chain away from us.

Cradling her in my tentacles, I rose and gathered every piece of fabric I could find in the abandoned bunkhouse. To my surprise, I located a mostly intact medical kit in a dented locker. I did not trust its contents to be viable or labeled correctly, even the painkillers that might have given my Calla some relief, but the scanner worked and the bandages were sealed and clean.

When everything was ready, I sat on a thin mattress in the center of the dirt floor with my supplies around me and my mate in my lap. Even unconscious, she smelled of pain.

N'Mora was very lucky I treasured my Calla's love and counsel above my own monstrous needs.

Carefully, I coiled the end of one tentacle around the bomb's bolt-like top, braced myself, and pulled it from her flesh. Blood gushed from the wound. My Calla made a pitiful sound that seemed to shred my hearts. My tentacles thrashed in grief and rage.

Cooing, I pressed a handful of cloths soaked with my own blood to the injury. I held her close as my blood went to work trying to heal her. Finally, she stopped groaning and went quiet again.

I understood how need for vengeance warped a person's

mind, but I could not comprehend how N'Mora could inflict torment on someone so good, who had done nothing to deserve it. And even after all her suffering, my Calla had put herself between N'Mora and me, knowing she risked death to do so, for N'Mora's benefit. She wanted N'Mora to have peace, perhaps because we had known so little of it in our lifetimes.

"You are far better than either N'Mora or me," I murmured, kissing my Calla's cool, damp brow. "And yet you love me. You are a wonder and a miracle I will never take for granted."

Her capacity for kindness was not the only wonder and miracle of the day. Within the hour, the wound stopped bleeding. Another hour later, she had healed enough that I felt I could bandage her wounds and move her.

Before leaving the bunkhouse, I burned everything that had our blood on it. I washed Calla's blood from the bomb in the sea, destroyed the detonator, and left the inert device in the broken locker where I had found the medical kit.

Then I dressed my Calla in her flight suit and myself in my own clothing, put her pack on my back, and carried my mate home.

CHAPTER 27

CALLA

MORE THAN A WEEK AFTER N'MORA'S ATTACK, VOS AND I returned to our inlet.

I'd wanted to go sooner, but Vos insisted we wait until I'd recovered enough to protect myself in case something attacked us. Nothing did, however. Nothing even came near us as we made the journey to the shore. No snakes, no kaory, no...nothing. Even the carrion birds in the trees made themselves scarce.

During one of our rest breaks, I sat on Vos's lap, pressed my lips to his ear, and murmured, "Where are all the predators?"

"I think I scared them away, my Calla." He kissed my temple and smiled to show all his sharp teeth. "I roared very loudly when I found you gone."

I recalled the bellow I'd heard just before he crashed through the bunkhouse door. To my surprise, far from eliciting fear or sadness, the memory caused a gush of wetness between my legs.

Vos's nostrils flared and he inhaled deeply, his eyes glowing softly with desire.

"My scary monster," I said, kissing him lightly. "I love you."

"I love you, my Calla." He rested his forehead against mine and pressed a peeled, sweet vinefruit into my hand. "Eat."

He gave me food as if I hadn't fed myself all my life until I came to Iosa. I sighed and accepted the fruit, and let him kiss me before I took a bite.

The walk took much longer than usual because I needed three rest breaks and couldn't walk quickly. Vos would have happily carried me, but I needed to make the journey on my own two feet. He seemed to understand that.

Vos had stayed busy caring for me and our home during my recovery, so he hadn't been back to the inlet since my kidnapping. When we arrived on the grassy bank, everything was just as he'd left it to track me.

At the sight of the scattered shells stained with my dried blood, my hand flew to the back of my neck.

"What is wrong?" Vos asked from behind me. His tentacles wrapped around me and drew me close.

"I just remembered," I said softly. "Not very clearly, but now I remember I was sitting here looking at the shells, and waiting for you to come back so we could go to the grotto, and something stung me in the back of my neck. Then everything went dark."

"It was a dart, I am sure." He kissed my hair and exhaled against my shoulder. "My Calla..."

I knew from his tone what troubled him. I squeezed his hand where it rested on my hip. "You have to forgive yourself, Vos. You *have* to. The attack on me was not your fault. I didn't see or hear them sneaking up on me, and if anything it was *my* job to watch my back. I let myself get complacent. What happened was N'Mora's doing. Actually, arguably, it was the fault of whoever tossed that bomb into the Bordian embassy and killed N'Vors. It wasn't your fault. You did nothing wrong."

Judging by the tension in his body and tentacles, he didn't believe me any more this time than the last seven or eight times

I'd made this argument. And I supposed seeing my blood on the shells didn't help. He would blame himself for what happened for a long, long time. Possibly forever. And maybe I would have too if our positions had been reversed, but I didn't want him to carry that burden. We had burdens enough.

So I did the only reasonable thing I could.

"All right, Vos. If you really want me to forgive you, carry me into the water, take me to the grotto, and give me the three best orgasms of my life *before* you fill me with your knot." A tall order, since the moment we were in the grotto his need for me made him start to knot almost immediately, but I had to make it at least somewhat of a challenge.

Just as I'd hoped, his tension melted away, and his chest shook with silent laughter.

"While we are bargaining, what else would you ask of me?" he asked finally, still chuckling.

"The prettiest purple and red shells in the inlet for me," I replied with a smile. "And two full sacks of big, fat sea enni for Poe."

Vos's arms tightened around me. "You demand a high price, my love, but very well. I agree to all your terms but one."

I frowned. "Which one do you not like?"

He turned me in his embrace and smiled down at me, his eyes glowing. "Three orgasms are not enough. And I do not want to wait to hear you scream for me until we reach the grotto."

Oh, gods above. My knees nearly buckled.

I reached for the collar of my flight suit, but he brushed my hand aside and unfastened it. "Allow me, my love," he murmured as he opened the top of the suit and slipped it down over my shoulders to my waist, baring my breasts. "I do not want to rush."

I thought he would continue removing the suit, but he left it around my waist and cupped my breasts in his hands. With the pads of his thumbs and his gaze locked on mine, he stroked my nipples until they formed hard, sensitive points, and then he lowered his head to suck my right nipple into his mouth.

I clung to him, one hand on the back of his neck and the other on his hard cock through the soft material of his pants, as he sucked and nibbled at each of my breasts in turn. But when I started to slip my hand into his pants to stroke him, he stopped me.

"No, my love," he murmured. "Not yet."

I let out a sound that was almost a whimper.

He helped me remove my boots, and then he slid my suit down over my hips and legs and off. I felt self-conscious being fully naked while he still wore all his clothes, and I was pretty sure he knew that.

He kissed me gently. "Do not move," he said, his lips against mine.

And then his hand slipped between my thighs. I quivered.

"Do you feel yourself dripping for me, my Calla?" he asked, his fingertips brushing lightly over my slit, gathering up my slickness. "Tell me how you feel."

"I feel wet," I said, and mewled as his thumb ghosted over my clit. My pussy gushed and clenched on its own emptiness. "I'm ready for you."

"Yes, you are." He raised his hand so I could see my wetness glistening on his fingers. Two of his tentacles slipped between my legs to coil around my thighs, tugging gently. "Open your legs a little more, my Calla."

I obeyed. His hand returned to my aching pussy, his fingertips gliding along my slit again. "So wet," he murmured. "I have barely touched you. Do you want me to touch you, my love?"

"Yes, please, Vos. Please."

He slipped one finger inside me, sliding it in and out. "Like this?"

I arched my hips toward him. "Yes."

He rubbed my clit with his thumb. "And this?"

"Y-yes." I began to tremble. "I can't stay standing."

"Yes, you can." He added a second finger, pumping them in and out of me, and moved closer. "Put your arm around my neck."

I did, and hung onto him desperately.

He put his mouth against my ear. "Did you know that when you come, you taste like honey to me?"

"No," I gasped. Oh, gods. A coil of heat and tension grew low in my belly.

"The sweetest honey." His teeth nipped my earlobe. "I have never tasted anything sweeter. Do you know what else I love about your orgasms?"

I shook my head, my chest heaving and my nails digging into the back of his neck.

"I love the way your cunt feels when it squeezes my fingers or my cock." He curled his fingers inside me and brushed them lightly over my G-spot. I cried out. "I love how perfectly you take me, how perfectly you come."

Another gentle brush. My knees gave out, but his tentacles and my arm around his neck kept me upright.

"I confess that as much as I enjoy seeing you make yourself come on my hand and my cock," he murmured, "what I love most is when you ask me to make you come."

There was no way he loved that more than I did, though. "Make me come," I pleaded. "I want you to make me come."

His teeth on my shoulder for pain and his fingers on my clit and G-spot for pleasure, he gave me what I wanted.

"Then come, my Calla," he rasped.

The orgasm rolled through me in a wave. I wailed and collapsed against him, trembling and shaking, but he held me up with his arm and tentacles. His fingers stroked me until I came undone again with a weak cry.

My Vos laid me gently and lovingly on the grass. Two of his

tentacles spread my legs and held them open, and he raised my hips to bring my quivering, dripping pussy to his mouth.

He licked me slowly from my asshole all the way up my slit, his tongue delving everywhere, drinking in my slickness, before he closed his lips on my clit. I grabbed his hair and thrust my hips against his face, almost sobbing in my desperation for another sweet release.

He licked his lips, his eyes glowing. "My mate," he said, and slipped his fingers into my pussy. "Do you have more honey for me?"

"Yes." My head fell back and my back arched as he fucked me with his fingers.

Two gentle tentacles roamed my body, tasting me and leaving little red marks everywhere they sucked.

"Give me every drop, my Calla," Vos murmured, his lips on my slit. "Every drop."

He tongued me as his thumb rubbed my clit, and I came on his face with a ragged cry, my fingers twisted in his hair.

We had never made love on the shore of the inlet. Too many dangers lurked around. But Vos had scared them off with all his beautiful, terrifying monstrousness, and now the bank was ours.

This was about much more than that, though. We were staking a claim on our special, sacred place, taking it back from the ghosts of the attack that had nearly ripped everything away from both of us. And maybe that was what Vos needed to start to let go of his guilt—to replace the memory of walking out of his beloved sea to find me gone with the sounds of me crying out his name.

When my Vos was satisfied with the number of orgasms he'd wrung from me, he discarded his clothing and finally, *finally* carried me into the ocean—but not before I threw all the bloody shells as hard and far as I could into the water without caring where they ended up. I couldn't fling them all that far, given my body felt weak and nearly boneless with pleasure, but I did the best I could.

I also couldn't get as deep of a breath as usual for a long underwater swim, so Vos brought me to our grotto in three shorter dives before swimming through the moss curtain on his back with me lying on his chest listening to his hearts beating. He loved taking me to the purple depths, but I could tell he didn't dislike this way of reaching our special place. If his rock-hard cock hadn't clued me in, the pleasant rumbling in his chest and the way his eyes shone would have.

As much pleasure as he'd already given me, my pussy ached for him—most especially for his knot. He swirled his tentacles in the water, keeping us afloat, as I stroked the frills and ridges of his cock languidly with one hand, my other arm around his neck while he pressed his lips into my hair.

It stunned me that for all the comfort and security it had given me in the beginning, how little I cared about the science of being Vos's true mate anymore.

Everything about our coupling was wondrous and magical to me now, from how his blood and cum healed my physical injuries to his sweet cooing that soothed my heart and body. And in the sea, when his cock transformed before my eyes, swelling with bumps that increased both our pleasure, all thoughts of science washed away like a receding tide and left me with only awe and peace in my heart.

"What makes you smile, my love?" Vos asked softly.

What could I say? Him? What my life had become? Our growing garden? Poe's happy trills? This grotto? The way I felt so safe and treasured in his arms? I chuckled to myself. His cock?

"Everything," I said, and kissed his chest. "I don't know how you've been so patient."

He nipped my ear with his teeth. "An assassin never forgets

his training, my Calla. Patience is a requirement of the trade. But if I may be honest, my patience wears thin."

"Mine too."

The words had scarcely left my mouth when he rolled us over into the water, turning me so my back was to him.

He wrapped me in his arms, his tentacles swirling around us. "My Calla," he said, one hand slipping between my thighs to stroke my clit as his cock head pressed into my aching pussy. "Take my cock, my love."

I closed my eyes and arched my back as he thrust, gasping and moaning as each bump slipped inside me. He echoed my groans, his body quivering, until I took in his knot and he was sealed fully inside me. It fit easily for now, but soon it would swell.

He cupped my breast in his hand and stroked my clit with the other, slipped from me one bump at a time, and then thrust again. "Vos," I gasped, trembling in his arms. "Yes. Oh, gods."

He pumped in and out of me slowly, his ridges and bumps stroking over my G-spot and his swelling knot bumping me until the sheer pleasure and thrill of knowing he was about to give me his knot pushed me over the edge.

I came undone with a wail, shuddering hard in his arms as his fingers plied my clit to draw out my pleasure.

"My mate," he murmured. And then he cooed.

Another, much softer orgasm swept through me unexpectedly. My pussy relaxed for him in the way I only did when we were in the water together. I let out a sound that was half groan, half sob.

His cock thrust into me, wrenching cries from me with every bump, and then his knot slipped inside me with that blissful sensation of pure completion I'd never known until the day we'd first knotted together.

Vos didn't stop rubbing my clit even as his knot swelled

inside me, sealing us together. His body spasmed and his arm tightened around my chest, his gills fluttering against my back.

With groans and spasms that shook us both, he spurted inside me, filling me completely one hot pulse at a time.

"Calla," he breathed, his lips against my ear. "I love you."

His twitching cock gave me another soft orgasm. I did sob that time, safe and treasured in his embrace. "I love you, my Vos," I rasped.

He was *mine*, this beautiful, monstrous man. He belonged to me—body, heart, and soul. Everything that made him Vos was mine. And everything of me was his. I had given him everything, and received the world in return.

I was his Calla and he was my Vos, and that was all that mattered to me.

EPILOGUE

VOS

THE SUN HAD NOT YET RISEN WHEN I WOKE ALONE IN BED. As they always did, my tentacles reached automatically for Calla. But this time they found only cool bedding and an empty pillow.

After a lifetime of never sleeping soundly, always ready for danger to strike, I slept well now, and had for a long time. I had found peace with my mate at my side. My weapons remained within easy reach, but I no longer slept with them beside me.

Silently, I rose from our bed and slipped into the front room of our house. The odors of construction hung in the air. We had purchased a second housing capsule, an expansion that doubled the size of our home. I took great pride in the work we had done. Calla had worked as hard as me, perhaps even more so. Our gardens had expanded as well, and blooming plants now filled flowerbeds on two sides of our house.

My Calla stood at the front window in her nightgown, looking out through the rain toward the swamp. I could not see her face from this angle, but her hunched shoulders and the smell of tears caused a knot of worry to form in my stomach.

I reached her in a heartbeat. "What is wrong, my mate?" I asked, wrapping my human arms around her. My tentacles plucked at her nightgown in worry.

She turned in my arms to face me. Tears streaked her cheeks, but she smiled. "I was just thinking how quickly three years have gone."

"Three years tonight." I kissed her forehead. "I wondered if you would remember."

"I do—at least, I remember the date." She rested her head against my chest. "I remember so little of that night."

"I remember every moment, every detail." I held her gently, my hand on the back of her head to comfort her. "I struggle to recall anything before that night, but every day after you fell from the sky, I see clearly."

"Good answer." She smiled up at me, her eyes shimmering. "You've always got the right answer, don't you?"

"Always." I wiped her tears away with my thumbs. "What keeps you awake, my mate? Did Poe shut the door too loudly going outside?"

Calla shook her head. "No, the usual."

"But which usual?" I asked, frowning. I rested my hands on the swell of her belly, still three months from term. "Our child is restless? Or…?"

"No, the other thing." She sighed. "Both you and the doctor said it's common in pregnancy, especially with a half-human, half-Fortusian child, but I miss getting a full night's sleep without waking up desperate for orgasms." Her sweet lips turned up in a wry smile. "And I'm sure you miss uninterrupted sleep too."

I cupped her cheek with my hand. "My mate, I have told you: nothing about you could ever be a burden to me, least of all your pleasure."

Her eyes lit up with hope. "Then you wouldn't mind...?"

In answer, I led her back to our bedroom. We left our nightclothes on the floor and settled on the bed with her on her back and me between her thighs, my hands under her hips and my tentacles caressing and then coiling around her legs to hold her gently but firmly. Her hands and arms, I allowed to be free.

My Calla already dripped for me. Lovingly, I delved my tongue into her slit. Sweet as honey, my mate. Ambrosia. She grabbed me by the hair, her fingers twisting through the strands for a better grip.

When I slipped two fingers into her beautiful cunt, she gasped and trembled. "I'm almost there already," she panted. "Gods, I need you so badly."

"I know, my love." As my tentacles pushed her legs wider for me, I sucked on her clit, flicking the sweet nub with my tongue, while my fingers stroked within her, seeking and finding the place that made her thrash in my embrace. As she had predicted, she came in moments, grinding against my face and fingers and calling my name.

I took advantage of her relaxation to coat the tip of one tentacle with my slick precum and press it into her asshole. She cried out as it dipped inside her just enough to make her pussy flutter around my fingers.

I gave her two more orgasms like that, with my fingers in her cunt, my tentacle tip in her ass, and my mouth on her sweet clit, until she had screamed my name and begged for mercy and my cock was hard as stone and aching.

When she had caught her breath, I rolled to my back and used my tentacles to lift and then settle her facing me, knees astride my hips.

"Put your tentacle back in my ass," she said, her pussy poised over my cock head, her sweet juices dripping onto me.

Gods above, my Calla.

I swirled my tentacle tip around my cock to gather up more

lubrication. And then as she took my cock into her cunt, I slipped it into her ass.

Her eyes rolled up and she moaned. "Yes," she breathed. "Fuck my ass, Vos. Please."

I did—or rather, she fucked my cock and my tentacle, riding them as I held her with my hands on her hips and my tentacles teasing her heavy breasts and swollen clit. I drank in her taste, her scent, her cries, and let her come as many times as she pleased because she was so beautiful when she came with her sweet pussy stretched around my cock.

Eventually, she grew tired. Sweat shimmered on her face and body in the moonlight that poured into our room through the window. I wrapped her in my tentacles and eased her off my cock.

"Will you come on my face tonight, my mate?" she asked, breathing hard in my embrace. "Mark me as your own?"

Few things pleased me more than doing so, but tonight I wanted something else.

"On your hands and knees," I told her, rising and moving her into position with the help of my tentacles. "I want to come in your beautiful cunt."

I went to my knees behind her, stroking my cock as I rubbed its head in her slit, over her lovely ass, and back, leaving trails of glowing precum. I rubbed her clit until she screamed my name and came once more, grinding against me.

"Give me your cock," she pleaded, trembling in my tentacles' embrace. "Please, Vos."

I fucked my mate with love, watching as my cock pumped in and out of her sweet cunt, making sure my precum dripped from her asshole and her slit, mixed with her slickness. Beautiful.

Finally, she quivered and came one last time, softly this time, her cunt fluttering around my cock. The sensation was enough to push me over the edge as well, and with full-body shudders I came in a dozen spurts that filled her and then over-filled her, my glowing lavender cum streaming down her thighs.

I rolled us very carefully to our sides and wrapped my arms around her as she quivered.

I kissed her sweaty temple. "Was that enough to ease your need?"

"Oh, yes." She snuggled back against me, making my spent and sensitive cock twitch inside her. "Thank you."

"There is no need to thank me. I had my fair share of our pleasure too."

"On the contrary." She chuckled, still breathless. "I got the better end of the deal."

"We will call it even," I countered. "As I cannot yet feel my legs."

My Calla laughed. I loved that sound as much as when she screamed my name. She had laughed so little during our early days together.

"You are happy, my mate?" I asked.

"Happier every day." She craned her neck to kiss me. "You know that, don't you?"

"I must ask sometimes, so I know this is real." I rested my head against hers. "It seems like a dream, and I fear I will wake."

"Well, if it's a dream, don't wake up, because I like it too." She took my hand and pressed it to her belly, where I felt a tiny flutter. "I think we woke him up," she teased. "Speaking of which, once he's born and old enough to understand what's going on, will we have to be quieter?"

"I will soundproof our room," I said, very seriously. "I cannot live without hearing you scream my name."

"Ugh, right answer *again*," she said, feigning exasperation. "I swear, Vos Turek, if you don't stop saying the exact right thing every damn time I ask you a question, I will—" She gasped, breaking off mid-sentence.

"You will do what, my mate?" I asked innocently, my fingers teasing her clit.

"I will do…something!" She whimpered. "You aren't getting hard again, are you?"

"I will let you guess whether I am." I kissed her shoulder. My tentacles tugged on her legs, encouraging her to spread them wider. "What is your guess, my mate?"

Calla sighed. "That I won't get to work on the baby's room until midday, *again*."

"You guessed correctly," I murmured into her ear. "Now, tell me what I may do for my Calla."

"Let me rest for a bit," she said, and smiled up at me. "And then…well, I'd like you to make me come with your cock in my ass, if that's not asking too much."

My cock twitched. "It is not too much to ask," I said.

Gently, I withdrew from her and laid her on the bed. I rose, went to the washroom for hot, wet cloths, and returned to clean her and myself.

That done, I formed a nest with my tentacles and arranged her with her head against my chest above my primary heart. It was how I had first cradled her in the sea after rescuing her from the raiders, and it would forever be my most favorite way to hold my mate.

I tucked her head under my chin and cooed. "Rest, my love."

She closed her eyes and settled in with her hand on her belly. I covered her hand with mine and hummed a lullaby. In moments, my Calla was asleep, a smile on her lips.

I drew a blanket over us and opened the window to let in cool night air, the smell of rain, and Poe's quiet, happy trills as she tended her garden.

What joy to no longer need to swim in the ocean's depths or escape into dreamless sleep to find perfect peace.

My thoughts drifted to a long-ago moment: the day Calla

first woke in my home and I had cradled her in my living room by the fire as the rain poured outside.

Had I gotten my wish to freeze time that afternoon, when my mate lay so badly injured in my arms and I had hoped for a chance, no matter how slim, to persuade her to stay, I would not have found this moment, nor any of the moments between then and now, nor any of the moments we had yet to share. I had dared to hope, despite every instinct and lingering doubt that warned against it.

Hope had led us here. Hope had brought us home.

THANK YOU FOR READING

Thank you for reading *Sheltered in the Storm*, the first book in the Fortusian Mates series! I hope you enjoyed the story.

More novels featuring Fortusian males and the fierce human women they love are coming soon.

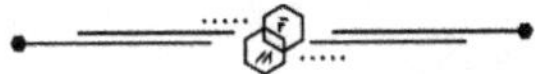

Reviews are very much appreciated by all indie authors, if you have the time to share your thoughts.

ACKNOWLEDGMENTS

First and foremost, thank you to my editor, Friel Black of Grey Moth Editing, who went from editing the ninth book in my Alice Worth urban fantasy series to eighty thousand words of alien smut without batting an eyelash. I cannot express how wonderful and reassuring it is to know that no matter how messy my drafts are, I have your help to whip them into shape and turn them into books I can be proud of.

I owe a huge debt of gratitude to Lindsey, aka @honeyy.fae, for this gorgeous cover and a boatload of bookish art. Many thanks also to Flavia and Bojana of FlavulousArt and Carly at Bookish-Beasts for their gorgeous art and contributions to this book's interior. Enormous thanks as well to Megan Van Dyke for the cover typography, which I love so much, and for your friendship.

A very special thanks to my Discordant Owl Squad for cheering me on during this project, particularly during bouts of crippling imposter syndrome and all the times I almost chickened out on publishing a book full of scenes and lines of dialogue that make my face turn bright red.

Thank you to all my close family and friends, all of whom I love to the moon and back. Please don't read this book. There's tentacle spice in here.

A very special thanks to my sister Michelle and brother-in-law Josh, my sister-in-law Amy, and my cousins Antoinette and Felicia, for your love and support. You are also all excused from reading this book. Go read something more wholesome, or not wholesome. Just…not this. Or its sequels.

And all my love to my wonderful and long-suffering husband Bill, who had to put up with a lot of mostly one-sided conversations about alien…um, appendages…and is still hanging around. You must really love me.

ABOUT THE AUTHOR

Lisa Edmonds was born and raised in Kansas. A graduate of Buhler High School, she studied English and forensic criminology at Wichita State University. After acquiring her Bachelor's degree, she considered a career in law enforcement as a behavioral analyst before earning a Master's in English from Wichita State and then a Ph.D. in English from Texas A&M University.

For ten years, she was an associate professor of English at a college in Texas, where she taught a variety of writing and literature courses. Now a full-time author, she shares a cute Victorian-style home called The Storybook House with her husband and their pets, and enjoys writing, reading, traveling, spoiling her niece and nephew, and singing karaoke.

Don't miss new releases or announcements! Visit https://linktr.ee/edmonds411 for all the links.